TRAIN RIDE TO DEATH

They started to count to fifteen before using the whistle again. At twelve the lavatory door buckled, the wrench clanged to the floor, and Dermot, scarlet-faced from heat and exertion, exploded from his imprisonment. Dermot's body was wholly in motion; he seemed to be executing a dance, behind whose gyrations Sammy emerged sheltering himself.

Hartley shot at Dermot's right leg, but missed. He fired again at Dermot, but splintered the cover of the toilet seat.

Three feet behind Hartley a fire extinguisher hung in a bracket on the forward wall of the generator area. Hartley transferred the revolver to his left hand. With his right, he pulled out the fire extinguisher, pressed the control, and sent a stream of foam against Dermot.

Gasping, Dermot dropped his shield, clawed at his eyes, staggered back, and fell through the opening into the laboratory. Before the fire extinguisher was empty, Hartley directed the stream against Sammy.

"You are going overboard. Off this train if you don't give up," Hartley told him.

"I'll never give up," Sammy gasped. "Damn your soul, Hartley. You've blinded me."

MURDER ON THE LONG STRAIGHT

CHARLOTTE YARBOROUGH

To R

Book Margins, Inc.

A BMI Edition

Published by special arrangement with Dorchester
Publishing Co., Inc.

Printed in the United States of America.

MURDER ON THE LONG STRAIGHT

1

START OF THE LONG STRAIGHT

The longest straight run of railroad track in the world begins about 720 miles east of Perth, Australia. It continues east through the Nullarbor Plain for about 300 miles across the almost ruler-flat henna-colored treeless plains of Western Australia and South Australia.

After a Sunday night departure from Perth, the Indian-Pacific train of the Railways of Australia, eastbound for Sydney, was due to enter the Straight on Monday afternoon at 2:47.

At 6:00 on that Monday morning Hartley Rhys was wakened by the car conductor, Albert Hawkins, bringing tea and biscuits.

"Thank you, Mr. Hawkins."

"This train is due at Kalgoorlie at six-thirty. We'll be there in a half-hour. I thought you might want to go out to look over the passengers we'll be taking on."

"Yes."

"I hope you were comfortable."

"Excellent train."

"None better," Hawkins said. "I've been chief conductor on this train for seven years. We haven't been late more than an average of four minutes a year in all that time. But that's the Indian-Pacific for you. Do you have anything like it in America?"

"I doubt it," Hartley said. "But I haven't spent much time in America lately—I've been in Singapore for the last eight years." He drank tea, appreciating its hotness. After Singapore, which he had left on the preceding Saturday, Australia's early October spring felt chilling.

"Even so, you'll be noticing differences," Hawkins said.

"Yes. We don't have car conductors, for one thing. Or two shower rooms in a car. Or this!" He raised the teacup. "And the roomettes are palatial, compared with the ones on American trains."

"I've traveled on American trains," Hawkins said. "And I must say I wasn't impressed by their equipment. Or with the system of car porters. Of course, they do the heavier chores, but we do a better job looking after our passengers."

"I believe it," Hartley said. "And thanks again for the list of passengers you gave me last night."

"Glad to help. I'll try to complete it as soon as I can." Hawkins took the empty teacup. Looking back from the doorway, he said, "Maybe you'll wonder why I have my office here in Car 2 instead of Car 1. Reason is that we try to put the families with children in Car 1. Nearest the dining car. So Car 1 tends to be noisy. Well, sir, I'll see you on the platform."

Hartley shaved, took a shower, and was dressed by

8

the time the train reached Kalgoorlie. He walked forward along the platform past the silver-colored shining cars to the silver and crimson diesel electric engine. Against the grayness of the misted morning and a background of dun-colored buildings, the train looked as brilliant as a spirited, quiescent dragon.

Five or six passengers were debarking; a few more than that number of newcomers were moving toward the opened vestibules of the five sleeping cars. Outside Car 2, Hawkins, erect with the pride of a hunter who has tamed a mythical beast, touched a hand to his uniform cap as Hartley approached him.

"On time, to the second."

"Good show," Hartley said.

"And now, sir," Hawkins said, "you'll see the Indian-Pacific's most loyal passenger. There he comes—and he still has that ruddy bird with him."

An old man in a wheelchair, stiff and alert, bearing a kookaburra on the left shoulder of his dirty bush jacket, was being propelled by a dark, wide-faced aborigine toward the vestibule of Car 2. Behind him three station porters pushed a hand truck loaded with gray canvas bags.

Under the brim of a savaged, grimy gray hat, the old man's steel-gray eyes met Hartley's. They were neither hostile nor friendly; inquisitive, perhaps, and ready to find in the stranger a new audience for stories, for boasting which age and wealth would justify. Hartley recognized the mingling of caustic humor in the eyes and the harsh, lean jaw. This old man was used to being listened to; he needed to be heard by more listeners than the small town would provide.

Hartley nodded to him, one passenger greeting

another. He nodded also to the great wide-faced aborigine servant, who stared back as if surprised at being noticed.

The bird on the old man's shoulder gave a creak of a half-laugh as the aborigine lifted the old man and carried him up the steps into Car 2.

The porters tugged, lifted, and finally loaded the gray sacks into the car.

"That," Hawkins said, with satisfaction, "is Cyrus Macrimmon."

The name brought to Hartley some memory of bloody Highland warfare.

"One of the few gold-mine operators left in Kalgoorlie," Hawkins said. "A pioneer, really. Every year he makes the run from here to Sydney with his gold. He wouldn't trust any other transportation."

"You mean he takes the gold with him on this train?" Hartley asked.

"Why not?" Hawkins demanded. "The Indian-Pacific is safer than armored vans."

"But still—security problems, insurance!"

"The Indian-Pacific is secure," Hawkins said loftily. "Every year Mr. Macrimmon takes two double compartments, one for him, the other for the Abo, with the gold sacks stowed all through. Sometimes he takes three compartments. And he always brings Kooka. Neat bird, I must say—though that jacket—oh, good morning, Lady Mary! Your father looks very fit."

He turned to speak to the tall tawny blonde whom Hartley had seen on the platform the night before. By daylight he saw her aggressive Arabic nose. She wore a lion-colored pant suit, black boots, and a black velvet ribbon defining the descent of her hair over a martially

10

poised head. She looked capable of taking on any beasts untamed by Hawkins.

"Lady Mary Richland—Mr. Hartley Rhys," Hawkins said.

"Morning," Lady Mary said. She did not have the cold coloring of her father—her eyes were chestnut—but with her thin lips and the aloof lift of her nose she faced outward in a more chilling impact.

"Yes," she said to Hawkins. "Fit enough. But he could stand a good hosing. Soaping."

Hawkins looked taken down. But he rallied and inquired for Sir Ian. "We rarely see him," he added.

"He's very fit too, and considerably cleaner." She climbed the steps vigorously as if practicing for mountains and disappeared into Car 2.

The porters emerged from the car with their empty hand-trucks. After them came the Abo to fold and carry on board the wheel chair. This time in passing he gave Hartley a nod. Hartley liked him.

"Lady Mary," Hawkins said, "takes the Indian-Pacific when her father goes to Sydney. She missed only one year after a horse threw her and she broke an arm."

Hartley wondered what happened to the horse.

"Do you go with us all the way to Sydney?" he asked.

"Only to Port Augusta. You'll be having a new crew there. Of course, the engineer and his assistant make shorter runs." Hartley imagined an unspoken "and why should they." Something here, he thought, similar to the centuries-old rift between deck and engineering officers on a ship.

Hawkins drew out his watch. "We leave in one and one-half minutes." He frowned as a girl with long bright

11

hair ran toward them carrying a suitcase and dragging a fair-haired boy, who carried a skateboard and towed on leash a young dog who looked like an incipient sheep-herding dog.

"The dog must travel in the baggage car," Hawkins said. "Please board. We're about to take off."

"All right," the girl panted. "I can't pay extra for the dog, but my husband will meet us in Sydney!" Her voice sang. "Will they feed him? My husband will pay!"

"He'll be taken care of," Hawkins said. "Don't you worry." He took the suitcase, and Hartley unwound the dog's leash from the ankles of the boy and his mother.

Holding his watch, Hawkins frowned toward the baggage car where the porters were still loading crates.

"They get slower and slower—all right now." He raised his arm in a signal to the engineer. From the lowest step Hartley said, "What about the girl's tickets?"

"See to that later. In with you, sir."

The bright dragon was in motion by the time Hartley entered the dining car. The time was 7:00 A.M. and Hawkins, behind him, was explaining: "I've seated you at the table with Mr. Macrimmon. Always expect Lady Mary to sit with him, but she never does. So it's you and Mr. Macrimmon and Mr. Merriam, the director of the tour group. Satisfactory, sir?"

"Entirely."

A flurry occurred in the aisle when the fair-haired girl and the boy came pulling their dog toward the baggage car. The boy looked miserable. A few minutes later Hartley was glad to see them, minus dog but smiling. They sat at a table near his.

"Everything all right with the dog?" he asked. The

boy brandished a spoon in a sign of victory. "They'll take care of him, all right. They gave him a steak!"

"You eat a good breakfast now," Hartley said. "Your dog would expect it."

"Yes, Davy. If you don't eat well, your father will be cross with me."

The boy laughed. "You fooling me? He's never cross." His mother hugged him.

A waiter brought Hartley coffee and fruit juice, and within a few minutes, eggs, bacon, an Australian breakfast steak, hot rolls, and marmalade. His shortage of sleep—he had spent a good part of the preceding night studying the partial passenger list that Hawkins had given him and roaming through the train, familiarizing himself with its physical features—was obviously going to be compensated for by Indian-Pacific food.

He was halfway through the steak when he was joined at the table by a brisk young man, darkly tanned, with gray-blond hair. He carried a briefcase.

"Name's Merriam. Don. Good morning."

Hartley recognized the name; Merriam was manager of the escorted tour whose members occupied the last cars.

"Name's Rhys. Hartley. And good morning to you."

To the waiter Merriam said, "What my neighbor has is fine. I'll have the same." He turned to look through the car, seemed to count, waved greeting to passengers at forward tables, and turned back, frowning amiably. "Jam-up later. A lot more of my people were booked for this sitting. Oh, well, the poor things have been on the go for over two weeks. Need these three days to rest. Unusually big crowd, but another man takes on half the group in Sydney. Less baggage to count—and passports—" He tapped the briefcase on his lap. "Tour manager's nightmare is losing a passport."

"You've never lost one?"

"Only in dreams, when there's time to sleep. But I don't believe in jet lag, do you? Why's it so important to sleep at exactly the same time? Normal people don't always go to bed on schedule."

"You're right," Hartley said. "But I imagine you get complaints. Maybe an occasional hypochondriac."

Merriam poured cream into his coffee. "Once in a while. This group I have now is pretty good. Some rather tottery old people, but they don't make a profession of frailty or age. When we have to take a plane at 4:30 A.M., they're up to it." He tasted the steak that the waiter had brought. "Jolly good food, as you English would say."

"I'm American," Hartley said. "But I live in Singapore."

"Wonderful city," Merriam said. "My company scants it. Never allows enough time there."

"Look me up when you do. I'll give you an address later."

"Glad to," Merriam said.

"Have all the members of your party been traveling with you right along?" Hartley asked.

"From the morning I met them in Manila. The tour started in Los Angeles. I picked them up at their first stop the next day. From Manila we went to Japan, then to Hong Kong, Thailand, Malaysia, Singapore, Java, Bali—now here. Only real setback was in Jogjakarta, where two gals tried to buy out the stores. Sarongs, batik, the half-face leather puppets, krises. They had

14

them all mailed to France, and I thought the rest of the party would flip at the time it took. But they were great. Of course it helped that the two gals were very pretty Frenchwomen. Everybody liked them and hoped they would see them in sarongs. They had to settle for the bastard sarong dresses the tourists buy. But those two—" Merriam laughed. "Wonderful girls. But devils. At the Ambarrukmo hotel they made a date with their room boy—boys are used there, not maids—and said they wanted to learn Indonesian. Wrote down words on the back of laundry slips."

"There's one old man," Merriam said, "delightful—former professor of history—has a heart condition. I worry about him. He gave me a raft of prescriptions in case he had an attack. But he told me the doctors said he'd be better off enjoying himself. And of course, I've got the route covered. I can whisk anybody into a hospital with good doctors all the way through the tour."

"Except on this three-day trip?" Hartley said.

"Yes. But what could happen on this civilized train? He'll just get a good rest. He's reasonable. I asked him to stay in bed and have his meals sent to him. Right now he's probably reading histories in three languages. He's all the more amenable because the French girls visit him. Lord, who wouldn't be!"

"He's in Car 4 or 5?"

"Yes. Car 4. The French girls are in Car 3. So am I. Not that it means anything, unfortunately. They try, bless their hearts, but I've got company rules."

"Still, it sounds like an interesting life," Hartley said.

"You can say that again. But you—how is your life?"

"Transportation survey," Hartley said.

"What have you surveyed so far?"

"Just the geography of the train."

"And the passengers?"

"The chief conductor promises to take me on a tour through passenger quarters this morning. But I won't have to bother the people in your party." At Merriam's questioning look, he added, "I could get your people's reactions—from you."

"Oh, sure," Merriam said. "Where are you—" He broke off. "We're getting company."

The Abo was wheeling Macrimmon into the dining car. Opposite Hartley and Merriam the old man with the bird on his shoulder, easily seated, grunted a greeting. The Abo folded the wheelchair and took it away.

"Well, boys. How about a drink?"

"A bit too early," Hartley said. Merriam agreed to have a bloody mary. Macrimmon ordered Scotch for himself."

"Kooka," he said, "has to start off with his Scotch. Eh, Kooka?" The bird winced, closing one eye as Macrimmon tapped him with a folded napkin.

A waiter came back with the drinks. "Usual—oh, you're new? Well, two steaks, no eggs. Fried potatoes. Bacon. And porridge to start with."

"Watch this." He poured Scotch into a spoon and fed it to the kookaburra.

"Gosh," Merriam whispered. "The bird's going to faint."

But the kookaburra rallied, ingested more Scotch, opened the closed eye, and peered sharply at his master.

"Does he like it?" Hartley asked.

"He'd better!" Macrimmon said. "It makes a man of him."

"Does he have to go through this at every meal?" Hartley asked.

He did not hear Macrimmon's answer. Merriam was whispering: "Wow! Open the barn door—look what's coming out!"

Behind Lady Mary and a squat man whose forehead was hidden under a mat of black hair, who wore canvas shorts and shirt and thongs, came a tall girl, dusky-haired, white-complexioned, with black eyes; a girl who carried herself regally. A rich, deep beauty with luminous, intelligent eyes.

"Not one of your party?" he said to Merriam.

"If she were, I'd give up the job and break the rules."

"What are you two muttering about?" Macrimmon demanded. "I may be beat with arthritis, but there's nothing the matter with my hearing. And it's not just arthritis—I was checking the mines. We have surface deposits—placer mines—and shaft mines for quartz. Heard a moaning—went down a ladder into an old shaft—it broke. And what was there? Our ruddy house cat with five new kittens. Broke two legs. Abo found me. Damn him, he took the cats up first. Loyalty, eh?"

"Did the legs mend?" Merriam asked.

"Damned bloody legs never did come around. Oh, I can hobble about. But it's grotesque."

"What happened to the cats?"

Macrimmon glared at Hartley.

"Don't know how to take you, boy."

"You won't take me," Hartley said.

17

Merriam, laughing, said, "He's not hard to take." He stood, saying, "Excuse me, I have to see some people in my party."

"What kind of party is *he* running?" Macrimmon asked.

"A tour group, mostly from the United States, I imagine."

"Just my luck it isn't poker."

"You might build up a poker game. Aren't you Australians pretty fond of gambling?"

"You could say so," Macrimmon answered, feeding the Kooka a crumb of toast. He laughed. "Not only us Australians. Would you believe it, the Abo plays poker?"

"You don't count him as an Australian?"

Macrimmon glanced sharply at Hartley. "At least we've never wiped them out—like Indians—or made slaves of them. You American?"

"Yes," Hartley said. "But living in Singapore."

"You can't shake off your spots that easily."

"What spots?"

Macrimmon laughed, slapping the somnolent kookaburra again with a napkin. "What are you doing out here?"

"Transportation survey." Hartley expected a quizzing, but was saved by Hawkins, who belatedly made introductions. He flicked a finger at the Kooka, who promptly bit it.

"Great sense of humor, that bird," Macrimmon said.

"I thought you'd like newspapers," Hawkins said.

"What for? More propaganda about your precious Labour Party rogue of a prime minister? Ah, he got kicked out all right. We have a conservative regime, and

18

by ruddy God, we deserve it. And you and your unions can pack up and go to hell!"

Hartley saw anger smoulder under Hawkins's urbanity.

Macrimmon folded his copy of the paper and struck the kookaburra. The characteristic kookaburra laugh came out more like a plaint.

"Most of us Australians," Macrimmon said, "know when we're well off. Not like you, Hawkins." The latter, again in control, nodded.

After the Abo had wheeled away his master and the bird, Hartley, over a final cup of coffee, lingered to enjoy through the window the meadowland of this part of Western Australia. For more than a year he had not traveled away from the tropics. He found himself thoroughly enjoying the towering gum trees with bouquets of leaves which reminded him of Mediterranean pines, and the rich lower growths of mulga and mesquite, the yellow and orange wildflowers. And this is all we need, he thought with delight, when in a clearing he saw a pair of tall kangaroos, bronze in the sunlight, leaping toward the next grove of gum trees.

"Beauties," he said to Hawkins who had come to stand beside the table.

"There will be more. And keep a watch for emus."

"Splendid country," Hartley said.

"Yes, well, no matter what Mr. Macrimmon says, plenty of us think highly of our former Labour Prime Minister. I don't know what your opinions are, Mr. Rhys."

"They're like yours. I admired the man. And you took Macrimmon's onslaught very well, I must say."

"Part of my job," Hawkins said. He gave Hartley a

neatly typed sheet. "This about completes the list. Not quite. Afraid I haven't been able to make many notes. I didn't include the names in Mr. Merriam's tour group."

"Quite right." Hartley took from a pocket the two other sheets that Hawkins had given him and added the new sheet to them. He had been amused to notice that on the first page the entries started with a group of six names in capital letters: Lady Mary, General Owen Percy, Glendon his granddaughter, Macrimmon, a British Consul named Armitage, and Thomas his nephew.

"If it suits you," Hawkins said, "I will be ready at ten to visit the passengers."

"Very good. What's your cover on this tour?"

Hawkins looked startled, then laughed. "Oh, I'll be wanting to know how they're enjoying the trip and, of course, explaining the survey you are making."

Hartley went to his roomette and resisted a desire to lower the bed from its lair in order to take a nap. He spent a few minutes looking over Hawkins's list, then at a station he left the train and walked along the platform vigorously, to wake himself. He saw a family— husband, wife, two young children—leave the train. Behind him, Hawkins said, "Railroad personnel. This town is a railroad center. Only about thirty people. All of them connected with the road."

Hartley saw nine or ten small brown houses, a building that looked like a store, and freight cars on a siding. An isolated life this young family would find.

He mounted the steps into his car and the train resumed its smooth passage. Recorded music played through the cars: oldish American songs for the most part, and "Hello Dolly" at least once every half-hour.

He had turned off the switch that poured the recordings into his room, but still found them annoyingly loud.

"There's only one thing I don't like about your train, Mr. Hawkins," he said when he met the latter at ten. The train was stopped at a station, but Hawkins was off-duty.

Although Hartley had spoken half-playfully, a fissure showed in Hawkins's urbanity.

"Something you *don't* like, sir?"

"The music is too loud. Do you ever turn it off?"

Hawkins looked affronted.

"Turn it *off*? Altogether? But you can control it by the switch in your room."

"Only in the room. It still pours in from all around."

"But the music is one of the services of the Indian-Pacific. It is never turned off until after midnight."

"Not even 'Hello Dolly'? I'm going to dream that tune, if I ever have time to sleep."

"You'll get used to it," Hawkins said, obviously sympathetic with Hartley's wistful reference to sleep. "Tonight I do hope you *will* sleep. And why shouldn't you? Whatever it is you are concerned about, what could happen on the Indian-Pacific?"

"Nothing, I hope."

"Well now, where shall we start our tour?"

"Right here—with Macrimmon," Hartley said, as they flattened themselves against a wall to let the Abo, with a quest animating his heavy features, brush past them on the way to the forward vestibule He had left the room's door open. Macrimmon, in his wheelchair beside the window table, called a crusty hello.

"Come in, boys."

"Mr. Macrimmon," Hartley said, "I understand

you're carrying some pretty valuable baggage. When you're alone, wouldn't it be safer if you locked the door?"

Hartley heard Hawkins check a protest.

Macrimmon produced a laugh somewhat like his bird's and pointed to the kookaburra perched on a canvas bag near the door.

"Best watchdog I ever had. I've got a revolver, too. Anyway, the Abo's just gone out to buy peanuts. Kooka doesn't eat ones with skin on them, and that's all they have on the train. Have a drink." He reached for a bottle of Scotch.

"Thanks, not now."

"And why would you be caring about my valuable baggage?" Macrimmon said. "Hawkins will tell you—I've been making this trip with valuables for—how many bloody years, Hawk?"

"Many years, Mr. Macrimmon. I might say, sir, that Mr. Rhys is interested in all aspects of transportation, including security."

"Well, sit down. If you think it's secure here."

He swung his wheelchair to half-face them as Hartley sat on the cushioned seat, and Hawkins took the chair on the opposite side of the table.

"Tell me," Macrimmon ordered Hartley, "what you think you're doing and where you're going. No—you let me tell you—it's some goddamned money-spending scheme left over from the Labour people. Right?"

Hartley did not have to answer, for Lady Mary strode into the room carrying a small bag of peanuts. The bird screamed.

"He never did like me," she said. She tore open the

22

cellophane and offered the Kooka three nuts which he took but spat out.

From the doorway the Abo, returning as the train started, mumbled something in his own language. Macrimmon guffawed, gulped Scotch, and translated.

"He says, in his goddamned jargon, something like 'the gift without the giver' and so forth."

In an ungainly but understandable English, the Abo said, "Kooka no like this train. Me no like."

"What's the matter with the train?" Macrimmon demanded.

The Abo answered, again using his own language.

"Woman have baby!" Macrimmon exclaimed. "God, now?"

"Coming," the Abo said. "Not luck."

"He means there's a pregnant woman on board?" Lady Mary said, frowning. "How does he know?"

"Door open. Car over there." The Abo gestured toward Car 1.

"God," said Macrimmon. "You're as full of superstitions as your head is with lice."

Hartley thought this was unjustified, for the Abo's dense black hair looked cleaner and better-tended than Macrimmon's dank gray hair. Macrimmon slammed a fist against the Abo's left temple. The Abo, like the bird, looked resigned if unenthusiastic.

"Bullshit," Macrimmon said. "Eh, Polly?"

"Don't call me Polly!"

"So Sir Ian wouldn't like it?" her father sneered. "What's that husband of yours up to now? Last I heard, he was in Singapore shacking up with Communists or nationalists, or what have you."

"It's impossible to talk to you." She looked at Hartley. "Who are you?"

"Friend of mine," Macrimmon said. "What's the first name, cobber?"

"Hartley."

"He's your friend and you don't know his name." Lady Mary's scorn reached from her father to Hartley.

"Friggin' mother of God!" her father exclaimed. "What's a name got to do with it!" He grinned. "We can't all be lords and ladies."

"I rather think not," Lady Mary said.

"Take a drink, Mary, and cool down."

"I don't want a drink. Besides, there's no clean glass."

"Abo!" Macrimmon shouted. "Get a glass."

The Abo brought a glass from the bathroom and poured Scotch into it. Lady Mary took the glass, looking into it as if searching for floating spiders.

Macrimmon raised his glass. "Here's to horrors!"

"Why to horrors?" Hartley asked.

"Why not? Horror never hurt anybody. Eh, Kooka?" He thumped the bird's smooth rear.

"You can hand it out," his daughter said acidly.

"If you don't like that Scotch—my last bottle of Glenlivet—you're welcome to double horrors," Macrimmon said. "And maybe you've got them in that husband of yours."

"You've certainly done all you could to hurt him. Jobs he tried for—that loan that would have—oh, well, we don't need you now."

"Then what are you doing, following me?" her father asked. "Going to try for a loan for your husband, from some friend of mine in Sydney?"

"We don't need a loan! We own an island and live a

more civilized life than you!" Then, almost mildly, as if the Glenlivet had planed off the edges of her temper, she asked, "What are you going to do after you sell your bags of gold?"

"Hah! You wouldn't know me in Sydney. Not after I get a haircut and clothes. Go to see my friend—he's a brain, but too conservative for you. Old Jim-Jam Blake. Curator of a science museum. We spend the time drinking in our club and cussing out the old Labour government, rot their souls. If any. And we stow in oysters at the Coachmen's Inn. And I order a ton of tinned oysters and another ton of caviar and a case of champagne and ten cases of Glenlivet and fifty pounds of peanuts for Kooka."

"What does the Abo get out of all this?" his daughter asked.

"The Abo? That sod gets anything he wants—new clothes, food, all the beer or Scotch he wants. He gets a room in a hotel near a beach—the creature likes to swim. Doesn't even have to look after me. Jim-Jam has plenty of servants. Better trained than you, Abo."

The Abo, perhaps lost in envisioning the luxuries at Sydney, nodded. Hartley wondered if Kooka got a vacation. Or was he a masochist bird?

The kooka jumped from the sack on which he had been perching and took his place on Macrimmon's left shoulder. The Abo gave him a peanut from the bag that Lady Mary had dropped on the table. They had a bond, Hartley thought, watching Kooka crunch the nut and look at the Abo.

"Well, are you going to be on my tail in Sydney?" Macrimmon asked his daughter.

She shook her head, angrily staring into her glass.

"What the hell, then, Sir Ian got a rival?"

Lady Mary slammed her glass on the table.

"Hold on," her father said. "I don't know what you—or I—expect each year when you make this run with me. We don't like each other. That's for bloody sure. Haven't ever. You were a bleeding sly little brat, but your mother liked you as long as she lived. Liked you better, I guess, than anything else in her life. Even liked that son-of-a-bitch you married. Point is now I've got some opals I don't want."

"Opals—you don't mean that mass of opals you got from your brother-in-law?"

"They're mine," her father said. "Sure I got them from Hall as security when I lent him the money to save his sodding sheep station that bad year."

"Pardon me, Mr. Macrimmon," Hawkins said, "but we have a Mr. William Hall on board. From Kalgoorlie."

"Bill Hall," Lady Mary said. "Your sainted nephew."

Macrimmon scowled. "What the devil's that bastard doing on this train?"

His daughter shrugged.

"Abo," Macrimmon said, "bring that red-striped bag out of the duffel bag."

"Why can't you use decent baggage?" Mary asked. "Do you have to jam everything into those dirty brown duffels? Can't you buy some suitcases?"

"You know what you can do with your bleeding suitcases," her father ungently said.

He loaded his pipe from a grey leather pouch and assumed an indifferent expression when the Abo tendered him a red-striped bag.

"Catch," Macrimmon said, hurling the bag toward his daughter. He broke several matches in lighting the pipe. Hartley saw the steel eyes furtively turn toward Lady Mary as she opened the drawstrings of the bag.

Opals poured into her lap. There were black opals with fiery eyes, flame-centered dark blue opals, and milk-pale opals with rainbow iridescence. The stones were large, excellently cut and polished, some of them matched, many of them set in gold as earrings, brooches, bracelets, and rings.

Lady Mary fixed her eyes on the flow and mystery of the jewels. A bracelet fell from her narrow lap and was picked up by Hawkins who murmured, "A fortune, a fortune."

Hartley, watching Lady Mary's face, saw a puzzling mixture of expressions pass over it. He would have expected her to show excitement, even rapture at the beauty of the gift. But it was nothing that simple.

"You don't like them," Macrimmon said. "Well, I never did like opals, either, but I thought they'd suit you. Something tigerish in them."

"No, no. I—they're overwhelming," his daughter said. She picked up a fire-hearted black opal. "Don't you even like this one?"

"Oh, I suppose it's one of the best of the lot. Have it made into something you can wear. Go to that jeweler in Sydney and have him send me the bill. And get any others set."

"I'll have something made for you. Cufflinks?" Her voice was faint, as though she foresaw what her father would answer. And he did.

"Yes, I suppose I could wear black opal cufflinks in a

27

dirty bush jacket when I go out to look over the mines.
Dammit, Mary, I don't like opals. Can't you get that
through your head? If you don't want the ruddy things,
we'll throw them away."

"I do like them. I'm grateful—"

"Stow it," Macrimmon said. He had recovered from
whatever he would not have admitted as a setback
during the minutes when he had thought Lady Mary did
not like the gift. "I don't want any of your ruddy
gratitude."

Hartley heard her gasp as though she had been
struck.

She said coldly now, "It's real, if you can recognize
it."

Slowly she replaced the opals in the red and white
bag. A small bag, Hartley thought, to encompass what
Hawkins had accurately characterized as a fortune.

Someone was standing in the doorway to the aisle.
Lady Mary raised an arm and a half-upturned palm
toward the squat, dark man whom Hartley had seen in
the dining car. "Coming, Dermot," she said.

"Who's that?" Macrimmon said.

"Michael Dermot. Man who works for my husband.
Purchases supplies in Sydney." She stood, moved
toward her father, and in her act of giving him the bag
of opals something passed between them which
Hartley felt embarrased to witness. Some communication from a source underlying words, deeper than and
less affected by divergences of opinion, of action, of
feeling.

"Father, please keep the opals for me. I'm out of my
room much of the time. They'd be safer with you."

It was the first time Hartley had heard her use the word *father*.

She rose and stood for a moment beside Macrimmon, who thrust the bag into a pocket.

The Abo, holding Kooka, must have pressed the bird too tightly, for it emitted a muffled protest. The wide, dark face of the Abo was turned toward Lady Mary; and even in his rudimentary features, Hartley saw a curious tension: a longing, a kind of hunger—not much to go on, Hartley thought, but he looks as if he would vote pretty hard for a family reconciliation, if that were necessary or possible.

After Lady Mary had joined Dermot at the doorway and left, Hawkins and Hartley took leave. Hawkins was still dazzled by the display of jewels.

"You know opals?"

"Yes, more or less."

"Fabulous. Those were solid opals, the first grade. No layering. I'd say thirty thousand dollars worth. And the gold in the settings—they would have paid for a lot of sheep. Well, where shall we start?"

"With the pregnant woman in Car 1," Hartley said.

"Oh well, yes. Foreigner. Malay or something."

"Foreign or not, she's pregant, if the Abo is right. Anybody in your crew with medical training?"

"No," Hawkins admitted. "But those Malays—or whatever—they drop babies the way cats drop kittens."

"How do you know it's that easy for cats?"

Hawkins looked at him with astonishment. "Why—always—it *must* be."

"Did you ever see the results of a poll on how cats suffer?"

"You're serious, sir?"

"Yes, but well, never mind."

Hawkins collected tea equipment.

In Car 1 a clatter and a crash met them. A small figure hunched on a wheeled board sped forward in front of them; a compartment door sprang open; the young blonde woman from Kalgoorlie leaned out screaming, plucked her son from the skateboard, and pulled him into the room. They heard her voice through the closed door: "Don't you ever—"

Hawkins stood the skateboard on end outside the door.

"Shall we cross them off our list of visits?" he asked.

"Yes. A lethal child."

The so-called music, indispensable according to Hawkins, pounded and swirled into the air. Maybe it will help to keep me awake, Hartley thought, as Hawkins tapped at double roomette 5 in Car 1.

"Ali Soto," Hawkins read, from the duplicate he had kept of the sheets given to Hartley. "Bound for Port Augusta. Is Soto Malay?"

"Probably half-Portuguese, half-Malay," Hartley guessed.

The door was opened by a dark-skinned, excessively tall, rail-thin young man in shorts and a flowered shirt, whose orange and purple gayety went strangely with his somber, hostile face.

"Well sir," said Hawkins, falsely jovial, "how's the wife?"

Hartley looked at the lumpish figure on the lower berth, but saw only rumpled blankets and a tangle of black hair on the pillow.

"All right. What you want?"

"To see how your wife is. Tea?" Hawkins carried the tray, although this car was not his to serve.

Ali shook his head. "No tea."

"You going to Port Augusta?"

"Why you ask? I have passport."

"I'm sure you have. Only inquiring. I am the chief conductor. Like to know how the Indian-Pacific passengers are enjoying the trip."

"Who's he?" Ali said, staring at Hartley.

"Oh, he's helping me serve tea," Hawkins said. "And I wanted to tell you that we are now in the Long Straight."

Ali looked as though he couldn't have cared less.

"When is the baby due?" Hartley asked.

Ali shrugged. "Today, tomorrow, next day. Why?"

"I'd have thought you'd fly," Hartley said. "Much faster."

"Air company say no. Wife."

"But you didn't have to take your wife with you when you went for flight tickets."

"Where leave wife? Stay with. Baby come any time."

"Well," Hawkins said, "I hope you'll like Port Augusta. You staying there?"

"Have friend. Job on ship."

"Where did you come from?" Hartley asked.

"Why matter?"

"No matter," Hawkins said silkily. "Just interested. If you have a job on a ship, what about your wife? And what ship?"

"Indonesian tanker. And wife stay with friends."

"Your first child?" Hartley asked.

Ali scowled. "Yes. Why ask?"

"Because it would make a difference if the baby

came while we're on the train."

"All right, Ali." Hawkins turned toward the door. Following, Hartley glanced at the figure mounded on the berth. A pair of piercing black eyes stared at him through a mat of black hair. The eyes closed when he met them full on.

In the corridor Hawkins was wiping his forehead with a white handkerchief smelling of lavender.

"Not," he said, "a remarkably warm reception."

"What happens if the woman decides to have her baby before Port Augusta?"

"We've never had a baby born on the Indian-Pacific. Or a death."

"The woman looked near popping," Hartley said.

"Oh, natives do."

"Look, Hawkins. Native or not, this isn't a joke."

"Of course not. What would you suggest? Have you had any experience with this sort of thing?"

Hartley hesitated. "Well, yes," he said reluctantly. "Once I was a passenger on a Company ship. Going to Penang. A Malay girl was having a baby. The purser was supposed to have medical training but panicked. I did what I could. There was a Filipino nurse on board. Luckily, it ended all right." The incident was all the more painful to remember because his wife Jewel had died while having a baby, and the baby had died too.

Hawkins, sensing his distress, said, "Maybe there will be a doctor or a nurse in the tourist group. Don't worry, Mr. Rhys." He was knocking at another door.

A man's voice—deep, toneless—said, "Come in."

"Mr. Hall?"

Hall carefully inserted an evelope in the book he had been reading, and his place secured, looked uncuriously at the two visitors. He was a tall, lean man whose clipped hair and eyes were the color of his gray suit and tie. His left eye had a slight cast.

Hawkins introduced himself and Hartley.

"Mr. Rhys, are you with the railroad?"

"No, I'm making a transportation survey for an independent organization."

"And what is the organization?"

"SEAOTO, Southeast Asia and Oceania Transport Organization." And I hate every false word of it, Hartley thought.

"Indeed. And may I ask what you survey?"

"Rates of carriers, security, economic soundness."

"And the Australian Railways subscribe to this survey?"

"A mainstay in our work." Somebody stop this, Hartley thought, before I have to invent a constitution and by-laws. Hawkins elaborately was not meeting his eyes. And somebody, Hartley thought, give me an excuse to laugh, for this rather stony-faced, saturnine sheep breeder obviously doesn't believe a word I'm saying.

"What," Hall said, "would you estimate to be your yearly budget? And by whom paid?"

"Easy to ascertain. The treasurer of the organization is T. L. Farnsleigh of the Sword Shipping Line in Singapore."

"Oh, Mr. Farnsleigh."

"A talented young man," Hartley said. Now, he thought, we'll see who else is bluffing.

Hall shook his head. "A nephew, perhaps. The Farnsleigh I knew was a commander in the Royal Navy in World War II."

33

"Of course," Hartley said. He'd had and would have differences with Hawkins but would always be grateful for the Hawkins intervention.

"I believe you come from Kalgoorlie?" Hawkins said.

"Near there."

"In mining, then?"

Hall shook his head. "Sheep."

"You probably know Mr. Macrimmon?"

"Yes." The voice was expressionless, but Hartley thought the already narrow lips became narrower. He could not see the title of the book Hall had been reading, for it had been turned front down, but he made out a few words, including "sheepherding" in the text on the back of the dust jacket. Hall impressed him as a man accustomed to being alone.

"Tea, Mr. Hall?"

"Thank you." The words might have meant yes or no. However, Hawkins poured the tea, saying, "I came along here to tell you we are near the start of the Long Straight."

"It looks familiar."

Three words—and if irony lay behind them, Hartley could not detect it.

"I trust everything on board the Indian-Pacific is satisfactory, Mr. Hall," Hawkins said, "and that you're enjoying your trip."

Hall seemed to be considering the implied questions.

Let well enough alone, Hartley thought. But Hawkins pressed on, as if needing an answer.

"Have you traveled with us before, sir?"

Hall set down his teacup, looked at Hawkins, and

moved his head in a motion which might have been negative.

"Am I correct in understanding that you are related to Mr. Macrimmon?" Hawkins asked.

"Mr. Hawkins, are you, like Mr. Rhys, making a survey of some kind?"

Hawkins chuckled as if the intent of the curt question had been humorous. He gathered up the teacup and his tray, and at last moved toward the door. By the time he and Hartley had closed it behind them, Hall was already immersed in his book.

"Not exactly an outgoing type, what?" Hawkins asked. He refilled the teapot and the hot-water jug. "Aside from Mr. Hall, the other passengers in Car 1 are families with children. Except, of course, Ali Soto, whom we've seen."

"How did Mr. Hall happen to be billeted among the families?" Hartley wondered.

"Can't always understand the way the office books passengers. He doesn't exactly look like a family man. I have nothing to do with that, but the office does usually hold the spaces in Car 1 for the screamers, which is what we call the children."

In contrast to Ali's semi-hostility and Hall's frozen indifference, the other passengers whom they visited briefly in Car 1 responded with the immediate friendliness of most Australians, which Hartley found endearing. "Back to finish in your car now, shall we?"

The roomette next to Hartley's was empty, its occupant not yet listed in Hawkins's sheets. The next two, Hawkins announced with unction, though they too were empty, were the compartments allotted to

General Percy and his granddaughter. In Car 3 Lady Mary's roomette and that of Michael Dermot were also empty. Across the aisle was a double compartment whose occupants were laconically listed by Hawkins as "Malays."

What Hartley first noticed about Daoud, the student who opened the door at Hawkins's knock, was the harmonious proportioning of his features. Above the slight narrowing of temples the forehead was high, the cheekbones were more defined than those of most Malays, and the eyes were quickened by hazel lights in the dark irises.

Hawkins introduced Hartley to Daoud, and he in turn introduced Kasim, who lay in the lower berth.

"My friend is not well. His meals are sent here," Daoud said with an apologetic gesture toward a tray of empty dishes in front of the bathroom door.

"We have some medical supplies on board," Hawkins said. "If Kasim needs anything?"

"I believe he needs nothing, thank you."

Hawkins, obviously impressed by Daoud's urbane courtesy and his faultless English, offered tea, which was politely refused, and said, "If you aren't familiar with this route, you may be interested to know that we will soon be traveling through the Long Straight, where we will continue to be until 11:10 tonight."

"Thank you for telling us," Daoud said.

Hartley noticed a textbook on political science, in English, on the table in front of the window.

"Are you planning to continue your studies in Sydney?"

"Perhaps, although I may go back to the university

where I have been studying in Singapore."

"And Kasim?"

"He will accompany me, either staying in Sydney or returning to Singapore, where he will be starting his first year at the university."

"I hope he will recover soon." Looking at the dishes piled on the tray, Hartley thought that Kasim's illness could not be serious unless he had been suffering previously from undernourishment.

"If we can send him any special food—" Hawkins said.

"You are very kind. And yes—if he could receive chocolate bars, nuts, biscuits, milk—I do not mean to be too demanding. I think his hunger is part of his recovering."

"You shall have them," Hawkins promised. "Tea now?"

Daoud carried a cup to Kasim in the berth.

"We thank you," he said.

In the aisle when they had headed back toward Car 2, Hawkins said, "Remarkable. How well he spoke English."

"Part of an Arab heritage. There's an old Arab saying, 'The angels touched the brain of the Franks, the hands of the Chinese, and the tongues of the Arabs.'"

"Indeed," Hawkins said politely. "And now, Mr. Rhys, I'm afraid it's late for lunch. But you can still have whatever you'd like to order."

"No lunch after that mammoth breakfast. But I'll go along for coffee."

Before going to the club car, Hartley stopped in his room. He tilted open the narrow blades of the blinds at

37

the window and, leaning with an elbow on the table, watched the serene flow of green and shadow-dappled land under the gum trees.

In the well-filled club car, passengers at tables and the bar faced windows, as if watching for a demarcation that would show where the Indian-Pacific entered the Long Straight. Hartley remembered the massing of passengers on a ship about to cross the equator. Here perhaps the transition would be visible. He took the last free table, a small one near the rear vestibule. Not far from him Lady Mary sat with an elderly couple and a younger man, whose pleasant Scotch accents he had heard at breakfast. Merriam sat a few tables away with a pale old man and two young women. Were they the devilish French girls? Evidently the tour rules did not prevent fraternization in the company of another member of the group. Beyond Merriam's table, an almost skeletal man, well over six feet in height, white haired, with military bearing, sat beside a dark, pansy-faced girl. They were the General Percy of the list and his granddaughter, Hartley thought. The girl was listening with obvious delight to what the old man was telling her. At another table Hartley saw a boy he had met on the plane from Singapore. The boy, looking sullen and bored, sat opposite a somnolent prim-faced man with a tucked-in mouth. He must have been the Consular uncle, Hartley thought, whom Hawkins had honored with capital letters.

At a table near the bar the uncordial Ali poured a soft drink from a can. He was sharing a table but nothing else with two attractive young Australians and what Hawkins would have called a screamer.

The rear door opened and the beautiful dusky-haired girl whom Hartley had seen at breakfast entered the car. Lady Mary hailed her, but Lady Mary's table was full, as were all others except Hartley's. The girl looked through the car and took a few steps forward. She looked unselfconscious, poised, lonely, Hartley thought as he rose and said, "Would you use this seat? I am alone."

"Thank you, yes." She took the chair opposite him.

"May I order something for you—a drink, coffee?"

"Coffee, yes. Thank you. I wanted," she said, "to see the start of the Long Straight. I suppose I could have seen it from my roomette, but I didn't know exactly when it would start. Do you?"

"In a few minutes, according to my timetable. Take a last look at trees and bushes."

"They're practically melting away, on schedule," she said.

The waiter brought her a cup of coffee and refilled Hartley's cup. She concentrated on the scene from the window.

"It's like New Year's Eve—waiting for the ball to drop in Times Square."

"Except," Hartley said, "that you'll see no crowds here."

The Indian-Pacific was running through a dull, rust-colored plain whose horizon was almost invisible against a sky that looked flattened and seemed hardly brighter than the empty earth. In that emptiness nothing alive, vertical, or in motion signaled the train's movement. The effect was like the apparent motionless of a plane flying over a uniform floor of clouds.

"It's eerie," the girl said. "As if anything might happen where nothing *is* happening. Just waiting."

I hope nothing *does* happen, Hartley thought.

His companion turned her lovely face toward him. He saw that she looked tired, worried. At close range her eyes, which he had thought were black, were curiously irradiated with violet. The thistle-colored suit, the silver-set amethyst earrings, the amethyst ring on her right hand, caught light from somewhere—perhaps from those deep-set eyes—or was it an interaction? Her naturalness, her poise, made her oddly restful to be with, despite the potential excitement of her beauty.

They hadn't at first bothered to exchange any of the usual trivia of strangers. But now, as if honoring a convention, the girl said, "You are English—or American?"

"American. But I have lived in Singapore a long time. And you—you are American?"

"Yes. A student at Columbia University."

"A long time ahead of you, I went to Princeton," Hartley said.

"It couldn't have been so very long."

"Long enough."

"Long enough for what?" she asked, smiling.

Long enough, Hartley thought, for me not to think I could interest a beautiful young girl like you. He passed off her question with a smile, which he hoped relegated him to something like an uncle. At most, she could have been no more than twenty-two or twenty-three. He was thirty-one.

From questioning him, she turned toward the train's gliding through the Straight.

"It was always smooth," she said. "But now we seem to be slipping over ice."

"We'll be doing that until after eleven tonight. And my friend Mr. Hawkins tells me the Indian-Pacific loses only about four or five minutes in a year."

"Then you must be in Car 2 where I am."

"Roomette 1," Hartley said.

"My number is 3. There's something odd in that car. A kind of weird laughing. Have you heard it?"

"The kookaburra," Hartley said. "Maybe you saw at breakfast the old man with the bird on his shoulder?"

"Yes."

"The kookaburra laughs, though without real amusement. He's Macrimmon's pet—the old man in the wheelchair with the Abo pushing him."

"The sounds I heard didn't seem amused."

"Oh, well, I think the kookaburra is masochistic."

"I suppose animals are, especially domesticated ones. An acquired characteristic."

"Not necessarily. Could be an adaptation—an exchange of independence for security, and a kind of brutish affection."

"And the aboriginal servant?"

"Something different," Hartley said. "Real affection for the old man. Of course I could be wrong. But the old man is likable. Or maybe I'm going senile and liking too many people."

She laughed. "I doubt it very much. Senility doesn't set in until one is 60 or so. If ever. I don't believe it's inevitable."

She looked again through the window.

"Awfully the same. Plus ça change, plus c'est le même. But it doesn't change."

"And it won't," Hartley said.

She looked through the car. After the first excitement

at entering the Long Straight, the passengers had resumed their idling over drinks.

Lady Mary, whose table now held two empty places, was signaling.

"I must go."

"Now?"

"Yes, Lady Mary—" Some swift feeling swept over her face. "She seems to be, well, haunting me. Or do I imagine it? Does she really want to be kind, as if I minded being alone?"

"Do you?"

She considered the question. "No. But I could have wished—well, I will go."

"She won't always monopolize you. I'll want to know how you like the Long Straight. Couldn't you have a drink with me at five and tell me?"

"Yes. At five. My name is Darya Javenel."

Hartley hoped that his immediate alertness was not noticeable. The name Javenel was too familiar.

2

MISSION

Two days earlier, Friday morning, after three hours of sleep, Hartley had been wakened in his Singapore apartment by a telephone call from T. L. Farnsleigh, president of the Sword Line, for which he worked as investigator and troubleshooter.

"Yes, Mr. Farnsleigh. I'll be in your office at eleven."

While water for tea was heating, Hartley looked through his windows at the blue arabesques of the harbor that merged with the golden-green of trees, the magenta masses of bougainvillea, the citron Chinese temple half-hidden by palms, and the more distant blue-grey dome and minaret of a mosque. Underfoot the russet and gray hemp mats were still cool, but the wooden slatted blinds, when he drew them closed, were already hot from the well-risen equatorial sun.

Under a flowering ilang ilang tree in the garden below his windows, a Chinese boy and his little sister were teaching two gray kittens to jump over their small hands. Hartley called good morning to them, and they threw him kisses. The little girl held up one kitten and made it sketch a flying kiss.

What a morning it would be, he thought, to watch the light deepen over the Singapore hills, to imagine that he could feel the vibrations of the ships entering the harbor, to assimilate the rhythms of this whole marvelous mingling of light and color and motion that was Singapore. And to sleep. He had spent most of the night at the Sword Line piers in quest of cargo pilferers.

Hartley's apartment, in a Chinese residential area, was smaller than the home he had left after the death of his beautiful half-Malay, half-English wife, Jewel, three years ago. This morning it would have been good to stay here for a slow breakfast, for a game with his young Chinese neighbors and later, drinks with their parents.

Hartley thought that he could get used to living somewhere else in the world, but he doubted it. Singapore was his city, discovered during a vacation from the Viet Nam War, and immediately seized on as the place he would come back to. That had happened even before he knew Jewel and had spent the two treasured years with her as his wife.

At eleven he entered the Farnsleigh office and as always was amused at its hybrid furnishings: the massive dark desk and bookcases and cabinets, the steel engravings of English scenes brought halfway around the world from a Victorian London by the founders of the Sword Line, the mats on the tiled floors, the revolving fan on the ceiling, and the wicker chairs. Farnsleigh himself was one of the few men in Singapore who had not adopted shorts or slacks and open-necked shirts. He wore starched linen suits with a collar and tie. With his stern face, steel-colored hair, and sideburns and mustache, he looked rather like a martinet, but was not. He was dedicated to ships and seas, and after the Japanese occupation of Singapore and his own service as a commander in the Royal Navy, he had laboriously revived the war-ruined shipping company.

"Good morning, Hartley. Tea? Coffee?"

"Thank you, sir. Coffee."

"You're looking fit." Farnsleigh pressed a button twice. Tea would have come after one ring.

"Yes. With some luck. I'll have a report to make shortly."

As usual they waited to talk until a secretary had served coffee and biscuits.

"You got back from Penang last night? I found the message you called in to our night people."

"I'll have a report to give you today. No evidence of a large or well-organized ring of pilferers and smugglers. But enough for you to proceed with arresting two or three leaders. Hindus. Although the physically active role is not customary for them."

Farnsleigh took several slow sips of coffee, broke a raisin biscuit, and studied it. "Maybe we are developing a new strain of Hindu," he said. "After all, they can't always ignore the example of the energetic Chinese and the inventive Malays."

In Farnsleigh's half-hearted digressions, Hartley recognized an unwillingness to broach the matter on which he had been called to the office.

But he did not have long to wait.

"Have you seen the newspaper or heard the radio

news this morning?" Farnsleigh asked. "No? Then I'll have to be the one to tell you—about Welles. You know he was in charge of the search for our missing junk the *Cutlass* for almost three months?"

"Yes," Hartley said apprehensively. "*Was*, you say?"

"Was. Around four this morning the police found his body in an alley near the main harbor. He had been strangled."

"God—no!"

Welles had been his friend.

"Aisha knows?"

Farnsleigh nodded. "I telephoned her, then went to see her."

"Do you know how it happened?"

"Not yet. We are trying. The alley was near a cantina at the waterfront. Mostly used by Malay seamen."

"You've called in the police?"

"Yes." Farnsleigh got up and brought from a cabinet a bottle of cognac and a liqueur glass, which he filled for Hartley.

"We think Welles may have been going to meet an informant at the cantina."

"Had Welles been at home? Did Aisha know anything about his movements?"

"I have never—" Farnsleigh, still holding the bottle of cognac, paused, went back to the cabinet to bring another glass and fill it for himself. "I have never enjoyed anything less than questioning that girl at five this morning. Nobody could have done better than she did. Wiped out, Hartley. Crushed. You can imagine."

I can imagine, Hartley thought. And if you just hint that you are surprised that the Eurasian mistress of one of your employees could be ravaged by the murder of her lover but still stand up to interrogation, by God, I'll throw this cognac into your plump, pink-pork face.

Farnsleigh, tasting his cognac, nodded. Hartley uncomfortably felt that Farnsleigh knew what he was thinking.

"Aisha had just returned to the apartment. After the dancing performance at the Hilton roof restaurant, she goes on to a night club, as you know. I don't know whether that made it any better than if she'd been waked up. Anyway, she still wore a bird costume of crimson and gold. And the Chinese maid was bringing her some breakfast."

"Could she tell you anything about Welles?"

"He had telephoned her yesterday afternoon. He said he probably couldn't come home. Had to meet somebody. Then he called again. The maid took the message around 3:30 A.M. He said he was flying to Australia tonight. Taking a train from Perth tomorrow."

"And so?"

"And so, Hartley, you will fly to Perth tonight and tomorrow take the Indian-Pacific train to Sydney. You will take over Welles's assignment in search of the *Cutlass.*"

Hartley nodded, resigned to what he had foreseen from the moment Farnsleigh had told him of Welles's death.

"I'll need to be briefed."

"You shall be. And let me say that I strongly considered assigning you the Cutlass search at the outset. You are our most valued investigator in all respects but one."

Hartley knew what was coming. His superior was not given to commendations. Even now, when trying to smooth Hartley's acceptance of a so-far failed mission, Farnsleigh would have to qualify his praise.

"The one weakness in your performance is that you are reluctant to meet violence with violence, despite all your experience in United States Naval Intelligence. The Cutlass case looked as though it might develop violent aspects."

"I am not," Hartley said, "a hired killer."

"Hardly." Farnsleigh stroked a smile under his steel-gray mustache.

"Not," Hartley added, "that Welles was, either."

"No. Merely—shall we say faster to draw?"

Say whatever you like, Hartley thought.

"Well, as to the briefing." Farnsleigh drew four different-colored folders toward him. "We have here reports from Welles. Up to yesterday. Nothing about last night's meeting. The police reports of their findings are in this green folder. Welles's reports are in the yellow folder. With background. The *Cutlass* was bound for Penang when she disappeared.

"She never got there. Four days after she was due at Penang—you know this, I think—the whole complement except the second mate and one steward were found adrift in a boat in the Riau Islands. Nothing to tell. The *Cutlass* was boarded at night. Masked men. They drugged the officers and crew on the *Cutlass*. Welles, with help, combed through the Riaus. Snaked around other islands where some kind of pot might be boiling. Even went to Bulan—that's where Sir Ian Richland holds out. By the way, we had a kind of reunion here last week—those of us who had served in these parts. Old Ian—mostly intelligence jobs—and Owen Percy—you've heard of him?"

"Who hasn't?" Hartley said. "General Percy of Malaya fame. He was here?"

"Yes. Taking a trip with his granddaughter and several others. Seemed a good idea to get together. Old Ian had given Welles a real bash on Bulan, a little island over near Borneo. Sound fellow, old Ian. Got fond of this part of the world and didn't go back to Britain after the war."

Hartley remembered, from Conrad's *Lord Jim*, a characterization of the young officer who was to have such a tragic destiny: "He was one of us." Not, he thought, that there was any resemblance between Sir Ian and the anticlimactic and ill-fated Jim.

"I'll need," he said, "a listing of ports visited by the *Cultass* before her last voyage."

"All here." Farnsleigh tapped a blue folder. "Also all cargo manifests. You won't find much that's helpful there. Routine general cargo to the islands. The *Cutlass* was making short trips before she went out on long ones. As you know, she was our newest and biggest junk. Named after an earlier *Cutlass* that burned. Some superstitious talk circulated: bad luck to name a new vessel after one that came to a bad end. Can't think anybody would have wanted to prove the superstition. No. But with such a routine cargo, why would the ship have disappeared? No storm. Pirates. Not anymore."

"Pirates," Hartley said. "That reminds me—the second mate on the *Cutlass* was Sammy Javenel, right?"

"Yes. And he and a steward disappeared."

"Javenal had a run-in with pirates on another ship. Beat them off."

"Pirates," Farnsleigh said scornfully. "Not in this age. Maybe some Indonesian foray. Yes, I grant you, Javenel came through. Well, you'll find personnel records covering him and all other officers and crew on the *Cutlass*." He tapped a red folder.

"I suppose," Hartley said, "Javenel is under suspicion along with the missing steward. Anything helpful from the captain or other men from the *Cutlass*?"

"There's a summary of their interrogations in this red folder. The captain stated that he'd had no trouble with Javenel. Didn't like him—thought that the boy felt superior. But no trouble."

"And the steward? Had he and Javenel been close?"

"Only insofar as Javenel had a waspish way of taking up with underdogs. The steward was a one-eyed Malay. Nose ran constantly, the captain said."

"His nose—" Hartley laughed.

"Yes, well, at table and all. Wasn't endearing. Nor was the missing eye."

"Then why was he signed on?"

"One of those times—men hard to get. This man with the nose had satisfactory recommendations—he'd worked for the owner of a fishing fleet in Malaysia. His home address was in Kuala Lumpur. We investigated. No one living at the address. One neighbor thought he remembered him. And a boy ran up and said, 'You mean the man with one eye?' So the Malay hadn't lost an eye fighting guerrillas. The boy said the steward had stolen his—the boy's—uncle's wife and the uncle had taken a fish-scaling knife and gouged out the eye."

"God," Hartley said. "What ramifications. But back to Sammy Javenel. No trace of him here?"

"No. His quarters were searched. We couldn't turn up friends. You, Hartley, probably were the best friend he had."

"I hope he had better ones. I wasn't exactly his friend. There was something about him—some drive, enthusiasm, some promise of unusual achievement. He had a real feeling for navigation. You remember the time he cleared that reef? A minute later the tide would have been too low and he'd have grounded, but he got to the island and the cargo of copra before the Indonesians."

"We don't encourage that kind of competition," Farnsleigh said grayly.

The hell you don't, Hartley thought, maybe not overtly. All right, he thought, let's get on with it. Farnsleigh will bring up the matter of the employees' fund. And Farnsleigh did.

"As I remember, you bailed out Sammy Javenel, repaid the money missing from the employees' fund. You must have believed his story."

"I did. There was a stevedore crushed under a fallen boom and Sammy got him to a hospital. Took three hundred dollars from the fund."

"You might be interested to know," Farnsleigh said, "that we can't find any record of the accident or of the admittance of the stevedore to a hospital."

Hartley shrugged. "The stevedore was a Hindu. Difficult name."

He lighted a cigarette.

"In the red folder on personnel," he said, "I suppose I'll find records concerning Javenel's hiring."

Farnsleigh nodded. "You'll find—perhaps you already know this—that his uncle is a friend of mine. An archaeologist. Under cover of some digs, he helped us substantially during the Malaysian action. About two years ago he wrote, asking me whether I could give

Sammy a post here. Lines weren't hard to read between. He'd had problems with the boy, whose parents were dead. But Sammy had rather creditably completed his training at a Merchant Marine Academy and come out with a third mate's license. Had some sort of fixation about the Far East. So I took the boy on. Before long we moved him up to second mate—needed one. Very presentable boy. Took to Singapore as if he'd been starved for it. Odd thing. Sometimes I thought he should have been an engineer. Had an addiction to machines. Bought a boat. Rebuilt it."

"Has his boat been found?" Hartley asked.

"Yes. At the dock where he kept it. He had no record of dubious associates. No troubles with women, drink, drugs. But I felt he had a wild streak."

"Yes, I felt that," Hartley said. "But nothing that seemed to involve money. Once I suggested we have a drink. He said no. He was out of funds, as usual. And he laughed. All he wanted to talk about then was something to do with a ship's engine. He was off base, of course, even if his idea was good. He did say his uncle was going to give him a goodish sum of money if he kept a job for—I forget. Two or three years."

"Did he ever mention a sister?"

"Not that I remember."

"Well, a girl who said she was his sister turned up here last week. Claimed to be looking for him. He hadn't been heard from for months, she said."

"Claimed—you didn't believe her?" Hartley asked.

"Well, I can't imagine sending a young girl halfway around the world alone to look for a brother. No friend of mine would do that."

"Did she establish her identity?"

"Oh, she had a passport. Talked with reasonable familiarity about the uncle."

"Did you get in touch with the uncle?"

"I've written to him. No answer yet."

"Tell me about the girl."

Farnsleigh refilled the cognac glasses.

"Cool as they come. Eyeshadow. Green."

Hartley checked a smile. He knew Farnsleigh's disapproval of maquillage, but only for those whom he would have classed as "nice" girls, or "ladies." For others, Hartley had gone out often enough with Farnsleigh in groups to know that the stricture did not hold for dancers or actresses. The more vivid the enamelings and shadings, the more appreciative Farnsleigh had shown himself. He had whole-heartedly admired Aisha and had never criticized what he must have considered the "irregularity" of Welles's relationship with the lovely Malaysian dancer.

"If this girl wasn't Sammy's sister," Hartley said, "what did you think she was doing here?"

"She might have been an accomplice. Trying to find out what *we* were finding out. We talked an hour or two. The girl seemed to think I wasn't being candid with her."

"Were you?" Hartley asked.

"No."

"Did the girl meet Welles?"

"No. I wouldn't have agreed to such a meeting, even if Welles had been in Singapore. Which reminds me—on this trip you are to be a representative of a mythical transportation association making a survey. The chief conductor on the Indian-Pacific train knows about you—Hawkins is his name. No one else is to know what your mission is, but it's all right, if pressed, to say that you have a connection with our company."

"But what about the girl? Sammy's supposed sister?"

"We had her followed. She was staying at the Hilton. No discovered connections. Made one trip—sightseeing coach to Johore. Left Singapore—two—three days ago. Flew to Perth. No traceable reservations from there."

"Her actions seem harmless enough," Hartley said.

"Yes. By now let's hope she is on her way back to New York. If that's where she came from."

Farnsleigh aligned the four folders and placed them in a large manila envelope.

"You can mail this back to me tomorrow from Perth. We've engaged a day room for you at the Parmelia Hotel, since the Indian-Pacific doesn't leave until nine tomorrow night. You'll have to confirm your train reservation and pick up your ticket."

"There's nothing more you can tell me about why Welles was going to take that train?"

"Nothing. But he must have learned something, probably from a first meeting with the informant."

"Any idea what happened to the informant?"

"A Malay was found murdered near Welles. Unidentifiable because of face and head injuries."

"Well, I'll go along—must write my report on the cargo-theft job."

"Dictate it to my secretary. She will give you your plane ticket, and the cashier has a check for you for expenses. If you go as far as Sydney, you can draw more money from our office there."

"If the train goes to Sydney," Hartley said, rising, "I should get there too."

"Logical," Farnsleigh said. "And in your role as transportation investigator, try to overcome your lukewarm feeling about trains. I realize you are an out-and-out shipman, luckily for us." He stood up and shook Hartley's hand.

By the time Hartley had dictated his report and picked up plane ticket and expense check, it was almost five o'clock. He wrote and mailed a note to his faultless Chinese housekeeper, of whom he had been deprived for almost two weeks while she cared for a sick daughter. He considered his accumulating problems of laundering and dry cleaning, and decided that he would have to buy clothing in Perth tomorrow. He sent, then, two dozen white roses to Aisha. They were her favorites.

It was early for a drink, but he went to the Hilton where, at his usual table midway along the green-toned cool cocktail lounge, whose walls were hung with British hunting scenes, his favorite waitress brought him Scotch. A tiny pixie of a girl, she looked no more than fourteen; but he knew that she had four thriving children and a husband on the Singapore police force.

"Oh, Mr. Rhys," she said, setting down a bowl of macadamia nuts, "I am so sorry about Mr. Welles. About that poor Aisha—oh, too bad."

"Yes," Hartley said.

"And so sorry for you—you were his friend. My husband is sorry too. He was there—at the harbor where they found poor Mr. Welles."

Hartley looked keenly at her.

"Were there indications that anybody else had been with him, perhaps killed with him?"

"Yes. My husband thinks someone else had been

with him. The bloodstains, they are being checked. And there was a Malayan dagger—my husband found it out almost where the tide would have reached it."

She left him to answer a call to another table. On her return, she brought another drink, and to divert him, said, "Over there, by the wall, there is Sir Ian Richland. Perhaps you know him?"

"No," Hartley said. He followed the direction of her gesture and saw Sir Ian's jovial, ageless face—fair, scarcely tanned, the neat, medium-long cropped grayish hair clearing by inches the collar of his shirt which somehow suggested a military tunic. Opposite him, at the banquette, Hartley recognized the Chinese owner of a large provisioning firm from whom Hartley's company bought supplies. Even if he had tried to hear what they were saying, Hartley was too far from them, but he did notice the curious little ticking cough which punctuated every few statements that Sir Ian made.

He recalled hearing someone compare Sir Ian with the White Rajah Brooke of Brunei.

"No more, thank you," he said to the waitress, who was offering to refill his glass.

"Would you like to meet Sir Ian?"

"Well—how?"

"Oh very easily. On your way to the door, I will follow with a tray—between us the drinks will be spilled—and you, covering my awkwardness, will offer to replace the drinks. Yes?" Her eyes gleamed conspiratorially.

He laughed, and for the first time in long hours felt warmth in his heart. But he declined the offer and left the lounge.

Now, at six, the punctual equatorial dusk was dimming Singapore's day brilliance. In a half hour the jeweled sky would dome over the nearer constellations of lights on the harbored ships and the leaf-softened glalaxies of color in the streets.

He had almost reached his parked car when he heard a small, moaning exclamation and saw a Chinese boy of five or six bending over a broken and dropped bag of groceries.

"Wait a minute." He returned to the cocktail lounge and from his waitress brought back a new bag, which he helped the child repack.

"But the milk—the eggs—gone!" the boy mourned.

"Never mind." Hartley put some bills into the pocket of the boy's shirt. "You take this new bag home. Then you can come out again to buy eggs and milk? And buy something for yourself."

The child laid his cheek against Hartley's hand.

Three hours later Hartley watched the gemlike lights of Singapore fall and fade and disappear as the plane swept over the Straits and across the Indian Ocean on the flight to Perth. And in Perth he would travel even farther, three thousand miles, in a pursuit based on the tenuous legacy of a dead man.

Around three the Chinese stewardess bent over Hartley, who sat next to the window. The aisle seat was not occupied.

"You are not sleeping, sir."

"Hardly ever on planes." He had been studying the contents of the colored folders.

"Would you like coffee? Rolls?"

"Coffee—yes, please. I could use several cups."

She brought a pot of coffee with cream and sugar,

placing the cup and bowl and pitcher so quietly on the shelf-table of the aisle seat that Hartley was not interrupted as he neared the end of the red folder. When she returned with a fresh pot of coffee, Hartley looked up and said, "I don't know what your rules are, but could I buy you a drink?"

"No, thank you, sir. If I had a drink I would fall hopelessly asleep, but soon I must be ready to serve breakfast."

A few minutes later Hartley was aware of someone moving in the aisle and thought it was the stewardess, but looked up to see an agreeable-looking boy of perhaps twenty, whom he had noticed in an aisle seat two rows forward.

"I beg pardon, sir—didn't mean to interrupt you. But would you mind if I sat here beside you just long enough to have a drink?" He gestured toward an elderly man, whose face, half-turned toward the window, held an expression suggesting an unsavory dream. "He's my uncle, and if I start a drink over there next to him, he'll wake up and go into a flap."

"Sit down," Hartley said, ringing for the stewardess. "What will you have?"

"Oh, not from you, sir. Let me buy *you* a drink."

"No, thanks. Must do some more reading. But you're more than welcome to sit here."

The stewardess returned with the boy's ordered Scotch, acknowledged his approving smile with one of her own, and went back to her post.

"Name's Armitage, Tommy," the boy said. Hartley introduced himself.

"Very kind of you, Mr. Rhys. Long night, yes?"

"Especially if you don't go in for sleeping in planes."

"Don't stop your reading, Mr. Rhys."

"Oh, I need a break. Almost finished anyway. You been traveling far, Tommy?"

"From Kuala Lumpur right now. My uncle is consul there. I came out for the long holiday—I'm reading at Christchurch, Oxford. Malaysia's all right. But as soon as I get something interesting going, like this trip, the old man pulls me away. Three days on a train to Sydney. God. We could fly in a few hours."

"Why does your uncle want to go by train?"

"He has some kind of hallucination about getting information on foreign countries, not that Australia's really foreign. I think the old boy's a bit of a masochist. And you, sir, you're American?"

"Yes, but living in Singapore for years."

"What kind of city is Singapore?"

"The greatest. But don't start me on the subject of Singapore. Order another Scotch when you want to."

"Sure you won't have one?"

"Thanks, no."

"You staying on in Perth?"

"No. As a matter of fact, I'm taking that three-day Indian-Pacific train trip."

"Well, I'll be damned! So civilized people do—I don't mean my old boy isn't civilized."

"Does he have any interest in shipping?"

"No."

"Any warm relations with Malaysians?"

Tommy laughed. "Warm relations? Not with anybody, I'd say, except Kit, an old white bulldog, short for Kitchener. The old man does his job competently.

59

Soul of conscientiousness. May I ask, sir, why are you taking this Indian-Pacific train?"

"I'm with a transportation survey group," Hartley said. Foolish-sounding cover, he thought. No wonder the boy shot Hartley a quick and rather searching glance.

Lowering the glass, Tommy said, "I'd have thought you were onto something more, well, active. Can't tell, right?"

"Can't tell," Hartley agreed.

Two hours later Hartley had finished his study of the contents of the folders, Tommy had returned to his seat, and the bleak gray line of the West Australian coast ahead of the plane was beginning to liven in still scant washes of opalescent rose and aquamarine. Opals, Hartley thought. He had intended to give his wife opals from Australia—and other gifts, now forever ungiven. Not much help in remembering what he *had* given her. Thank heaven he had found jade that she delighted in.

The stewardess, her face freshened with pleasingly eloquent makeup, was beside him. "We're going to be late, sir. Gale winds over Perth. Would you like tea now? And then breakfast?"

"Thank you, yes. Very late?"

"Perhaps an hour."

Hartley sealed the envelope that enclosed the colored folders.

He had brought no hand baggage, so he could not shave. The face that he looked at in the lavatory mirror was not prepossessing. Somewhere, he thought, other passengers bound for the Indian-Pacific, shaved or unshaved, would be waking. With what purpose would they be facing this new day, the upcoming night's start of the train's journey?

Once he arrived at the airport of the windy, sunlit city of Perth, he mailed the thick envelope to Farnsleigh and then took a cab to the Parmelia Hotel. A call brought no answer from Hawkins, the senior conductor on the Indian-Pacific. The Australian Railways Company warded him off—no use to try to see the train. It was being readied for its next trip. Yes, if he insisted, he could go on board and look over the train when he picked up his ticket at eight or so tonight.

His transportation survey story went down, but not easily. In the end he had to use the Sword Line as a sponsor. They gave him no help with a passenger list.

Now, temporarily halted, he would at least have time for a shave, a haircut, and the purchase of clothing to replace the accumulations of his laundry at his apartment in the absence of his housekeeper. He went through these errands and found that he needed a new suitcase to house the new clothes, for which, he thought, Farnsleigh ought not to boggle in paying.

The long, curiously narrow-looking line of the Indian-Pacific's silvery coaches, with lighted windows and the scarlet locomotive at the head, impressed him with its restrained and straining immobility.

He saw with satisfaction that station guards were on duty at all vestibules. Whatever message Farnsleigh had sent to the chief conductor would, Hartley thought, have ensured a thorough search for a possible if not highly improbable bomb.

At the ticket office when he picked up his ticket, he had inquired about Hawkins and had learned that the chief conductor had his office in Car 2, the car in which Hartley's roomette was located. Now on the platform at the entrance to Car 2, Hartley saw what he thought of as a kind of father-figure, a sturdy middle-aged man, broad-shouldered, faultlessly uniformed, holding himself with important erectness.

He gripped Hartley's hand and greeted him warmly. "You are welcome on board the Indian-Pacific, Mr. Rhys. I will show you to your room. Here at the end of the car," He said as they entered Car 2, "is my office, and next to it the compartment I use. Yours is directly opposite."

"Very comfortable," Hartley said. "Walkway even after the bed is lowered, yes?"

"Yes. And this cabinet houses all lavatory facilities."

On the top of the cabinet, between glasses and racks of towels, Hartley saw a thermos jug and a tray of mangos, oranges, and bananas.

"I don't know what your favorite drink is," Hawkins said, "but I have Scotch and gin in my office, and of course the means of producing tea and coffee. The thermos jug is full of ice. As a shipping man, you must be used to such amenities. But I trust the Indian-Pacific will serve as ship away from ships." He closed the door of the compartment and said, "I received the confidential message from the president of your company and have acted on it to insure security."

"Very good," Hartley said. "I'll appreciate your giving me a passenger list, if you have one."

"I will compile one, as best I can," Hawkins said. "I can't give you much tonight, but will try to produce something tomorrow, when the tickets are all in."

"You're probably busy," Hartley said. "I needn't keep you. But I would like to wander through the train to get the geography clear."

"By all means." Hawkins hesitated, then added, "From the message I am not clear as to what you are looking for."

"Neither are we," Hartley said. "We have had only an indefinite lead, a suggestion that someone on board the Indian-Pacific may be connected with our loss of a ship."

"Dear me," Hawkins said. "It doesn't seem likely, now, does it?"

"No," Hartley said. "And I appreciate your help—all the more in such a vague cause."

On the platform a passenger was being paged.

"Excuse me, sir, there is a page for Lady Mary." Hawkins spoke with unction. Hartley followed to the vestibule and saw him steering a messenger toward a tall, striding woman from a rear car, a tawny-haired woman in a chestnut-colored pantsuit and boots. Moving aft, Hartley reached Car 3 in time to see the woman enter a roomette and to hear her speaking—in Australian not British accents—to someone inside.

A few passengers had moved into Car 3. Cars 4 and 5, at the rear, were still empty. A placard at each of the rear vestibule doors announced that these cars would be occupied by members of the New Horizon tour group.

Hartley wandered forward through Cars 3, 2, and 1, in which aisles were crowded with arriving passengers, porters, and baggage. Beyond Car 1 in the club car, a few early arrivals sat with glasses at tables. The dining car, farther forward, was dimly lighted.

He had returned to his roomette by the time the Indian-Pacific, released from immobility, glided past the illuminated platform into the night beyond.

3

THE KOOKABURRA

Was Darya Javenel the sister or the wife of Sammy
Javenel? Was she a possible accomplice, as Farnsleigh
had suspected?

He watched her moving toward Lady Mary's table in
the club car. For the first time since he had left
Singapore, he felt a tightening of nerve and muscle.
Despite all his doubts and misgivings, this journey on
board the Indian-Pacific was to be connected with the
search for the missing junk.

When he met Darya at five, the questions that he
would put to her would be more searching than the
casual, acquaintance-forming conversation between
two strangers. Purposely he had not given her his name,
for there was a chance that Sammy might have
mentioned it. Lady Mary, however, knew his name and
might have told her. The anticipation of seeing her
again was gone; he would have to interrogate her—one

of the least savory parts of his job. And if Darya were the cool, self-sufficient partner in a scheme of Sammy's, she might recognize the techniques of interrogation, no matter with what long-experienced skill he used them.

He paid for the coffees and was about to leave when, looking up, he met the eyes of Hall, the owner of sheep, who was passing on his way to the rear vestibule of the club car.

"Hello, Mr. Hall. Sit down and have a drink?"

"Well." That word only. But the curtailed answer might have been due to Lady Mary's approach from her table, now occupied by Darya, the dark Dermot, and a comfortable-looking, oldish Australian woman. Somebody, then, Hartley thought, had time to be comfortable.

"Bill Hall," Lady Mary said. "Can we sit here, Mr. Rhys?" She did not wait for an answer. A waiter brought another chair, in which Hall seated himself warily, as if he thought it might throw him. If Hartley had been traveling as a tourist unencumbered with the responsibilities of his mission, he would gladly have left them to talk in private. As it was, he could not go, unless they demanded his leaving, which did not seem likely. Lady Mary, leaning forward with her elbows on the table, was rather fiercely scanning Hall's indifferent, half-averted face.

"Bill. You and I have never had any trouble."

"Or anything untroubled," Hall said.

"Oh shut up," she said. "All right, I won't bring up Angus the collie. We shared him—or other things—animals mostly."

"Please don't," Hall said. "It's too late."

"It's not too late to establish some kind of—"

66

Hall interrupted. "It's too late for any kind of—whatever you had in mind. I have nothing to talk about with you, Mary."

"But I have—with you. The opals."

Hall shook his head. "You'll have your father's story. That the opals were given as part payment for the loan. My father and I understood they were collateral. The loan has now been repaid in full, without considering the opals. My father hasn't much longer to live. The opals—well, let's say he was fond of them, apart from their value. The repayment didn't include the opals. At present appraisals, their value would be about twice the amount of the whole loan. Over a quarter of a million dollars."

Lady Mary groped for something to hold. Hartley signaled the waiter to bring coffee.

"I know they're enormously valuable," she said.

"But," Hall said, "I'll repeat: their value for my father has little or nothing to do with their market value."

"My father wants to give me the opals. I don't have them. He's keeping them for me."

"They'd be a tidy help in some of your husband's schemes," the cousin said caustically. "He could buy another island."

Lady Mary bristled.

"He has enough islands."

"I thought he was insatiable about islands."

"Leave him out of this." Aggressiveness and hostility had replaced the calm with which she had started the talk with her cousin.

"Why do you have to be so bloody difficult to talk to?" she demanded. Hall, looking through the window at the Long Straight, ignored her question and said as if to himself, "Amazing. Not a twig to make a shadow."

"Who gives a damn about a shadow!" Mary cried angrily.

God, Hartley thought, I wish they'd get this over with.

"All I wanted to do when I flagged you down here," Mary said, "was to talk about returning the opals to you."

"At what cost to me?" Hall said, still looking through the window. "What do you want?"

"Damn you, Hall—I don't want anything except no trouble for my father!"

"A new stance, Mary. You've obviously built up an exaggerated idea of my capacity for making trouble."

"I don't think so—not when it's for your father. I could—"

"Don't tell me what you'd spare *your* father," Hall said.

Hartley couldn't help feeling sorry for Lady Mary, although he had never expected to.

The door from the vestibule opened. The Abo wheeled Macrimmon into the car. The kookaburra sat on the shoulder of what Hartley recognized as a clean jacket. Lady Mary's doing? Oh, don't stop here, he prayed. Not at this table. The Abo pushed on to a table recently vacated, seated Macrimmon, and bore away the folded wheelchair.

Macrimmon beat on the arm handle of his chair with a spoon from the table. "A drink for everybody!" he cried. "We're in the Long Straight. Who'll be first?" He glanced through the car and raised a hand to salute his daughter, who looked at him with a fierce look in her eyes. He also looked at Hall and grimaced. He recognized Hartley with a pointing of his pipe and a grin, which showed yellowish fangs.

All we need, Hartley thought, is for the old boy to tangle in this talk. But the old boy did not tangle, because Hall, without a word, stood and walked toward the rear vestibule.

Mary pounded a fist on the table. Hall's untasted coffee spilled, filling the saucer and pooling on the tiled surface of the table. The imperceptible motion of the train kept the spilled coffee to a neat circle.

"You can't win them all," Hartley said.

Lady Mary looked at him with hatred, got up, and stalked out of the car. Her booted feet ground on the aisle as if she were treading on tarantulas.

Hartley paid for the coffees and went to his roomette. Not so hard now, he thought, to resist a nap. He could even ignore the eardrum battering of the taped melodies. The train's motion, always even but with occasional quirks caused by rises and curves, had become a glassy gliding. He thought of Darya, whose name did not appear on Hawkins's incomplete lists, and of the other passengers whom he had met. On his mind anxiously was the pregnant wife of Ali. He went back to Car 1 and rapped at Ali's door. No answer. Perhaps Ali was still in the club car. The woman would not be opening the door. But he called: "Mrs. Soto, are you all right?"

A faint grudging answer sounded: "Yes. Please go away."

All right now, but for how long? And what would Farnsleigh say if Hartley had to report helping to deliver one Malaysian baby? At least Farnsleigh would not have to approve the payment of any costs for delivery. He would merely drill into Hartley, at the next conference, that his duties did not include midwifery.

In his room again, Hartley shaved for the second time since early morning and looked with displeasure at his face, which was grim and gaunt. It didn't even look particularly honest, and probably wasn't. It was easier to look honest after you've had at least half enough sleep, he thought. Not that sleep seemed important now, when he was beginning to feel hunger pangs, the small gnawings that foreran the coming to grips with action in an assignment.

He dressed in dark blue slacks and the navy blue blazer which he had bought expensively in Perth. He inserted securely his revolver in the belt of his slacks, and put the derringer, which he carried as a spare arm, in his jacket pocket. Good thing, he thought, I don't rattle when I walk.

It was still too early to meet Darya, but he wanted to escape the limited space of the roomette. Ahead of him in the aisle were the two attractive women who had been at a table with Merriam in the club car. He was still holding open the vestibule door between Cars 2 and 1, when one of them, a gold- and silver-dusted blonde, said, "Monsieur, would you join my sister Laure and me for a drink?"

The sister nodded, smiling. She was darker, perhaps younger, though he could not tell. She said, "What a handsome jacket, monsieur. N'est-ce-pas, Thérèse?"

"Véritablement," Thérèe said.

Who, Hartley thought, could have helped feeling set up by such appreciation from two charming women? Farnsleigh? Maybe so. They wore heavy eye shadow.

"I have a business engagement at five," he said, "but

nothing until then."

Thérèse pressed her fingers against her ears. "Quel bruit affreux!"

"Yes," Hartley agreed. "The so-called music makes it hard to concentrate."

"To concentrate—no matter, that—but for other pursuits—"

"Tais-toi, chérie," Laure said.

The club car was half-empty. Siestas being taken, Hartley thought. Australian mothers doing a bit of laundry. Conductors and stewards having a brief rest.

"And now," Thérèse said, when they were seated and Hartley had ordered wine for the sisters and Scotch for himself, "we will tell you that we are going to *use* you."

"How?"

"You see, we have a problem. Monsieur Merriam—is he shy? Or do the rules of his employment force him to be monastic?"

"Probably the rules," Hartley said. "Deplorable," he added, laughing.

In French, Thérèse said to her sister, "It may be that the one who helps us, helps more than we foresee."

"So," Hartley said, "you think Merriam needs a male chaperone to encourage him?"

"Admirable!" Laure exclaimed. "Oh, but there are more serious things to address ourselves to. It is a good train and comfortable, and there is good scenery. But a strange train. We see you—you move—not as a traveler who rests."

"Perhaps it's my restless face, which I can't help," Hartley said.

The sisters laughed.

"A charming face," Thérèse said warmly. "No. We think you have more than kangaroos and miles to cover. We would like to help you."

"I'll remember that," Hartley said. "What is strange about the train?"

"Next to our room in Car 3," Laure said, "there are Malays. We like Malays. Ordinarily they like us." Parenthetically to her sister she murmured, "You remember Jogjakarta?"

Thérèse laughed tunefully.

"But these Malays," Laure continued, "are *atroces*! One is ill, perhaps, though enormous trays of food go to that room. When he comes out, he does not look ill, not even from overeating. You see, we are accustomed to living where much happens. So we keep open our door, watch for diversion."

"And for Monsieur Merriam," Thérèse added.

"So you watch. And the Malays are grim. Maybe they're naturally grim Malays," Hartley said. "What else?"

"People come to their room. The one we call the Amazon—we expect her to carry a whip."

"Lady Mary?" Hartley asked.

"Yes. And another. When we were children, we lived in a French colony in Africa. We saw fighting. We came to recognize mercenaries."

"How do you recognize a mercenary?" Hartley asked.

"By his feet and his eyes," Thérèse said. "The feet are dirty; the eyes do not look at you. And of course the hand, ready to draw a revolver from a belt or a holster."

Hartley nodded. "I have seen your mercenary," he said.

Over the rim of her wineglass, Thérèse, unsmiling, looked at him.

"I think," she said, "that you have seen more than that."

"Right now I see Merriam coming into this car."

Merriam sat between the sisters, and Hartley ordered drinks for the three. Then, since it was almost five, he left them. He had claimed a table for two by the time Darya Javenel entered the car.

"Have you decided—do you like the Straight?" Hartley asked her.

"Yes. I think so." How long does it continue?"

She wore an ivory-colored dress, gold-loop earrings, and carried a flame-colored scarf.

Outside the window, the plain had dulled to brownish gray under a sky whose rare cloud had caught some of the earth's drab coloration. But even reduced to color, without the variation of any form of life, the Straight had begun to develop personality.

"Did you have some rest?" Hartley asked.

"Not much. I don't sleep, really, on anything that's in motion."

"But here, the motion is minimal. Something else wrong?"

Darya sipped her sherry. "Plenty," she said. She put down the wineglass and looked earnestly at Hartley.

Hartley allowed her a minute or so of respite. He offered her a cigarette.

"Rothman cigarettes," she said. "English. And no ice in your Scotch. Are you sure you aren't English?"

"I'm sure."

"Your name is Hartley—Hartley Rhys?"

He nodded yes. Unless she were acting, she spoke his

73

name with no indication that she had heard it before today.

She turned from Hartley and watched the night filling the Straight.

"You said you thought you liked this plain. What do you think now?" he asked.

"It looks as if it were waiting for something to happen."

"What do you think might happen?"

"I don't know. But the Straight seems to ask more questions than it answers. Why is it here? How did it get to be what it is?"

"God knows."

She smiled. "Profanity or religion?"

"Neither intended—I only meant to say that I'm as puzzled as you are. But to go back—how could anything happen?" He wanted to further sound out her apprehension. What she said might indicate her conscious or unconscious knowledge about this trip. But she merely shook her head.

"At least the Straight doesn't make any pretense," Hartley said. "When it's dark, you won't know it's there."

"But I want to know what's there," Darya said.

"You're used to cities."

"Yes."

"Tell me, Darya, do you like traveling alone on vacation?"

"Vacation?" She set down her glass. Hartley saw the paleness of her face, the fatigue shadows under her eyes. "It isn't a vacation, though I'm taking a semester off."

"What are you studying?"

"Archeology. Sort of inherited it. My uncle is an archeologist. Turkey, Persia. I took a year off from Columbia to work with him on a dig. In Turkey. His last. He's not very well—doesn't do field work—just writes." She added with enthusiasm, "He's a wonderful man. He and my aunt have raised my brother and me."

I mustn't push too hard, Hartley thought.

The club car was filling again. At the forward end, Macrimmon was haranguing a new audience. A little girl reached up and stroked the Kooka's head. Watch it, Hartley thought, but the Kooka, apparently respecting children, did not nip her fingers.

Merriam, from the table where the two French sisters lavished their attentions on him, caught Hartley's eye, raised an accusing finger, but grinned.

"If this trip isn't vacation," Hartley said to Darya, "does it have anything to do with your work or with your uncle's?"

Darya took a silver cigarette case from her bag and accepted a light from Hartley. "No," she smiled. "You ask a lot of questions, don't you?"

"I'm interested in the answers. Here you are, almost halfway around the world from your family and university. Maybe I could qualify as a substitute uncle."

"I doubt whether I would feel I were your niece." Darya laughed. "At the most you must be—twenty-six?"

"Thirty-one."

"I am twenty-two," Darya said. "So you couldn't be an uncle. Not in that blue jacket, anyway."

"Well, my status can be determined later, in whatever jacket." He returned to questioning her. "You already have a brother?"

Darya frowned. "My brother, Sammy. That's why I flew to Singapore. I hadn't heard from Sammy for months. Nobody in the family had heard. He wasn't a very dependable letter-writer, but somebody always heard from him by post card at least once a month or so. We tried to telephone Sammy's apartment in Singapore, but he had moved. My uncle cabled the company Sammy worked for—got a vague answer. I don't know whether I would have come, except that our aunt was ill and kept worrying about Sammy. So my uncle said pack up and go to Singapore. He told me it was a place I should see, anyway."

"Then you came. Did you find your brother?"

"No. The head of the shipping company he worked for was as vague as his cable. He was a kind of emperor of an old man, very polished. Seemed to think I was a crook. Voyages among the islands could be long, he said. Some of the ships apparently run like tramps, not on schedules."

"A runaround?" Hartley said. "So you left Singapore?"

"After two weeks. No luck at all. And I get awfully— well, homesick, though Singapore would have been marvelous at any other time."

She opened her cigarette case. It was empty. Hartley offered her his pack and lighted her cigarette. "You didn't get any idea where your brother was?"

She hesitated. "One thing. In Perth at the hotel—I flew there last Thursday to take this train—I got a message Saturday morning."

"From your brother?"

"It was supposed to be—maybe was. A telephone message. I was out, but the message was there when I got back. It said, 'Don't take train to Sydney.'"

"Why would he think you would take the train?"

"Oh, because we loved trains, always took them when they went where we wanted to go. But if Sammy knew where I was—oh, why didn't he come *himself*?"

"But you took the train," Hartley said.

"Of course I did. I wanted to go to Perth Friday but couldn't get a flight. So I had to go on Thursday, and stay there two nights. I didn't see why I shouldn't take this train. If Sammy had wanted to bother seeing me, explaining anything—"

"You could have flown back to New York from Singapore."

"Yes. But while I was out here, I wanted to see something of Australia. And the flight home from Sydney will be shorter than the one to Singapore." She added, "I hate to go home without anything to tell my aunt and uncle."

"Did you know Lady Mary before this trip?"

"No. I met her on the plane from Singapore to Perth. We were staying at the same hotel in Perth. The Parmelia. Why?"

"She seems to have adopted you."

"Yes," Darya agreed, without enthusiasm. "She's all right, I suppose, but I don't like the Irishman that follows her around. Dermot. Why can't he wear socks?"

"Did Dermot materialize, sockless, in Perth?"

"Yes. Looked even worse there. Oh, Hartley—" she halted. It was the first time she had used his name. "Uncle Hartley?" Her eyes gleamed with amusement.

He shook his head. "It's all right if I say it, but I don't like it when you do. How about having dinner with me?"

"I wish I could have dinner with you! Lady Mary arranged to have them put me at her table. With the Irishman. Damn. There's a sweet little old Australian woman, but Lady Mary isn't very nice to her."

"You could miss the first sitting. Wait and have dinner with me. Though Macrimmon and the bird might be there."

"You don't eat at the first sitting?"

"I'm an irregular," Hartley said.

"Lady Mary would pry me away."

"I'll fight her off."

"By asking questions? Hartley, what about you—you're not just traveling on vacation? Somebody, a boy I met named Tommy, said you were making some kind of travel survey. Are you?"

"In a way, yes." Everything about her, and what she had said rang true. All right, T.L., he thought, so I'm backing a hunch.

Darya frowned. "Are you some kind of detective?"

"Officially, yes. Right now I'm your friend. I hope."

"You mean, for a while you were—"

"I had to make sure you weren't involved in what I'm investigating."

A glitter of resentment shone in Darya's eyes.

Hartley placed his hand on the tense white fingers that gripped her cigarette case.

"Darya, I work as an investigator and troubleshooter for the Sword Line in Singapore."

"Sword Line—that's the company Sammy works for! You know him?" She withdrew her fingers.

"Yes."

"You might have told me."

"No. I had to find out who you were. What you were doing."

"You found out," she said coldly. "It's my turn to ask questions. Are you investigating my brother?"

"I am trying to find out what happened to one of the Company's ships, the *Cutlass*. It has been missing for almost four months. Sammy was first mate on that ship. He and one other crew member have been missing since the disappearance of the ship."

"Was there a storm?"

"There are no reports of storms or even rough seas in the areas we have been searching. The ship was bound for Penang in Malaysia. She often sailed to Penang, but sometimes was routed to other ports, depending on what cargoes were available."

"The other crew members—what about them?"

"They were found adrift in a small boat, not far from Singapore harbor. They were still recovering from being drugged. All they could tell us was that masked men had boarded the *Cutlass* at night and had overpowered them and drugged them. They knew nothing about Sammy and the missing crew member."

"But what are you looking for on this train?" Darya spoke without anger but with grave distress.

"I don't know," Hartley said. "The man, Welles, who had charge of our search was murdered. His body was found last Friday."

Darya gasped.

"I was assigned to the *Cutlass* job. Welles had planned to take this train. No reason given. But he must have had some reason for making the trip. So I am here."

"But Sammy couldn't be on board!"

"Not as a legitimate passenger. We haven't made a thorough search for a possible stowaway."

"*Sammy*—on this train! And not letting me know!"

79

She reached for Hartley's hand, all antagonism replaced by distress. Hartley took her hand.

"We don't know, Darya."

"But what could happen on the train?"

Hartley shook his head. "I don't know."

"That tragic man—Welles. Did he leave a family?"

"He had been living with a dancer in Singapore who was devoted to him. It was she who told us he was planning to take this train. She had a telephone call from him before he was murdered."

"Oh, poor poor girl!"

"And poor Welles. Stabbed to death in a Singapore alley. He was—a friend of mine."

"Hartley. I can't believe—can't believe Sammy has anything to do with this. But—" she shook her head. "If he has, he wouldn't have anything to do with murder."

"That," Hartley said, "is what I've always thought about Sammy. Whatever else."

"But what else was there?"

"Darya, Lady Mary is coming through this car. Play up."

Darya locked her hands in her lap as Hartley motioned to the waiter. "Another round." The waiter interposed a brief barrier as Lady Mary marched past the table.

"Hartley, I'm sorry I was angry. This is nothing whimsical."

"Very far from it. If you can tell me anything about Sammy that could help—"

"We've always been fairly congenial. Our parents have been dead for eighteen years." She opened the empty cigarette case, and again Hartley gave her a Rothman and lighted it. "If only he could have waited another month."

"Another month? Why?"

"Our uncle promised to give Sammy ten thousand dollars if he would stick to one job for three years. It would have been three years if Sammy had held out. Just one more month. From the time we stopped hearing from him."

"Sammy," Hartley said, "always seemed to live it up. Was there an inheritance?"

"Yes, but Sammy, well, you knew him. He was reckless and impulsive—borrowed on the trust fund."

"Anything else you can tell me about Sammy would help. I didn't know him well. I know he had made a good showing at the Merchant Marine Academy—got through fast. He was a good navigator but reckless. Once he took a shortcut through reefs. Came within a hair of cutting the junk in two. He almost lost his job over that."

"Yes. It sounds like him. He's always been machine-mad. And speed-mad. He's had sailboats and outboards and racing cars and a racehorse. Sometimes—" she hesitated. "Sometimes he has seemed to enjoy destroying things."

"Why did he go to Singapore?"

"I don't know exactly. Sammy and I were friends. Maybe we weren't close enough to have family friction. He was away so much, and I was plodding through school and and the University. He's three years older than I am. He left school and spent about a year traveling. He even did some camel racing in Arabia. One time he told me he wished he had been a bedouin. He went to Singapore on that trip. I think he found it exciting. He stayed until his money ran out. My uncle has friends there—they lent him money to come home. My uncle paid them because Sammy had borrowed all he could on the trust fund. And from me. Not that that's important. Just a fact about Sammy."

"I can understand," Hartley said, "why anyone would find Singapore exciting."

In Singapore now, he thought, it would be dark, perhaps cooled by a shower; and the garden below his windows would be lantern-lighted and night-scented by ilang ilang. Here, in this latitude, the brown twilight sluggishly seeped through the Long Straight without setting a limit to its bareness and immensity.

In response to his signal, the waiter refilled Darya's daffodil-shaped glass with sherry and brought another Scotch.

"That," Darya said, "was before he met the girl. Munah. What was she—Indonesian? Malay? Sammy sent me a picture. He hadn't ever stayed fond of any girl, not longer than he stayed with any job." From her bag she took a wallet and gave Hartley four snapshots. One showed Munah in a sarong; a handsome girl, who might have been Balinese. In two other pictures Sammy and Darya were posed with a sheepdog, against palm trees and the distant rise of Diamond Head.

"Honolulu," Darya said. "The dog is Selby. I had to take him out there—Sammy wanted to see him. Sammy had some kind of job in Honolulu. For a few months."

In the fourth snapshot, Sammy, in uniform, stood on the bridge of a ship. The bridge telegraph, Hartley noticed, was set to Full Ahead.

"You didn't see Munah when you were in Singapore?" Hartley asked.

"No. I didn't know her last name. Mr. Farnsleigh

didn't know anything about her. I couldn't find any friends of Sammy. If he had any. Oh, one old Chinese, a caretaker at the apartment where Sammy lived for a while, looked at the picture and said he had seen Munah. But months ago. She is pretty, isn't she?"

"Yes."

"I suppose I'd better go in to dinner," Darya said. "Lady Mary is making motions."

"You won't tell her what we've talked about?"

"No. But do you think she has anything to do with Sammy or the *Cutlass*?"

"It's possible, Take care, Darya. Keep your roomette door locked and get some sleep."

"I'd like to. But the minute I touch the pillow I'm wide awake."

"Rest, anyway. And I'll see you in the morning. My roomette in No. 2—your car."

He stayed at the table after Darya had left, finishing his Scotch slowly and watching the passengers who filed through the club car.

"Coming?" Merriam asked.

"Soon. You'll have company." The Abo was pushing Macrimmon's wheelchair into the club car. As they went by Hartley's table, Macrimmon leaned over and picked up Hartley's glass.

"Come along, boy, and have a refill." To the Abo he said, "Speed it up, Abo." On Macrimmon's shoulder the sad-eyed kookaburra laughed dismally.

Forward in the car, the two Frenchwomen waved to Hartley as they went toward the dining car. A few minutes later the monosyllabic sheepherder, Hall, flicked by, as inconspicuous and unnoticeable as a man could be. The Malay student, Daoud, who had gone into the dining car earlier, came out bearing a large tray. His roommate, Hartley thought, must be retaining his appetite. The Abo returned with the folded wheelchair.

The Straight was entirely dark. On his schedule Hartley saw that the train had passed from Western Australia into South Australia. He paid the waiter and went to his table in the dining car.

A double Scotch stood at his place; and Merriam was fending off Macrimmon's peremptory offer of another drink. As Hartley sat down, the kookaburra beaked a ripe olive from a relish tray and spat out the seed, which hit Merriam on the right cheek.

"Help!" Merriam cried cheerfully.

"Perfect aim. Mind you, I'm not saying he doesn't like you." Macrimmon dragged a large gold watch from a pocket in a grimed vest. "On time. Sydney on Wednesday at 3:50. What are you going to do in Sydney, boy? I know he has to herd his bloody tourists."

Hartley finished ordering before he answered. "Oh, I'll be getting some sleep."

"Never sleep in Sydney. Not me." Macrimmon said. He squinted along the length of the car. He raised a hand in a half-salute and said, "What did you think of my daughter, boy?"

"A handsome lady," Hartley said.

"What did you think of those opals?"

"Splendid opals."

"If you go to Melbourne, I can tell you where to buy the best opals in Eastern Australia."

"That would be good to know," Merriam said. "Some of my people want to buy opals, and we're going to Melbourne."

Shakily, Macrimmon wrote a name on a menu card. The train had started as smoothly as it had stopped, but Macrimmon's arthritically swollen finger joints were not obedient. Merriman thanked him, and for a few minutes the table was quiet, until the kookaburra selected another olive and this time spewed the pit at Hartley but missed.

"The absolute bloody limit," Macrimmon said proudly. He whacked the bird with his napkin.

When Hartley left the table, the Abo had already wheeled away Macrimmon and returned for his own dinner. Merriam was standing at another table, talking with four members of his party. Darya's table was empty, and he did not see her when he went to the club car, where Hawkins was serving demitasses and chocolate mints. He looked flurried.

"What's wrong?" Hartley asked Hawkins as he set down a cup.

"They'll turn up. They *must* turn up!"

"What's lost?"

"Keys," Hawkins said. "Master set. All parts of train. Kept hanging on hook in my office."

"Could one of the other conductors have borrowed them?"

"Without asking me? No. And we should have reached Cook three minutes ago. Just now coming into station. We make a thirty-minute stop here, and set our watches ahead an hour and a half."

"An hour and a *half*? Unusual, that."

"Australia is an unusual country." The pride that might have sounded in that statement was dulled by Hawkins's worries. "Well, I'll be getting along to the platform."

Hartley set his watch ahead and exchanged comments on time zones with Merriam and several other passengers who stopped at his table on their way to their rooms. They were followed by Macrimmon, wheeled by the Abo. Few people were left in the club car. Some passengers might have gone out to the platform for exercises, but more likely, Hartley thought, the emptying of dining and club cars was due to the accumulation of travel-weariness or to the soporific monotony of the Long Straight. He finished his coffee, allowing himself to imagine the luxury of a night's sleep, for the passengers and the progress of the Indian-Pacific seemed orderly. He wondered whether Macrimmon and the kookaburra were asleep, and whether the bird was obliged to roost on his master's pillow, or was free to perch on a sack of gold and to brook about a greater freedom among gum trees.

The minutes remaining before the train's departure could well be used for a turn on the platform, Hartley thought. As he rose, several passengers came from the dining car, and behind them a nervous-looking waiter who started to speak cleared his throat and tried again: "Ladies and gentlemen, we're sorry but we have to ask you to leave. The club car must be cleared. A refrigerator is leaking—there is gas."

The passengers remaining looked at him, startled and annoyed.

"Please take your drinks with you, if you want to," the waiter said.

The tables were emptying as Hartley went to the rear vestibule and down to the platform. Although the time here was not quite 9:30, the station suggested that of a ghost town, if ghost towns had stations. A cluster of shops were dark, the platform was empty, and only one window in the station building showed meager light. He walked briskly a few car lengths and, on returning, came close enough to the lighted window to see Hawkins, watch in hand, bending over the stationmaster, who sat at a desk taking notes as he listened to a telephone. Hartley saw him replace the receiver and hand a sheet of paper to Hawkins. Stumbling over the doorstep in his haste to leave the office, Hawkins complained to Hartley, "Fifty seconds more lost. Last-minute dispatch came in by telephone."

"Your train will make it up."

"Well, yes—but there's something else offbeat. We had no passengers to discharge here, but just as the stationmaster called me to his office, a man carrying a suitcase got off at the rear of the train. I couldn't see him clearly—he went right off into the darkness. Well, you'd better board now, sir. I'm giving the signal for departure."

Hartley boarded at the front end of Car 1 and was moving toward the rear when the train started. As he entered Car 2, he turned to see whether Hawkins was following. Not seeing him, however, he went on into Car 2.

He had taken only a few steps when he heard Darya's voice. "Hartley! *Hartley*!"

In the corridor outside the room which connected with Macrimmon's, Darya, in a dark-blue dressing gown, cradled something in her arms.

What she held was the limp body of the kookaburra.

"I heard dreadful screams from the bird. I was coming back from the shower—it had been screaming when I went to the shower—and just before I got here, it stopped. I knocked but nobody answered. The door wasn't quite shut. I pushed it open. The kooka was lying just inside. The door to the next room was closed."

Tears ran down her cheeks. She held the kookaburra toward Hartley. As he took the small sad body, the train halted. He laid the bird on the bed in Darya's room and was turning toward Macrimmon's door when the broadcast music stopped. A man's voice began to speak. "Ladies and gentlemen, passengers on the Indian-Pacific, I am speaking for the new director of the train. You will stay in your rooms. Return *immediately* to your rooms if you are away from them. The lights will go out. Men in the corridors and on the roofs of the cars—armed men—will be on patrol. No one is to try to leave the train. The patrols will shoot anyone who leaves his room. No one will be hurt, not if you stay in your rooms."

The corridor lights went out.

"Hartley!" Darya cried. "That was Sammy's voice!"

4

BULAN FOREVER

Sammy's voice gave way to an outflow of Malayan music: gongs, drums, strings, and chanting voices. Hartley caught the name *Bulan* and the words for *freedom* and *forever* as he ran into his room to grope for a flashlight. He pounded on Macrimmon's door and shouted. He called for Hawkins to answer. Passengers, warned to return to their rooms, ran past. Macrimmon's door was locked, but the door to the connecting room, which Darya had entered, was not locked.

In Macrimmon's room, Hartley's torch beam showed the wheelchair overturned. He passed on to the lower berth. Macrimmon's body hung over the edge, his broken head inverted in a swamp of blood, some of it his, the rest streaming from the Abo, who lay on the floor at an angle with the berth. There was no possibility that Macrimmon could be alive.

Hartley was bending over the Abo when a shot

sounded from overhead. The roof patrol, Hartley thought, must be directly above this room. The firing angle would make penetration through the window impossible, but he jerked down the blind to hide the torch light.

The Abo was unconscious. Hartley found a weak pulsebeat, and blood was draining from a gash at the lower part of his throat. Arterial blood? Hartley snatched a towel from the bathroom and used a pencil to make a tourniquet. The towel was stiff, non-absorbent. He needed bandages.

A stir of sound at the door to the connecting room sent Hartley's right hand to the revolver in his belt. He aimed the flashlight at the door and saw Darya.

"How can I help?"

"Darya, can you stand blood?"

"Yes."

"I have to get through to Merriam in Car 3. He will have a medical kit. I need bandages and some kind of sedative—the Abo is thrashing around. I don't know whether the patrols are working, or the roof snipers. Wait a second." He lifted the poor body of Macrimmon into the berth and covered it with a blanket. "All right. If you could hold this towel—tight, not too tight, around the Abo's neck—I ought to be back in a few minutes."

A shot sounded outside the window.

"Down!" Hartley cried. He pulled tight the slatted blinds through which the flashlight's beam had shown. Darya crept toward him.

"You keep the flashlight. If the Abo goes berserk, hit his head with the flash. Use a pillowcase—anything—if the towel gets soaked with blood.

"I understand."

"If the patrols come in here, get them to take you to your brother."

He left through the connecting room and flattened himself against the wall of the corridor, listening. The train was still halted. At least one of the roof guards had taken his position, as the two shots had indicated. The aching urgency of the need to save the Abo's life outweighed everything that he would have to deal with later. He must get through to Merriam's room in Car 3.

If the patrols were in action in the aisles, how would he recognize them? Or how would they identify someone not of their team? They would carry flashlights, but might hesitate to use them if they needed to preserve secrecy against a possible opponent. But what possible opponents, probably none of them armed, would they have in this train except for him? If they knew who he was?

He heard footsteps which would have been inaudible if the train had not been stopped. Someone was coming toward him from the rear of the car. He heard a sound, the wedging open of the door of the vestibule? At the same time, he heard steps from behind him. Two patrols? How would they make themselves known? The two sets of footsteps, the two men taking them, stopped near him. A flashlight described a circle on the ceiling of the car. Behind him, another flashlight imitated the signal. So that would be their way of signaling each other.

He would have to wait for painful seconds, imagining the flow of blood from the Abo's neck.

The patrols passed each other. One, still ahead,

might have to be dealt with between here and Merriam's room in Car 3. Straining to listen, he could hear nothing at the rear of the car. He took a few steps toward the vestibule, holding his revolver in his right hand, and the flashlight, now darkened, in his left.

Merriam's door was near the forward end of Car 3. Hartley reached it, tapped it, and risked a low call. "Merriam." No answer came. Oh, where is Merriam? With the old man, the semi-invalid? But where was his room? Perhaps next to Merriam's. Hartley placed an ear at the juncture of door and frame of the next roomette.

He heard nothing from the room; but in the corridor there were steps. Was it the patrol returning from the rear cars? The man was sweeping his flashlight in low arcs.

Before the light could pick him out, Hartley with his flashlight traced a circle on the car's ceiling and whispered, "Bulan" and "Merdeka." The patrol traced an answering ring of light on the ceiling and proceeded forward. Hartley waited, counting seconds. How long would it be before this patrol would reach Car 2? Forty, fifty seconds?

He tapped at the door. With his lips pressed against the jointure of door and jamb he murmured, "Merriam."

The door opened. Merriam drew him into the room.

In the light from a flashlight held by Thérèse at the bedside, Hartley saw the pallid face of an old man. Next to Thérèse, Laure was fanning him with a magazine. The air conditioning had gone off with the lights.

"Merriam, you must help me. Medicine kit, ban-

92

dages. The Abo has been terribly hurt—Macrimmon killed."

Merriam's flashlight, turned off when he had opened the door for Hartley, showed his profile.

The old man raised a trembling hand. "Go," he said. "I'll be all right."

Laure stroked his forehead.

"The medicine kit—where—" Merriam began.

"Here," Thérèse said, giving it to him. "I have the special pills for our friend, if he needs them. Go, Merriam, we will stay here."

"God love you," Merriam murmured.

"So far off?" Thérèse questioned. "Couldn't it be someone nearer?"

"Or *two* people?" Laure asked gently.

"Hurry. Please hurry," Hartley said. "If we meet a patrol, signal with a circle from the flashlight on the ceiling. That's their signal. And you'd better take this." He gave Merriam the derringer. "I have a revolver."

Behind them, he heard Thérèse say, "The next time we travel, remind me to bring guns."

"An arsenal," Merriam muttered, pocketing the derringer, as he let Hartley and himself narrowly into the corridor.

Hartley took the lead, with Merriam pressing closely behind him. No patrols in Car 3. The door of the last roomette in Car 3 hung ajar. A face showed in the opening.

"Tommy," Merriam whispered. "Shut the door. Stay inside."

"What's all this about?"

"Hijacking," Merriam said. "Get back into your

93

room before we have to shoot you for a hijacker."

They pressed on close to the wall, and crossed the vestibule into Car 2. Outside the shower room on the starboard side of the train, whose door was partly open, Hartley's heel sloshed in water. Shielding his flashlight, he shone it into the room. A man, dark-suited, lay sprawled on the floor, over the loose-woven straw mat that covered the drain. Hartley checked the dripping faucet and turned the man's body so that air could reach the upturned nostrils.

"A conductor, I think," Hartley whispered. "Drugged? Knocked out? Will find out later—hurry now."

In Macrimmon's room they found Darya kneeling beside the Abo. Blood stained her hands and her dressing gown.

"I couldn't stop the bleeding," she said.

"We will," Merriam told her.

"First, though," Hartley said, "we must put him into a bed. He'll be trampled if they break in here."

Together he and Merriam carried the light body of Macrimmon into the connecting room, placed it in a bunk, and covered it with a blanket. Meanwhile in the other room Darya had torn the sheets from the lower berth and pulled down others and the pillow from above. Hartley and Merriam lifted the Abo into the lower berth, where Merriam treated and bandaged his throat and gave him a sedative. But the Abo, half-conscious, was flailing arms and legs under the sheet that covered him.

"Where Mac? Where Kooka?"

"We'll tell you later," Merriam said. "You sleep now."

"No sleep. Where Mac?"

"You sleep, damn you!" Merriam cried. "Mac would say sleep. We talk later."

"Who you?"

"Friend," Merriam said. Beside him, Hartley said, "Friend here. Two friends."

"Why need two," the Abo mumbled. The sedative was beginning to work.

"God," Merriam said, "I gave him a dose big enough to put a horse under."

"He *is* a horse," Hartley said.

"Horse or not," Merriam said, "the bleeding wasn't arterial. It was bad enough, but your tourniquet would probably have saved him. We'll have to keep checking the bandage. Must be tight, but not too tight. I've got to get back to my old man. Stay here until the Abo settles down."

"Here we go," Hartley said. The train had started. "Merriam, come back when you can. I need your help with something else."

He swept the beam of the flashlight through the room. Darya was not there. By now the hijackers must be in position, he thought. One man, at least, was patrolling the roofs of the cars. How many were there? Sammy had announced the takeover with the tones of leadership. Before the action started, he must have been hidden in the bathroom in Daoud's room, the trays of food carried to the room to be divided between him and the ill, or supposedly ill, Kasim. Three members of the group were accounted for. Ali, Hartley thought, was the fourth. Dermot and Lady Mary, so often seen together—were they the fifth and sixth members?

If Sammy was driving the engine, he would have

made the cab his command post. He would need another person to watch for signals of trouble to the rear. Flash beams? Was it Lady Mary's assignment to carry out that watch?

I must get into the cab, Hartley thought. Strike at the leader. Gain control of the running of the train.

The forces of the enemy, even if six, would be spread thin. But not thin enough. Not yet. Not until the patrols had been made inoperative.

Suddenly, unwillingly, he thought of the pregnant woman. A possibility of trickery? But she had looked pregnant, ill, miserable. Had she already gone into labor? Sitting beside the Abo's berth, Hartley lighted a cigarette. He knew he could not ignore the possibility of that Malay woman's agony and danger.

He touched the Abo's forehead and found it feverish, but the Abo was lying still. Then he spoke. "I want whisky," the Abo said.

The flashlight showed a light bloodstain that had seeped through the bandage. "You go to sleep, Abo."

The Abo tried to sit up. Hartley pressed him back against the pillow. "Abo, you sleep. Then whiskey."

"No!" The voice was strong. "Get whisky. No sleep. Whisky in bathroom. *Get.*"

Merriam should have given the Abo enough sedative for two horses. And what would it do to him to have whisky on top of the drug? Hoping that whisky would supplement the horsepower of the sedative, Hartley located the bottle of Scotch in the bathroom, found a glass, and poured an ounce, then another. He supported the Abo's shoulders while the Abo drank.

"Mean. Little. Where Mac? Where Kooka?"

Where indeed? Hartley thought, in misery. And

what would happen to this great, devoted man? He did not think of the Abo as a barbarian, but as a human being who had spent his life in serving and in loving a man now dead.

Hartley knew that other people, white people, would not share his feelings about the Abo. There would be suspicion, harassment. Not if I can help it, Hartley thought grimly, pouring another drink. "Now, you drink. Then sleep," he told the Abo.

The Abo drank, then, giving Hartley the empty glass, reached for the flashlight and traced the room, halting the ray at the empty wheelchair. He returned the torch.

"Mac not here. Me—in Mac's bed. No Kooka. Mac dead."

Hartley didn't need the flashlight to know what anguish contorted the Abo's face.

The Abo raised a hand and pointed a finger as if to accuse Hartley. Then the combination of sedative and liquor sent a quiver and a jerk through his hand muscles. Hartley, touching the hand, felt it relax. He listened. The Abo's breathing had become slow, regular. The forehead was still fever-hot. There were no more unbloodied towels. Hartley soaked his handkerchief in cold water and laid it on the Abo's brow.

At the moment, he thought, the Abo was safe. And when Merriam returned, he could replace the stained bandage. For a few minutes the Abo could be left alone.

And for himself, Hartley knew, it would be impossible not to make a foray into Car 1 to the room of the pregnant woman.

The room was hot. Both to cool it and to prepare for what he wanted to do later with Merriam's help, Hartley encased his right hand in a bath towel, rolled up the venetian blinds, and broke the window, which had been sealed shut. The night air that drifted in from the Long Straight was too still to be either fresh or cool. There was no greenness to liven the night's dankness. He went through the connecting room, opened the door, and listened. All he could hear were the Bulan song and in pauses the soft brisk click of the wheels, which sounded irrelevant and indifferent to the stresses and fears of the people being carried through the Straight like prisoners in narrow, moving cells; indifferent also to the menacing purposes of the small group of jailers.

He shut the door behind him and now, committed to the blackness of the corridor, moved past silent closed doors and came to Hawkins's two rooms. Here, from a faint change in the air and from touch, he could tell that the doors were open. Beyond, the vestibule doors had been wedged open; from the louder sound of wheels he could tell that the outer doors were also open.

Pressing against the wall, inside Car 1, he listened and strained to see a flashlight beam. Moving again, he heard near the middle of the car the sharp crying of a child inside a room which he thought was next to William Hall's. He couldn't remember the number of the Malays' room, couldn't have looked for it if he had remembered. 5 perhaps? He knew it was separated from the conductor's quarters by the room occupied by the girl and the child from Kalgoorlie. He would have to grope his way to the end of the car and work back. Looking forward into the club car, he thought he saw a point of light. A patrol? He waited. The light was shut off. No footsteps sounded. At the door to the Malays' room, with his lips against the crack between the door and the wall, he said softly, "Ali? Mrs. Soto? Are you there?" When no answer came, he tried the door. It was not locked. He went into the room, closing the door, and searched with his flashlight. The room was empty. On the lower bunk he saw what looked like a bird's nest with long matted strands of black hair.

All right, he thought, so it was a trick. But he could not help feeling relief at not finding a Malay girl alone and in agony. He had made a start toward his goal, the locomotive. But before he could go all the way, he would have to reduce the enemy's forces somehow. But now he must go back to Car 2 to look after the Abo.

No sound, no light warned him. Hands gripped his throat and pulled him down. With his flashlight he beat at the space where he thought an assailant's head might be, but there was only space. The grip on his throat tightened. Hartley drew his revolver from his belt, but could not fire, not without knowing who his attacker was and without knowing what passenger, emerging from a room, might come into the line of fire.

Then the grip seemed to relax. Hartley beat against the hands with his revolver butt. Although the pressure had slackened, it was forceful enough to drag him backward toward the vestibule of the car. In the narrow aisle he couldn't kick. He thrust the revolver into his belt, but still held his flashlight, which he shone on the other man's face. He was a Malay.

Using light that the momentary flash had shown him, he sliced again at the Malay's throat. As Hartley flailed, sliced, beat against the Malay's steel hold, the impulse of the attack was pulling him from the car. He reached for the door handle of a room and clung to it. Then his feet stumbled against something in the corridor: the skateboard, Davy's skateboard. He kicked the board away from the wall, kicking it toward the Malay. The Malay's hands were so entwined around Hartley's throat, that when the latter, lunging to break away from Hartley's attack, stumbled onto the board, lost footing, and began to coast backward, Hartley went with him into the vestibule.

They teetered at the left edge of the platform, then fell to the iron flooring. Hartley was underneath. He lost the flashlight, tore with both hands at the Malay's grip, and was thrown off-balance when the latter, releasing Hartley's throat, pushed him over the edge of the vestibule.

Hartley's feet missed the steps, but he caught hold of the right handrail. The track swirled below him. Above, the Malay had drawn a revolver. But Hartley found footing on the steps and lunged upward to the platform to make impact with the Malay at the moment of firing. The shot went out into the Straight.

Again they grappled, so tightly that the Malay could not use his revolver. An inch, two inches—Hartley was forcing the Malay toward the opening at the right. The train gave a shallow lurch, not from an alteration in terrain but from some impulse of the driver of the engine. God, Hartley thought, do they time these things? He lost the two-inch advantage, regained it, and heard footsteps running from the car behind. A man's voice half-whispered, half-called, "Hartley, which one is you?"

"At left—your left," Hartley gasped. Immediately the Malay squirmed, shoved, trying to reverse their positions, but he was not fast enough. Hartley heard an impact, then felt himself free. Where the Malay had been, there was space. From the club car he thought he heard footfalls diminishing in sound.

A voice beside him said, "God, what if I'd brained the wrong man?"

"Chance worth taking," Hartley panted. "Who're you?"

"Tommy. Do we pursue?"

"No. We don't know. Can't see what's ahead. Back to Car 2. Wait to talk."

Hartley heard the grating of metal on metal, and felt Tommy grasp his arms for balance.

"What the hell's *that*?"

"Skateboard."

"*Skateboard*! Games, eh?"

"Not exactly. Pick it up. Bring it along. We might use it."

Hartley opened the door of the connecting room and went ahead of Tommy into what had been Macrimmon's. In the darkness and without a flashlight, he could not see the Abo's face. But the Abo spoke.

"Who you?"

"Hartley, friend. How you feel?"

"Want whisky. You friend, you bring." Then he added, "Why no turn lights? Dark no good."

"Can't turn lights. No work." Behind him Hartley heard Tommy laugh at the pidgin English.

"Give him a tot," Tommy said. "Where's the ruddy bottle?"

They groped and ran against each other. Finally, Hartley found the bottle on the floor beside the Abo's bunk and a glass beside the bottle.

"Good," the Abo said, emptying the glass. "You friend."

Hartley felt through his pockets. "You have matches?" Tommy brought out a folder. The brief flame of one match showed the stained bandages on the Abo's throat.

"Tear up sheet. Fix neck," Tommy said, mockingly. He groped into the next room.

"My God, there's a stiff in here! What have we got, a morgue?"

"Never mind. Just tear up a sheet or something."

"You ever try just by hand? I'll have to go to my uncle—old woman, really. Never travels without medicines, sewing kit, what not. You know, Hartley, when all this bash started, I said, 'Well let's organize a counterblow.' Old chum yawned and said, 'Let this ridiculous Australian incident wear itself out.' And the old sod went to sleep!"

"How did you know where I was?"

"Thought you'd be with the Abo. Came out—heard that gunshot forward—came on the double. With golf iron."

"Handy of you," Hartley said. "Get scissors, and if you could find a flashlight—"

"Will try," Tommy said and was off.

Where, Hartley wondered, was Darya? And the Abo, Hartley thought. What to do about him? More whisky? He knelt beside the berth, in which the Abo's restiveness was already disarranging the covers.

The Abo held out his glass for more whisky.

If the whisky hadn't hurt him so far, why not give him more? Who knew what an aborigine could take? And what, he thought, would ease or defer the Abo's suffering when he learned of his losses?

He poured whisky into the empty tumbler and

supported the Abo's head and neck while he drank.

At the connecting doorway Merriam spoke quietly.

"Hartley, you there?"

Hartley answered.

"Careful about broken glass. Window's broken. Blind is down—flash oughtn't to show. I'll tell you what I want us to do, but first, the Abo's bandage needs changing. I've lost my flash—couldn't do anything in the dark."

"Everything's hard to do," Merriam said, locating the fresh bandages. "We go groping around like blindmen. Narrow thing on my way here just now. I ran into someone—thought it was a patrol and started to jump him. But it turned out to be Tommy."

"How's your old man?"

"Making out all right, thank heaven. How'd you lose your flash?"

Hartley told him.

"So what's next?"

"We'll have to work fast," Hartley said. "I think we'll be getting company. Three main things I need to do: get to the engine, delay the train as much as possible, and make it late reaching a rendezvous. They must have set up transport somewhere along here to carry off the gold. You've finished with the Abo?"

"Yes."

"Then help me."

"You bleeding?"

"No. Just help me get one of the sacks to the window."

Merriam swept the light over two sacks on the floor, laid the flash on top of the overturned wheelchair, and said, "What are you up to?"

"Diversion. Help me get this one on the table."

"God, it's heavy," Merriam said. "How much gold could the old man mine in a year?"

"Hard to believe. All right, I'm going forward to the vestibule. Give me about fifteen seconds. Then open the blind and show your flashlight. Push one sack through the window, count to ten, and push out the second one. Then come out to the vestibule."

The Bulan song had started again in its continuous exhortations. As he ran toward the vestibule, Hartley heard again the Malay word *merdeka*, which means *freedom*. Freedom, he thought, to kill and wound and cause panic and seize property? Oh Sammy Javenel, I will catch up with you.

Through the open vestibule door he saw light from Macrimmon's window and heard the first sack fall to the cinder bed beside the track; then seconds later, the second.

When Merriam came into the vestibule at a run, Hartley was already on the lowest step at the exit on the right side of the car. "Come down far enough to hang on to me when I lean out," Hartley said. He felt Merriam's grip firm on his belt and leaned out as far as Merriam's grasp could secure him. He couldn't remember ever seeing a night as dark as this. The ray from the sniper's flashlight cut thinly downward through the blackness outside the room he and Merriam had left. The cinder bed beside the track glinted like the points of dying embers from the light on the car roof. With the upper part of his body at an angle of at least sixty degrees with the side of the train, he fired the revolver at the beam overhead. An unlikely shot. One chance in—but the light disappeared.

"You hit!" Merriam's half-whisper was triumphant.

Hartley swung back to secure footing on the steps. "I hit the flashlight, anyway—maybe interrupted their warning signals." He regained the vestibule floor. "Patrol would have heard the shot—might have to go to the cab to stop the train if they're going to pick up the sacks. No, there's a flash signal farther forward—they must have had two men on the roofs. Hang on—the train may stop with a bang."

A few seconds later the train came to a rough stop.

"They'll be coming this way," Hartley said. "I'll go to the Abo—you'd better get back to your old man."

"But if they bring the sacks back there, the Abo's room—"

"Don't think so. Too far from both ends of the car. Train's moved past the sacks—oh—they're backing. Get going, man, while they're busy."

A minute or so after Hartley reached the Abo, the train had stopped backing and come again to a stop. He peered through the broken window. A momentary flash picked out figures beside the track. He heard the rasping drag of the heavy sacks over cinders, moving forward, he thought.

"Abo, you all right?"

"Yes. Turn lights."

"No lights. Can't. I told you."

"Bad train," the Abo grunted. "Bad luck. Woman."

"Woman was man," Hartley said.

"Worse luck if man have baby."

Of all times, Hartley thought. To the Abo he said, "Listen, if men come in here, you stay quiet. Like sleep. I cover your head." He drew the sheet loosely over the Abo's head. "No move, you understand?"

The Abo muttered a grudging assent. "Want food."

"Yes, of course you do. I try bring you food, soon as I can. You're a good, brave man, Abo. Just stay quiet."

How much did the Abo understand? No telling. But from under the sheet a thick hot finger came out and gently laid itself on Hartley's hand. No laugh, Hartley thought.

"More." The Abo nudged at Hartley who stood beside the bunk. Hartley poured about an ounce, justifying himself by thinking that if the horse-sized sedative hadn't worked, maybe the whisky would.

Above the half-gulp, half-cough of the Abo's drinking, Hartley heard another sound. Unidentifiable.

"Merriam? Darya?" No answer came. But moving away from the Abo's bunk, he collided with the overturned wheelchair and felt its wheels spinning. He reached for his revolver, but before he could draw it, he was struck on the head.

He staggered back against the bunk, seized the bottle that he had left on the floor, and hurled it toward the invisible attacker. But hands seized his throat and other hands grasped his arms. He swung away, battling. He kicked at them, felt the wheelchair beside him, freed his right hand, and fired a shot toward where the men seemed to be. Then he rammed the wheelchair into them, but something struck his forehead. He fired another shot, fell under another blow, and clung to the rolling wheelchair as he was drawn toward the window. Kicking his nearest assailant, he heard an acknowledging cry of pain. The two opponents seemed to fall back. Then hands taloned into his throat and a new weight propelled him toward the window. He felt the jagged shards of the glass and, as he fell, the sharp cinders beside the track.

When he came back to consciousness, he was lying face down, close to the car wheels on the cinder roadbed. He did not know how long he had been there. He rolled nearer to the wheels, dangerously nearer if the train started, as a flashlight from the car's roof searched along the roadbed. A second or two later he stood on legs that seemed about to fold. There was pain in his head and on his abraded face and wrists, but it was not severe as the urgency he felt to reboard the train. By now the enemy would have picked up and reloaded the two sacks of gold. There would have been a delay. The train was still halted.

I must get back on board, he thought, starting toward the rear of Car 2, which seemed to be the nearest entrance. He tried not to think of what would happen if the train started.

The train started. Still partly dazed, he began to run as if on showshoes over no snow. Under erratic guidance, the train jerkily gained speed, which was increasing faster than he could make his legs move. Legs, to hell with you, he thought. Hell, double hell.

Car 2 was moving past him with the false animation of carousel horses. At the moment when the handrail of the steps to the vestibule of Car 2 was almost near enough to grasp, a flash from the car's roof prodded downward and a shot struck the cinderbed a few feet to his left. He zigzagged, now with the problem of running closer to the edge of the cinderbed in order to avoid suction from the train's movement. He missed catching the handrail at the vestibule between Cars 2 and 3. But the sniper on the roof would have the double handicap of keeping balance and hitting a target not only moving, but moving unevenly.

Car 3 was now sliding past him. He stumbled on a

cluster of cinders. If he missed Car 4, there was only one more chance at the end car. And by then the train's speed would have picked up. Damn you, train, he thought. Damn you. And, foot-dragging, he caught the handrail at the steps of the rear vestibule of Car 4. He pulled himself to the plates of the vestibule floor, rested there briefly, then entered Car 4. Merriam's people here, he knew.

Car 2 seemed a home base. He made his way to the Abo's room and spoke softly to identify himself. The room reeked of whisky. He groped, made out the Abo's knees, legs, at the side of his bunk.

"Get back into bed. Nobody hurt you?"

The Abo grunted what could have been no, and seemed to sleep.

What time was it? It seemed as if they had been in the Long Straight, been hijacked, for hours. No way of reading his watch. He must go forward. To the engine. That was the center of this evil. And on the way, he must cause as much delay as possible for the hijackers.

So far he had accomplished nothing except one delay of perhaps a half-hour, but there was no reduction of the enemy forces, no rallying of help from the train crew. Where *were* they all—five conductors, two messmen, chef, and two men from the engine? Ten men? Drugged, bound, stowed—but where?

He edged from the connecting room into the corridor. To the rear a light flashed. A patrol coming from Car 3? Had they seen him board the train? He pressed against the wall, one hand tight on his revolver.

There was no steady show of light, and he could not hear steps until they were a few feet away from him. He could have shot then, but how could he be sure this moving figure was an enemy patrol, not Merriam or Tommy? There was no flashing circle overhead.

Through the door which he had left ajar, he backed into the room connecting with the Abo's and waited there until the patrol passed. If the wait lasted a minute, it was an immoderately long minute. He counted off an additional thirty seconds. Surely by now the patrol would have gone on into Car 1. He would move forward.

His hands found the open doors to Hawkins's rooms. From the precious folder that Tommy had given him he broke out a match and noticed the gold image of a peacock and the gold lettering that named a nightclub in Kuala Lumpur, something from another world, too far in space and in circumstance to have reality here. The match and a second verified what he had found earlier, that both rooms were empty. Before the second match died, it showed a pool of water on the floor of the office, tea leaves, and a broken ceramic teapot.

He remembered that there was a lavatory opposite Hawkins's office. He turned the handle and opened the door, which, in moving, released what seemed to Hartley in the darkness a falling mass, only later by matchlight identifiable as the body of a man whose arms and legs were roped. Hawkins. Incoherent sounds came from behind a gag or taped lips. Hartley had time only to drag Hawkins to a chair in the office before he heard steps in the vestibule. He crouched behind the sprawled figure of Hawkins in the chair, Hartley's fingers tight on his revolver. A flashlight beam swept the room, touching the bound figure, showing Hawkins's features. It showed also, about two feet from Hartley, a metal pitcher on a table. As the flash was turned off, Hartley grasped the pitcher and hurled it at the figure in the doorway.

He heard an impact and a woman's voice briefly reacting to the blow. He leaped toward the sound and seized the woman's wrist. Her flashlight and a revolver fell to the floor as he bore down upon her, shifting his hold from wrists to throat.

The pressure that he could exert with one hand—he still held his automatic in his right hand—was not strong enough to shut off her half-choked cry. "Stop—stop!" It was Lady Mary's voice.

"I will stop when you tell me where Darya is."

No answer.

"Do you know, Lady Mary, that your father has been murdered?"

His hand gripping her throat felt the tension rising in her body. But she uttered an almost unrecognizable sound, something like laughter.

"Talk," he ordered, easing his grasp.

"You are lying. My father has not been murdered."

"I have seen him. He's dead." He needed to be two people, or to have as many hands as a Hindu goddess. First he must quell Lady Mary. He increased pressure on Lady Mary's throat until her resistance weakened and dragged her nearer the sink and cabinet. He pulled open drawers, found towels, and bound her wrists, listening meanwhile for the opening of the vestibule door from Car 1. He tore the tape from Hawkins's lips, moistened a dish towel at the tap, and wiped the macerated lips. With lips free, Hawkins, semiconscious, muttered, "Tea—ready." Hartley turned to Lady Mary, pulled her to her feet. "You're coming with me," he said.

A great burst of Bulan music sounded. He lowered

Lady Mary to the floor and crouched behind Hawkins's chair. The outer arc of a flashlight beam edged into the room and picked out Mary's feet, blacked for a moment, then shone again, sweeping over her body, over Hawkins, through the room.

Again the light was turned off. Hartley could imagine what was happening: Mary was being found. She cried, "Dermot, look out, he's behind the chair!"

Hartley smelled sweat and rum. For a moment the room was entirely dark.

From the corridor he heard Merriam's voice. "Hartley!"

"Stay back, Merriam!" Hartley shouted. Dermot flashed his torch toward the corridor, then switched it off. Still crouching, Hartley fired. Then, overturning Hawkins's chair, he made a projectile of man and chair and propelled it toward the place where he now saw Dermot's light. The shot had missed, but the projectile had knocked Dermot off-balance, for he dropped the flashlight.

For a moment, before Hartley picked it up and switched off the light, the beam, washing across the floor, showed two squarish dirty feet in thong sandals, Lady Mary's brown boots, and Hawkins's black-shod feet under the chair from which he had fallen face forward. A shot exploded, another followed, and a third. Had Merriam been hit in the exchange of shots?

"Stop, Dermot!" Lady Mary screamed. "*No killing.* Ian ordered that!" Her voice was near Hartley. As he reached out to grasp her, she kicked his ribs hard and painfully, then kicked the revolver from his hand.

He seized her arms and held her.

"Dermot!" she cried. No answer came from Dermot,

but from along the corridor another shot sounded.

Hartley shook Lady Mary until she fell against him, gasping. Then he thrust her away and heard dishes and silver clash as she fell against the table at the end of the room.

He felt along the floor and found his own revolver, which Mary had kicked from him. He did not find Lady Mary's. Not knowing where Dermot was, he did not use the flashlight which he still had in his belt. He heard Hawkins groan, gave up the search, and crossed the room. With his pocket knife, he cut the cords that bound Hawkins and fumbled awkwardly in the dark to feel and remove the gag. He set the chair upright and lifted Hawkins into it.

"What," Hawkins mumbled, "is going on?"

"We're hijacked."

"No—impossible!" His speech was thick from the gag.

"Not impossible. It's real. You all right?"

"I could use something to drink."

"Hang on. I'll find something."

Stumbling over Mary's body, Hartley found a jug containing liquid. He gave it to Hawkins, who took two gulps and complained, "It's cream! Too expensive to *drink!*"

"All I could find. Drink it."

"What's that music?" Hawkins cried. "Nothing we had. Turn on the lights, will you?"

"Can't. They're off. And you stay here. There may be patrols in the corridors."

From the doorway he shouted, "Stop shooting! You'll hit Lady Mary! She is here. I am going to take her to her father's room. Keep the corridor clear."

Outside the room he heard footsteps and muffled voices.

To Hawkins he said, "Have you a flashlight?"

"Mine got broken. Men jumped at me—knocked me out. I came to, tied up, in the lavatory. There's another flashlight somewhere, if I could see. I must go to the engine—dispatch—"

"You can't go to the engine. The hijackers are running the train. Can you walk?"

"I think so."

Hartley heard Hawkins stumble over one of the objects that littered the floor. He risked a sweep from the flashlight he held and saw Hawkins staggering to his feet. Beyond him he saw the two canvas sacks that had been thrown from the train.

"Where," Hawkins muttered, "is everybody—the crew?"

"If they're on the train, they're tied up and stowed somewhere, maybe drugged. And Macrimmon has been murdered."

Hawkins gasped.

"Lady Mary won't believe me. You and I are going to take her to Macrimmon's room."

"I won't go!" Mary cried. She was on her feet.

"You *will* go. Hawkins—I have the revolver—can you make her come, carry her if you have to? Move fast—there'll be patrols through the corridor. I don't know if they'll hold off shooting."

"*Patrols!* What patrols?"

"Hijackers."

"Lady Mary, please—"

"For God's sake, don't waste time being polite! *Bring her!*"

"But why?"

"Because she's one of them!"

"You must be out of your mind, Rhys. Maybe *you're* one of them."

"I untied you, and I need your help. I'm going ahead—you come along after me."

Behind him in the corridor Hartley heard Mary cursing and heard Hawkins mumbling. But they reached the room next to the one in which the Abo lay.

"Bring her into the next room," Hartley ordered. He flashed the torch over the figure of the Abo, the bloodstains on the floor.

"Your father," he said, "was killed in that bunk."

"No!"

"Then come here. Come along—you'll see what your friends have done."

"My friends haven't murdered anybody!"

He put the revolver through his belt, and still holding the flashlight in his left hand, drew Mary into the connecting room. He flashed the torch on the lower berth and pulled down the sheet.

Macrimmon's daughter looked at her father's devastated face, screamed, and fainted. Hawkins caught her as she fell.

"Why did they have to kill one old crippled man if what they wanted was the gold!"

Hartley put a hand on Hawkins's shoulder.

"Yes. Why? But pull yourself together. We must take Lady Mary to her room—get her out of here. Just let's hope the patrols will let us go through." He drew his revolver again and preceded Hawkins through the corridor and into Car 3.

"Stop at her room—you know the layout. All right.

Put her down. Lower the bed. Lift her into it."

"We can't just leave her," Hawkins said.

"We won't. Get a towel, wet it, put it—"

"I know the procedure," Hawkins said stiffly.

"You have brandy in your office?"

"I will bring brandy."

"Take the flashlight. I'll stay here until you come back. Wait a minute."

To the patrols, which Hartley thought had followed them, he called: "We're getting medical help for Lady Mary. Hold your fire."

Would they? he wondered. Were they at all restrained by Sir Ian's supposed orders? Or had everything gone too far? Or not far enough?

He was no nearer the engine. He had a half-hearted ally in Hawkins, now on his way back to Car 2. Where was Merriam? He loosened the scarf that Mary wore around her throat, and tried to pull off her boots when Tommy's voice sounded at the open doorway.

"Hartley? You here?"

"Yes. You find a flashlight?"

"Tried all over. No go." He struck a match.

"My word, what have you done to Lady Mary?"

"Just convinced her that her father has been murdered."

"Have you raped her?"

"Not yet," Hartley said.

"Well, need any help?"

Hartley chose to answer the more reasonable of the two interpretations of the question.

"Yes. Help me get these boots off."

They were still tugging when the train stopped. Hartley heard a clanking noise from the direction of the

115

forward vestibule. Then a light showed at the door. Hawkins stood there holding a lighted candle. He looked as guileless as a choirboy. Under his right arm he carried a brandy bottle, and in his right hand a teacup and a spoon.

"What's going on at the vestibule?" Hartley demanded.

"Some men there, but they let me come through," Hawkins said. "I said I was coming to help Lady Mary."

"Then you take over," Hartley said. "I must see what's up. Tommy, did you see Merriam or Darya?"

"Darya, no. Merriam, yes. Hands full, that lad. Old lady, room next to old man heart case—she's sort of collapsed. And Glendon's uncle—he's having a malaria. Damned unhealthy train."

"In more ways than one," Hartley said.

"Merriam had the two French girls looking after the old lady. He was all set to go help you. I said I'd look in on the old man. Glendon's taking care of her grandfather."

"That will be General Percy," Hawkins said. He had managed to withdraw Lady Mary's boots, and now covered her with a sheet, lowered the pillows, and was using the teaspoon to try to make her swallow a few drops of brandy.

"There, now, good girl, you try this. Another go, yes? Maybe you'd like tea? I'm afraid it's not the hottest."

Tommy followed Hartley through the doorway.

"Nursie at work," he said.

"Never mind," Hartley answered sharply. "He's had an awful shock. Stay put, Tommy. Don't go anywhere until we know what those people are doing at the vestibule. I don't know where Merriam is. You look after the old man."

"All right, but he's due for another injection. How the bloody hell do I give an injection?"

"You'll have to," Hartley said.

"In the ass—or where?" Tommy's voice behind him was muted.

"Just get it into him," Hartley said, "any way you can."

Tommy disappeared beyond the range of a flash beam that now, in the hands of someone moving aft, flickered through the corridor. The engine, that compelling but evasive goal, was more than five cars ahead. I will get there, Hartley thought, if I can stay on this train.

Should I try to crash through—shoot through—whatever people there are in the vestibule, without knowing how many or how obedient they'd be to orders from the distant Sir Ian? Perhaps less obedient now that Sir Ian's wife was immobilized? Or would Hawkins bring her to consciousness and release her with his benediction? She would now, Hartley thought, be the weakest member of the enemy team, although his ribs still ached from her booted kick. But her grief and horror in that room beside the ravaged body of her father could not have been pretended. He remembered the emotions that had contorted her face when Macrimmon had tried to give her the opals. No, she had been in some hostile way close to her father, and he, in an even more hostile way, close to her. Waiting, listening to the sounds from the vestibule, wiping sweat from his forehead, he remembered Sir Ian as he had seen him at the Hilton bar in Singapore. A schemer, a visionary? All right. A man who would plot murder? No, he thought. And not only because Sir Ian was a friend of Farnsleigh. There had been no cruelty in that bland face. Ambition? Greed, even? Hawkins's had the face of a well-meaning man who was determined to carry out his obligations, his responsibilities to the train and its passengers.

Why had all this happened? And what would happen still? One thing that will happen, he thought grimly, is that I will face Sammy Javenel in the cab of the engine.

He wiped sweat from his eyes. When he withdrew the handkerchief, the flicker of lights at the vestibule had blacked out. As he moved forward, the train started. He heard wheels rotate but felt no motion. Nearing the vestibule, he saw stars over the Long Straight, stars as withdrawn, as indifferent as the sound of the wheels.

The vestibule was empty. He swept the flash over the iron plates, saw the black gap in the middle of the vestibule, saw the gap widening.

The cars to the rear of Car 2 had been uncoupled. And he was in Car 3.

5

MAD ENGINEER

What a miserably uncomfortable bed, Hartley thought. My bed? Why did I ever want to go to bed? Where was the gentle smell of the floor mats, the mysterious deep scent of ilang ilang outside his windows in the Singapore apartment? And why was this, whatever it was, *moving*?

Sit up, he ordered himself, and sat. A glint from an unbelievably near mass of stars picked out an echo below him, a brief shine of metal. A track? Then he remembered. Looking down, he saw that he was lying within a few inches of a descent toward those tracks.

Now as he moved away from the verge he remembered seeing a darker-than-dark gap opening between the car where he had been and what was ahead and moving away from him. Had stars helped then? Or had he felt the widening darkness? He remembered jumping. He did not remember reaching the platform where he was now. The distance had been quickly increasing. Unlikely that he could have passed over that space. He dragged himself farther from the descent. Safe? But, was this Car 2? Certainly there was nothing behind him except solid night, the night that inexhaustibly had filled the Long Straight. Was there ever so much of anything except night? Ocean, perhaps?

How far away any ocean was! Nostalgically he thought of the miraculous blue and green mingling of sea and inlets with the alabaster and purple and verdant colors of the city that was Singapore. Before he could return, he had work to do.

Something had changed. Light. That was it. Light over the open entrance to the car ahead. He stood up, moved through the open doorway into that car, which from where he stood held nothing to distinguish it from any of the other sleeping cars. But as his head cleared, he remembered. He had been in Car 3 when the last three cars had been uncoupled, so now he must be in Car 2. The return of lighting would be a help but also a hazard. How was he going to reach the engine through lighted cars? And how long had he been immobilized on the platform? His wristwatch was shattered during his fall. He had lost another flashlight, but could now do without it.

His allies, Tommy, Hawkins—he had lost them. His strongest ally had been Merriam. God, he thought, I hope Merriam, after the brave try at helping, had got back to his car safely before the uncoupling.

The enemy had lost one of their number. Lady Mary. His ribs still ached from her booted kick. From a cut on his forehead, blood trickled into his eyes; he must have cut himself on a plate when he landed after jumping from Car 3. Otherwise he assessed his capabilities as normal. And perhaps he had an advantage over the enemies—they must have been so sure that he was marooned with the others in Cars 3, 4, and 5, that they had not been on guard when he jumped.

He doubted whether the uncoupling had been aimed primarily at disposing of him. However, if Sammy had been listening from the bathroom when Hartley and Hawkins had talked with Daoud, Sammy, hearing his name, would have known that Hartley was a threat. The hijackers could not risk interference from a man who they would have guessed would be armed and trained professionally in combat skills. His presence on the train was a factor they could not have foreseen. What was likely, Hartley thought, was that he had been followed into Car 3, when he and Hawkins had taken Lady Mary to her room, and that the enemy had chosen that time for the uncoupling. If he had been nearer the vestibule and had tried to stop them, he might have found himself again lying beside the track or suffering from graver danger.

He remembered Lady Mary's impassioned outcry against murder and her stern reiteration of Sir Ian's orders, but how much authority could she have exercised? Now that she was not aboard the train, such authority might wear thin under the hijackers' zeal.

Although reasoning told him that he was in Car 2, he looked for confirmation as he moved cautiously forward in the corridor. Outside the last room on his right, he saw pieces of broken crockery and recognized them as remainders from the fighting in Hawkins's office.

Before seeing to the Abo, he entered his own room to get a handkerchief. He was not surprised to find the room disassembled. From the lowered bed the coverings had been stripped, and the contents of his suitcase and the smaller bag were piled on the floor, along with the clothing he had hung in the closet. On the cabinet top his shaving gear was tumbled, and a bottle of lotion was spilled, fragmented. Fruit was trampled on the floor. What had the enemy been looking for— weapons, papers relating to the search for *The Cutlass*? He picked up a towel from the welter on the bed and wiped the blood from the cut above his right cheekbone, then found a clean handkerchief under a tumbled pile of underwear, took a banana from the cabinet top, and crossed the corridor to the Abo's room.

The Abo, following instructions, lay motionless under the sheet which still covered his face. Spikes of glass shone on a canvas sack near the broken window.

"Abo. It's me. Friend. How feel?"

The Abo lowered the sheet to uncover his left eye. "Light came," he observed.

The bandage around his throat was clean, and his forehead was cooler than when Hartley had felt it before. Hartley gave him the banana, saying, "More food later."

The Abo peeled and ate the banana with the quick rapacity of a monkey, and as Hartley had expected, he asked for whisky.

"No more. Bottle broken. More later."

In the Abo's improved condition, Hartley thought that he could be questioned.

"Tell me what you saw. What happened when you came back from the dining car?"

"Came back. Soon. Felt bad luck. Opals no good. Train no good."

Opals unlucky? Some legend about that stirred in Hartley's mind. I'll sort it out later, he thought. He remembered seeing Lady Mary return the sack of opals to her father, who had thrust it into a jacket pocket. The jacket now lay crumpled in a corner of the room. A tobacco sack, a box of matches, a pipe, a dirty handkerchief, a large coin purse, a wallet full of bills, but no sack of opals.

"You find?"

"No," he told the Abo. "Go on. You come here. Get Mac ready for bed?"

"No. Mac *in* bed. Before. I eat. Come back. Kooka yell. Next room. Somebody turn off light. Dark. I put light. Mac—all blood. Light go off—somebody hit— feel knife—not know."

"You didn't see the man who stabbed you?"

"No see. Feel." The Abo tried to sit up. Hartley pushed him down.

"Just take it easy. If anybody comes, you act dead. Like before. I cover face. You understand? If they think you dead, they won't hurt you."

"Why kill Kooka?"

Macrimmon's death brought a grief too enormous for immediate reaction; the slaughter of the Kooka, following Macrimmon's, struck hard and perhaps more measurably.

"I kill," the Abo said. "I kill two kills."

Hartley patted a dark hand clenched on the top of the sheet.

"Want food." The Abo added.

"I know. I bring food. Soon."

"Where you go?"

"To engine. Try to stop men that stole train."

"Hijackers," the Abo said with sly impatience. Hartley wondered how much of his own grotesque try at pidgin English had been necessary. Like Macrimmon, the Abo could deliver linquistic surprises.

"Maybe you can go to sleep. If anybody comes, you play dead. You act dead. You asleep. You not snore."

"No snore," the Abo promised.

Hartley pulled the sheet over the Abo's face. Damn, damn, *damn*, he thought. He liked this dark, wounded creature. He had also liked Macrimmon, even though Macrimmon had been harsh, profane, uncouth. Nevertheless, the essence of the old man had won him. He had been counting on knowing Macrimmon, on seeing him again, and grieved, thinking of the poor slight figure of Macrimmon lying on the bunk in the next room.

Hartley turned off the light and went into the corridor. The train was moving over its track with less motion than would have been needed to stir whisky in a full tumbler. It was a deceptive motion, inviting, as before, Hartley's progress toward the engine. But that progress had become a Kafka nightmare sequence of movements forward and backward, within and outside the train. And denuded of weapons, what chance did he have of forcing his way to a confrontation with Sammy?

Where, he wondered again, was Darya? Lights, probably left with the switches on when the train was darkened, showed her door open, the room empty. On the bed the Kooka's body lay wrapped in a towel. Near it he saw the top of Darya's blue pajamas, stained with

124

blood—from, he thought, her help with the Abo—and her handbag. The room had not been vandalized. A book by Arthur Upfield, the Australian writer of mysteries, was sprawled on the floor near the bed. A smell of hyacinths was exhaled faintly from a perfume bottle on the top of the cabinet. He took her handbag. Now that the hijackers felt secure enough to reactivate the lighting, they might also feel free to pillage.

The room next to Darya's, he remembered from Hawkins's list, was General Percy's; the one beyond, his granddaughter's. Hartley tapped at the door to that room. The door opened far enough for him to see the dark face of Glendon, the granddaughter.

"Hartley. Where's Tommy? He was coming here—"

She opened the door wider, and Hartley entered the room.

"Tommy is in Car 3—marooned—with 4 and 5. Miles behind us."

"Left there—what if something runs into them?"

"Hawkins is on board. He—or Tommy—will think of lighting a fire to warn off traffic from behind. They're probably safer than we are, Glendon. Have you seen Darya?"

"No. Not since dinner. I've been—well, my grandfather had a malaria attack. He's going to be all right. He's had medicine, and he's reading his post-malaria cure, a Yeats play. Tommy came here—said he would come back. Hartley—your forehead—it's bleeding." She brought bandaids from a cosmetic case and covered the cuts and abrasions on his forehead and cheek.

Hartley held up Darya's bag. "Will you keep this? I found it in her room."

"Of course. Anything else I can do?"

"No. Unless you have a revolver. I'm out of arms."

"Wait." She went to the door.

"Careful—look down the corridor," Hartley warned.

"Empty," she said.

In a few minutes she came back with an automatic revolver, which she gave Hartley.

Hartley sighed with relief. "But this leaves you both without any arms?"

"Never mind," he added. "I'll collect something— bring this back as soon as I can."

"What are you going to do?"

"Get to the engine. Have it out with Sammy Javenel."

"Sammy—*Darya's brother*?"

"Yes."

"She told me she was trying to find him—but you—I know you've been helping everybody—Tommy told me—oh, if only he were here—to help *you*! Who are you, Hartley?"

"I'm trying to find a missing junk. Working for the Sword Shipping Company. Sammy sailed for them."

"And now he's running this train for the hijackers? I wish I could help you."

"You've helped," Hartley said. "I felt pretty naked without a gun."

"Have the hijackers killed anybody?"

"Macrimmon, the old man with the bird, was killed. And the bird. I don't know who did it."

"The dark man, his servant?"

"Almost killed too. I think we've saved him. You stay in your room. I think you'll be safe. And Tommy's all right. Keep your door locked." That, he thought, was a useless precaution. The hijackers had Hawkins's keys.

The corridor was still clear when he left Glendon. As he started down the corridor in Car 1, he heard a woman scream. The girl who had boarded the train at Kalgoorlie with her son stood outside her door. She screamed again as he approached her.

"Stop it," he ordered. "Go back into your room."

"But my boy is gone!"

"Quiet." He pushed her into the room. "I'll look for him."

When I came out, he was gone!" Her screams turned into hysterical sobbing.

He pushed her down on the lower berth. Poor, poor girl, he thought. But he slapped her cheeks and said with forced harshness, "Stop that noise. It won't help Davy. I don't think anyone will hurt him. I'll try to find him as soon as I can."

"Maybe," she cried, "he went to the baggage car to see his dog!"

"Well, do stop screaming. You'll bring patrols here." He took her by the shoulders and shook her. "Anything that can be done, I'll do. If you keep on screaming, you'll make my job harder."

She turned her head, trying to bury her face in the pillow, crying now, but more silently.

Hartley left her. From the club car he heard voices. But the corridor of Car 1 was clear. How many people were in the club car? His one gun against four?

At the door to the room where he and Hawkins had stopped to talk with Hall, Macrimmon's nephew, he stopped, tapped, and opened the door. With revolver in hand, ready for a possible attack if Hall were there, Hartley entered the compartment. It was empty. The closet door hung open, showing an orange dressing gown crumpled on the floor. A tin of shoe polish lay in front of the lavatory cabinet, on top of which stood a crystal bottle of cologne. Two orange and gold Moroccan leather slippers, as if escaping from their alliance, pointed in different directions under the chair. There was no baggage in the room. On the table an envelope marked a place in the book Hall had been reading. Hartley withdrew the envelope on which Hall's address was written in jet-black ink, the writing firm and sloped to the right. The envelope had been postmarked in Sydney eight days ago; no return address appeared on it or on the enclosed letter:

Dear Squinchy:

Big news—I've got a week's vacation for when you are here. Aunt Lynne says be sure to stay with us. So just as soon as you finish your sheep business—or sooner—come on out here.

Of course I understand about coming to Kalgoorlie for our wedding. I know your father can't travel to Sydney right now. I hope he's better, and you get his opals back from the crooked old uncle. Why won't he be reasonable? Maybe if you can talk to him on that train trip? I remember when your father was in the hospital here we talked so much about the opals. He loved them.

Give Blazer a werp-woof from me.

Love,

Morsel

P.S. Our Tomcat had three kittens. They're using your room. I didn't know what he was—is.

And what will I do about the cats when we go

*to Kalgoorlie! Bring them along and dress them up
as bridesmaids?*

The remote and uncordial Hall, Hartley thought,
apparently had unexpected qualities to rate a letter like
Morsel's. Would Hall, on his way to visit his fiancée,
have been likely to commit a murder in transit? Not a
premeditated murder, surely. Still, Hall was a mysterious man. And there were the opals. Wherever they were
now. And if, as seemed probable, Hall had been the
passenger who left the train at Cook Station in the haste
indicated by the condition of his room, was that action
consistent with innocence of involvement in his uncle's
death?

As he replaced Morsel's letter in Hall's book, Hartley
felt, as often before, how tantalizing it was, the way bits
of people's lives became real and appealing, although
the people themselves might never be known.

Under the onslaught of the Bulan anthem, he looked
through the corridor. He saw only the closed doors
behind which people and families, hoarding children
under coverings, waited out this ordeal as silent as the
residents of a bewitched castle.

And all of them, he thought, were being borne
forward through the dark plains in that snake-oily
motion of the train, that motion irrelevant to what
happened inside the narrow snake belly of its enclosing
metal sheath.

He looked toward his left and drew back a few
inches into Hall's room. Leaning against the inner side
of the entrance into the vestibule between Car 1 and the
club car, stood a man wearing a tan shirt and shorts and
red cap and drooping a revolver from his right hand.

His left hand, holding a cigarette, was raised toward his lips. His head was turned to look through the vestibule window, at the right-hand section of the night-colored area of the Long Straight that the train bisected.

Hartley covered the few paces between the doorway where he stood and the vestibule, and delivered a hard slicing blow at the back of the man's neck.

The patrol slid down over the door and fell backward, dropping both revolver and cigarette. The revolver slid across the plates and fell outside.

Hartley stamped out the cigarette. He pulled the patrol into the vestibule, and the latter's red cap fell off. As Hartley lifted the patrol's body, the meager body of a boy, and started to lower it over the steps, the boy's eyelids moved and his eyes met Hartley's. For a moment Hartley felt horror, for they were the black, feral eyes that had stared up at him through the tangled hair of the pregnant figure in the berth in Ali's room. But the horror was unreasonable: the body he held in his arms was hard and lean, unmistakably a boy's, and it smelled of whisky from the smashed bottle in the Abo's room. He lowered the man as easily as he could to the cinder bed beside the track.

The boy's red cap, which might have been a badge of the hijackers, he put on, pulling its visor over his eyes for whatever brief disguise it might provide.

The club car was empty. Inside, as he entered, he smelled the acrid fumes from a gas which he thought had been used to subdue the messmen. He remembered the nervous waiter who had announced that the car would be closed, and who, he thought now, had probably been threatened by an armed hijacker, perhaps behind the bar, or in the doorway from the dining car. Where, Hartley wondered, had the train's staff been hidden? Lavatories? He hoped fervently that they had not been ejected from the train. Hawkins, at least, was safe marooned in Car 3. Safe, yes, but Hartley thought with acute misgiving of the possibility of a train from behind crashing into the immobilized three sleepers of the Indian-Pacific. A fire beside the track might not serve as warning. It was unlikely that a passenger train would be on the track; but a freight train might bear down on them. He had faith in Merriam, if indeed Merriam were on board the marooned Car 3, or in the consular nephew, to imagine such possible collision and to guard against it.

He moved through the club car. At one table a liqueur glass lay overturned. From the vestibule between the club car and the dining car he caught sight of a spot of color, a red cap, and the shine of metal. He moved, crouching, into the shelter of an out-jutting sideboard at the rear of the car. The red cap was on the head of Daoud; the metal was the barrel of a rifle, leaning against the table, near the front of the car, where Daoud sat. His back was toward the rear of the car. He was rubbing a stick of butter on his right ankle. Near him, a little farther forward, Darya sat facing the rear. Her long dark blue dressing gown partly covered dark blue slippers. She looked unharmed. She might have seen him; for immediately she began to talk to Daoud. To distract Daoud? To give Hartley time—for what?

The heels of her slippers were raised, the toes pressed down in tension.

He was near enough to hear what she was saying.

Perhaps she was speaking loudly to let him hear.

"Daoud," she said, "please let me go to my room long enough to dress."

"Why should you do that?" Daoud asked. "You are decently dressed now. Your friend Hartley is not on the train. You couldn't hope to find him. We left him miles back when we uncoupled the rear cars. No. You will stay here, as your brother ordered when Lady Mary took you to him. They were not pleased. You had been seen with the spy Hartley."

"But if he isn't on the train now, how could I help him? And I am cold."

"I will bring you a jacket," Daoud said.

Yes, Hartley thought; do that and go far for it. But Daoud, did not leave.

"Where," Darya asked, "is Lady Mary?"

"In the part of the train that has been left behind us."

"But you will need her?"

"We would always need her, but I do not know how useful she would be now. She was much disturbed by her father's death."

"Her father's murder," Darya said. She added, conversationally, as if trying not to antagonize the Malay: "I do not see why it was necessary to murder Macrimmon. You could have got the sacks of gold—he couldn't have been much of a threat."

"We did *not* murder Macrimmon! The leader in our cause, Sir Ian, forbade murder or unnecessary violence. And we have obeyed him."

"But," Darya said, "Macrimmon was murdered. And his servant was violently attacked."

"The servant," Daoud said. "Have you thought that he might have rebelled, or killed his master?"

You, Daoud, could not then have seen the Abo as we found him, she thought. But peaceably she said, "I know you are supposed to guard me, Daoud. But you could go with me as far as my room. It wouldn't take me more than a few minutes to dress. And I would pay you five dollars for every minute you waited."

"We from Bulan," Daoud said haughtily, "do not take bribes."

"But you steal a train—and gold."

"We *borrow*."

"You mean you will repay the gold?"

"Yes. After it has served our purposes."

"And the train, the hardships to passengers, how return that?"

"They must undergo regrettable but minor trouble in the interests of our cause."

"Well," Darya said, "I want to go to my room. You don't take bribes, but how about gifts? Perfume for a friend? A bottle of wine for you?"

"I am a Moslem. I do not use liquor. You should know that from your brother."

"I haven't seen much of my brother lately," Darya said. "But please let me go. Allah values kindness."

This was something that reached the Malay. He held the half-wrapped bar of butter thoughtfully above his ankle.

"Miss Darya," he said slowly, "I have no desire to be unkind to you. But our purposes do not permit us to indulge in ordinary civilized behavior. It is shut away. It will have to wait until the larger ends are achieved."

"By then it will be rusty. Maybe you won't ever be able to reactivate it. You are a university student, Daoud?"

133

"I am a graduate of the University of Singapore, with postgraduate work in political science. I met your brother in Singapore."

"Then you know that civil rights, constitutional rights, are hard to resurrect, once they have been shut away. You must know a good deal of histroy."

Daoud laughed. "I also know when I see a clever attempt to sidetrack what I am trying to explain."

"You haven't explained very much."

"Didn't your brother tell you anything?"

"Almost nothing. He wasn't pleased to see me. So I would be interested to know more about the Bulan independence movement. If you would care to tell me."

"Yes! I would care. I was born on Bulan. I lived through abuses from Portuguese, Dutch, Indonesians, and Japanese. After the Japanese were cleared out, and the Dutch, the Indonesians and the Portuguese carried on a kind of joint control. Since the Portuguese have pulled out, the Indonesians are trying to swallow us. We will not be swallowed. Sir Ian is our leader."

"The people in Bulan," Darya said. "They are Moslems, like you?"

"There are Chinese, too. We find them sympathetic. There are also some Indians, as in all the islands. They are good bookkeepers, businessmen."

Daoud rubbed more butter on his leg and ankle.

"You hurt your ankle on the roof?" Darya asked.

"It is nothing."

"Ali is up there now?"

"Yes. He is better than I am. I lost balance."

"But," Darya said, "you were very clever. You kept Sammy hidden in your room. And who was the boy

134

who was ill—or was he ill?"

"Kasim. He was not ill, but we needed to bring food to the room."

"Where is he now—and the others?"

"Where they are needed."

"Where are we going?"

"As far as we need to," Daoud said.

Good try, Hartley thought.

She was trying again.

"Is Sir Ian converted to Islam?"

"Yes."

"Lady Mary?"

Daoud gestured with the bar of butter, and said indifferently, "She is a woman."

"What about my brother Sammy?"

"Another convert. Partly because of the girl. The girl—yes, a woman sometimes can help. But Munah is not for your brother."

"She is for you?" Darya asked.

He nodded.

"When this is all finished. Yes."

He applied more butter to the ankle wound.

"You must have missed a prayer up there on top of the train," Darya said. "Or did you have a prayer mat with you?"

"I have not missed a prayer," Daoud said.

"If you haven't missed a prayer," Darya said, "it must be time to pray now."

Daoud laughed unamusedly. "You are telling *me* what to do? It is *you* who should be praying, however you do it, for the success of our Bulan mission.

"Why?"

"You must have some feeling for your brother. You would always have a home with him in a new independent nation."

"I like the old independent nation I live in," Darya said.

"You should have stayed there. Sammy did not enjoy living there. He is unalterably one of us now."

"But Sammy is a highly alterable person, Daoud. Is he the leader of your group in this mission?"

"Yes. Dermot is second."

"How many others are working with you on this train?"

Daoud shrugged. "You ask so many questions. Stop talking, please."

"No, not unless you let me go to my room and get dressed."

"I could enforce my order, but I do not wish to offend Sammy's sister."

"What do you call *this*?" Darya asked. "I call it offense to be forced to stay here. Cold and hungry."

"What could you expect? Sammy warned you not to travel on this train. He has enough problems without worrying about a sister."

"Is that Bulan's idea about family loyalty?"

Daoud threw down the remnant of the bar of butter angrily, muttering a retort.

Hartley did not hear the words. He heard something else: the whistle of a locomotive. Not the one Sammy was driving, but another, forward on the track. Eerie, shocking in this broad flat stretch of empty space, the whistle brought him the memory of the whistle of a ghost train in a play he had seen as a child, a play in which the train materialized only in the chilling shriek of the whistle offstage.

This was different. A train was coming toward the Indian-Pacific whose speed did not diminish. He saw Darya's right hand grip the arm of her chair, and saw Daoud, tense, catch up his rifle.

Brake, brake, slow down, you bloody fool, Hartley thought. Was Sammy a madman?

Something Hawkins had told him came to Hartley. Normally the Indian-Pacific had open track all the way, but occasionally a signal by radio or at the Cook station would warn of an oncoming freight and the need to pull into a sidetrack some miles east of Cook. Why hadn't that dispatch received at Cook been radioed? He remembered then what Hawkins had told him earlier: there was a short-wave radio in the engine cab, but it had been unreliable.

Hawkins had not been seen after the stop at Cook.

And I, Hartley thought, was worrying about a collision with the uncoupled cars behind us. *Why doesn't Sammy stop?*

Another whistle sounded, much nearer, prolonged. Now Hartley could hear the pounding of wheels and the grind of brakes.

At the sound of the second whistle, Daoud caught up his rifle and dashed toward the engine.

Windows had been broken open in the car. Hartley ran to the nearest one and looked out. In the beam of the Indian-Pacific's engine he saw the brilliant headlight eye of another engine, and behind it, freights cars. He heard shouts from men aboard the freight train. Why doesn't the madman brake and stop this train? Is he going to try to ram the freight?

When Hartley leaped into the dining car toward Darya, she was standing, pallid, aghast, facing him. He grasped her and pulled her down under the table, covering her with his body.

"Close your eyes!"

"He won't stop!" Darya cried. "He is mad! Hartley—"

"Close your eyes and your mouth!"

The tablecloth unwrapped around his legs, and dishes and glasses slid toward the end of the table.

He braced for the crash.

6

JETTISON AGAIN

A shock emptied the table above them. Glass, china, crashed to the floor.

Hartley waited for the crumpling of walls, the overturning of the car. His lips were on Darya's hair.

The tablecloth muffled him. He tore it loose. Darya stirred; he moved to release her from his weight.

Silence, for a moment.

Then he heard shouts forward.

He crawled from under the table. The floor was pebbled with broken dishes, glasses. Chairs had overturned.

Darya came from the shelter of the table. "Hartley, did we hit the train?"

"No. Just a vicious stop. You all right?"

"But what happened back there?" she asked, pointing toward the cars behind them. "It was a killing stop."

"Only two passenger cars left. The others were uncoupled. Miles back. Stay here now—get down behind a table. Wait till we see what happens. Sure you're all right? They didn't hurt you?"

"No. Lady Mary—she had a revolver—she took me to Sammy."

He put his arms around her and drew her close.

"What did you say?" she asked.

"Malayan. Means something like darling."

She put her lips against his cheek, then quickly withdrew them.

"You talk to me in Malayan now?"

"No time before, in any language," Hartley said. "Safe now, I think—you can go to your room."

"And you?"

"I must get into the engine. Reach Sammy. Try to delay the train to spoil their schedule and get more time for any help coming to us."

"You're going to the engine with all those people there? Could I help?"

"Not unless you were bristling with guns. No. God, what's this?"

From the baggage car a wild small figure, half-shouting, half-whistling, ran toward them. In his arms he clutched a dog almost as large as he, a dog whose head hung away from its body limply and unnaturally.

Hartley reached for the boy.

"Let me go—I'm not going to be a hostage!"

"No. You'll be all right." Hartley touched the dog's head and saw the eyes obscured with blood.

"Davy." He held the boy's shoulders. "What happened?"

Davy looked at him savagely, with dread in his eyes. "In the baggage car—a big box fell on him." He held the dog more tightly.

"Leave him with me. I'll try to help him," Hartley said.

"No!" He tore away from him and ran toward the vestibule.

"Darya, on your way see that he goes to his room. It's the first on the left in Car 1, after the conductor's rooms. Hang on for a rough start."

"The dog is dead?"

"Yes," Hartley said.

"Oh, they are vicious—killing people, pets!"

He heard her sob as she ran after Davy.

From the rear of the dining car Hartley looked into the baggage car, where dislodged boxes and pieces of luggage blocked whatever passageway had been left along the middle of the car. None of the hijackers showed; they were, Hartley thought, massed around Sammy in the cab; and he himself had reached the point farthest forward in his tortuous progress through the train. With the concentration of the enemy in the cab, he could not hope to penetrate to Sammy's post, not yet, at least. He would try to hold his precarious gains. He stood near the forward end of the baggage car, ready to take shelter behind packing cases. From where he stood, he could see Sammy leaning through the window beside the engineer's seat. Dermot, Daoud, and Kasim flanked him.

From the ground came a voice, the freight engineer's, Hartley thought. "—fifteen minutes ago," the voice said. "Didn't you get the dispatch at Cook?"

"No dispatch," Sammy said coolly.

"Where's your head conductor? I'll talk to him."

"Hawkins was taken ill, had to be left at Cook," Sammy answered.

"Where are the other condcutors?" the engineer cried belligerently.

"Not my concern. I've got enough to look after right here. I can't go running around after the crew. But get this straight—*the Indian-Pacific goes through*. You'll have to back up to the nearest siding. Get moving. We have right of way."

"Back nineteen freight cars, some loaded with explosives for the mines, ten miles to the nearest siding behind us? No, you bloody fool! *You* back to the siding where you ought to be right now!"

"Not us," Sammy said, almost happily. "Get into your cab and start backing."

"Like hell, I will!"

"Like hell, you will be doing just that!" Dermot shouted. Hartley saw his arm rise. A shot sounded, an outraged scream from the freight engineer, and a shout from another member of the freight's crew. Sammy blew his engine's whistle with menace.

Silence. The engineer and crew of the freight, Hartley thought, were stunned by the shot from the sacrosanct Indian-Pacific. They would share the Hawkins syndrome of thinking that nothing like this could happen.

"What's your name?" the freight engineer shouted.

"Go to hell!" Sammy shouted back. "Just start backing."

Another shot grazed the engine of the freight train.

"You'll never run another locomotive. I will tell the company—"

"And you will never see another morning, unless you back—" Suddenly, a third shot followed by a scream from the engineer or one of his men. Silence again.

Then Hartley heard the reversing of the engine of the freight. He also heard Sammy's hysterical singing of the Bulan anthem. The light from the freight's engine receded.

"Kasim, bring me something to eat!" Sammy ordered.

Hartley retreated farther into the baggage car and took cover behind a massive packing case. While waiting for Kasim to pass, he glanced at the label on the case addressed to the curator of a science museum in Sydney, the sender's name an illegible scrawl, the sending point Kalgoorlie.

Sydney seemed as far away as another planet. If only, Hartley thought, I could have given some signal to the freight crew. The sound of the backing engine was dying. Hartley thought again of danger from behind to the marooned three cars on the track. And he saw in imagination the poor crumpled body of Macrimmon lying in that berth, with none of his plans for celebrations and pleasures ever to be realized in Sydney, or anywhere else.

Kasim was now coming into the baggage car slowly as if resenting his slave duty.

Hartley listened for any following footsteps. Then, regretting the need to yield even an inch of the hard-won territory, he retreated in a cautious, irregular path among and behind crates and boxes until he reached the last shelter at the rear vestibule, where he could look into the galley section of the dining car. He saw Kasim laying out slices of bread on the counter beside the stove, stooping to open the door of the refrigerator under the counter, bringing out a partial roast of lamb, and opening a drawer to find a knife, with which he sliced the roast. Then Kasim bent down again, opened the refrigerator door, and searched for something else. Before he could find what he was looking for, Hartley sprang through the vestibule and struck him on the back of the neck with the revolver butt.

As Kasim fell, a jar of cherries dropped from his hand and broke on the floor, splattering his khaki shirt and making his injury look like butchery. Hartley dragged Kasim's body to the rear vestibule of the dining car, removed the revolver from the pocket of the khaki shirt, and lodged it beside General Percy's in the belt of his slacks.

In the seconds that he waited, listening for anyone who might be coming from the forward end of the car, he saw with compunction the young face, the skin only a shade darker than Daoud's, not as dark as Ahmad's. The boy's long eyelashes reached down to his level cheekbones.

He heard himself say, "Kasim," and then lowered the boy's body through the open vestibule and let it drop the short distance over the steps to the cinderbed.

He must return General Percy's automatic, he thought. But not yet, not while he had a chance to preserve his position near the engine. He ran back to the baggage car and took shelter behind a case with only a minute or two to spare before Ali, dirty, scowling, swinging his rifle, came into the car from the rear and was met by Dermot and Daoud entering from the front.

Dermot was saying, "—in a black mood, ordering us out of the cab."

"You should know he cannot be criticized," Daoud said. "Especially when he is hungry."

"So you," Dermot said to Ali, "finally got knocked off the roof."

"No! Nothing knocks me off," Ali answered. He added words in Malay, which Daoud translated for Dermot.

"He says one of his ancestors was a panther."

Dermot snorted.

"Where's the girl?" he asked Daoud, who shrugged.

"She cannot go far."

As he spoke, the engine started with the violence of a dropped elevator.

"Mother of God!" Dermot roared. He ran forward into the engine."

Ali kicked at a suitcase that had come unstowed and lay in the aisle. Daoud raised his eyebrows when the suitcase broke open and ejected a doll, a toy koala bear, a green shoe, and a pair of compasses.

Dermot came back.

"By Jesus, he'll be murdering every last man of us if he rams that freight!" Dermot stamped on the doll and crushed it. "I told him to slow down, but would he? Not him! I told him I thought he knew how to run a train—it's all he's talked about for months."

Daoud's voice, following Dermot's, sounded cool and fatalistic. "Sometimes," Daoud said, "I have thought he cared more for running the engine than for helping Bulan become a free nation." He picked up the koala and set it beside him on the box on which he sat.

Ali muttered something in Malay.

"Ali," Daoud translated, "says that Sammy has brought us this far."

"And where indeed are we?" Dermot cried. "Late for our meeting with the Land Rovers, and maybe not getting to the coast until daylight. And not even then, if Sammy decides to take over the freight."

"Why would he want to take over the freight train?"

145

Daoud asked. "He has enough on his hands, and so do we."

"True," Dermot said. "In the islands near the country I came from there's an old saying: 'Providence takes care of drunken men and madmen.' Drink's not Sammy's problem; but about engines he's fey. You understand that word, Daoud?"

"I don't know the word, but I can guess. If Allah wills that we finish our mission, let us not tell Sir Ian about the freight train."

Dermot pulled a flask from his jacket pocket and drank. His voice became more jovial. "Who will be snitching?" Then he added, "After we finish, I might go home to Dublin to visit."

"You will not stay to help Bulan?"

"Oh, well, of course if Sir Ian makes a generous offer—and he's fair man, for an Englishman. Pays up what he promises."

"Sir Ian," Daoud said, "will be unhappy because there has been a murder. Lady Mary will be unhappy about the death of her father and because she has been separated from us."

Dermot drank again from his flask.

"Why do you think Lady Mary will be unhappy about the death of her father?"

"She is a woman and unpredictable. I knew that she suffered from the division between her father and our hopes for Bulan."

Ali, sitting on a carton near Daoud, unwrapped a cube of sugar and ate it. He spoke in Malay and Daoud translated.

"Ali reminds us that Lady Mary believed we could pay her father for the gold by selling the oil on our island."

"Don't talk about *that*!" Dermot cried. "Don't think it aloud. It's not for anyone to hear. What the petroleum geologists reported is the deadliest of secrets. Other countries, Indonesia, would swarm down on us, swallow us. Where would your freedom be? Or the money I'd get for helping you again?"

Ali set down his rifle which he had been cleaning. "Who killed the old man?"

"None of us," Dermot said. "We were all busy in teams taking over the train."

"Not," Daoud said, "until the action started a few minutes before the train left the station. I believe Macrimmon was killed earlier."

"Why?" Dermot asked.

"Because one shot was fired from Macrimmon's revolver which he kept under his pillow. It would have been heard if the train had been standing. And when the train stopped, even before we started our action, there were people in the corridors leaving the dining and club cars, some of them going down to the platform."

"And where were you seeing all this?"

"I was at the back of the club car, waiting. You know our plan. A few minutes before the train was due to leave Cook, Sammy and Lady Mary and you, Dermot, were to go to the engine. Kasim and Ahmad and I were to use the tear gas to immobilize the dining car staff. Ali was already on his way to the car roofs. Kasim and I were to deal with the conductor of Car 1 as he came on board, and then we were to take Hawkins in Car 2. Ahmad was our reserve. And we needed him, for there was a delay here. Instead of boarding the train at Car 2, as he usually did, Hawkins came on board with the conductor of Car 1, so we had two to deal with. Kasim and I were to go to Macrimmon's room *before* Sammy's announcement. We knew he and his servant were armed. We were to overpower them and drug them, but because of the delay, we could not reach Macrimmon's room until after the announcement. When we went to that room, the old man was dead, his revolver was on the floor, and the servant had been stabbed."

"When you and Ahmad got to Rhys later, why didn't you kill him, not just throw him overboard?" Dermot kicked the sandal from his right foot and scratched it.

"We are not here on this train to kill," Daoud said. "Or have you forgotten Sir Ian's orders and our own rules? Our independent Bulan will not be built on a flooring of dead bodies."

"Oh, crap," Dermot muttered.

Ali impassively munched a cube of sugar.

Hartley saw Daoud cross his left leg over his right with aristocratic grace, minimizing the gesture.

"I see," Daoud said to Dermot, "that your foot is not injured."

"My foot? Why should it be injured?"

"There was blood on your ankle when you passed me on the way to the engine earlier, at the start of our action."

"Some bit of glass. And you, son-of-a-bitch, want to tie me into the murder. I tell you, Daoud, if you try, the first night after we get back to Bulan, I'll carve your throat from ear to ear!"

"As Allah wills," Daoud said. "But I have not finished. Nor have we returned to Bulan."

Dermot shoved his foot back into the sandal.

"Finish, then. But with all your fine talk about principles, don't be forgetting the murder of the rat from the *Cutlass*, and the Sword Company spy, in

Singapore. What did Sir Ian have to say about all that?"

"I had nothing to do with that action," Daoud said. "I believe Sir Ian would not have ordered murder," he continued. "There is one other thing. From where I was watching just before the train left Cook, I saw a man leave the train at the rear. A very tall man in gray, carrying a suitcase. The train started within seconds after he left the train. He moved in haste. Almost ran toward the end of the platform."

"Tall, gray, if he was who I think he was," Dermot said. "He was the nephew of Macrimmon. Mary pointed him out to me. An enemy in some family feud. Was there blood on *his* ankle?" he sneered.

"Blood or not," Daoud said, "he did leave in a great hurry, and with no time to spare before the train started."

Dermot lighted a cigarette.

"He could have killed Macrimmon," he said. "Or the Abo could have."

"The Abo himself was half-dead," Daoud said. "Whoever killed Macrimmon, Sir Ian will be angry and saddened, and we will have trouble with Lady Mary."

"But," Dermot protested, "she didn't like the old man. She was willing for us to take the gold."

"But not her father's life."

"Well," Dermot said, "she's out of our hair now. Who uncoupled those cars?"

"I did," Daoud said, "with Ahmad's help."

"Did Sammy order that?"

"We talked about it earlier. We had too many cars to patrol, and the roofs. And there were troublemakers— Rhys and the man in charge of the tourists. And there was no reason to prolong any trouble for the tourists."

"Tourists," Dermot said scornfully. He lighted a

cigarette. "Who cares about them?"

"If," Daoud said, "anything goes wrong, we will have enough legal difficulties without involving people from the United States and Europe."

"Nothing is going to go wrong—not in the end!" Dermot exclaimed. "Only thing bothers me—fuel for the ruddy junk."

"Sammy," Daoud said, "knows a fueling station in the Bight. We'll have to pay extra because we haven't landing permits. But he says we'll get the fuel."

"Hope he hasn't dreamed it up," Dermot said. "How far from where the junk is anchored?"

"Near enough."

"We'll need a hell of a lot. Long voyage back to Bulan."

"Sammy had calculated the tanks' capacity."

"It was a close thing on the way over," Dermot said.

"Yes, but Sammy took us in at night to fuel at that yacht basin near Perth. You remember."

"I remember. Cost us a packet. Damn that Australian dollar. Still, we're behind schedule, but we have the gold, we have transport to the coast, and we have the ship. If you have any dark thoughts, Daoud, how can you be so cool?"

"The outcome will be decided by Allah," Daoud added, translating words spoken by Ali.

"He said all that? I don't believe it. Sounds more like you. Infidel, eh? My Church is six hundred years older than yours."

"I could ask you," Daoud said, "how faithful you are to your religion, when you sell your services to us."

"Well," Dermot said, "my Church isn't helping me make a living. Not at what I do best, having had much practice in fighting against the bloody English."

Hartley heard the whistle of the freight engine some distance ahead, but not far enough. He heard also, from Dermot, the question he had been expecting.

"Where's that sod of a Kasim with Sammy's food?" Dermot asked.

"And where is Ahmad?" Daoud said. "I haven't seen him since we uncoupled the cars."

"Maybe he took his pregnancy to heart, or whatever. Or maybe he and Kasim have defected."

"Never!" Daoud exclaimed. "Ahmad was the most bitter of all of us toward outsiders. And Kasim is as strong and as trustworthy as a water buffalo. Ali, will you go to look for them?"

"Don't ask me, Daoud," Ali said. He expanded his refusal in Malayan.

"Ali," Daoud responded, "does not want to go back to where Macrimmon was killed."

Around the edge of his shelter Hartley saw Ali still holding the rifle and stretching out his long, thin body on top of two packing cases near Daoud.

"Well, then, I'll be going myself," Dermot said. "But I cannot understand you Malays. You're so fancy against killing. Sure you aren't Buddhists with all that crap about sparing bloody beasts and bugs?"

"No religious faith," Daoud answered, "has a monopoly on mercy."

Dermot ground out his cigarette on the floor and stood up.

"You missed your calling, boy. You should have been a ruddy priest. Not a revolutionary."

After Dermot left, Daoud went forward into the engine. Hartley heard Ali snoring.

The Abo, Hartley thought, would be vulnerable to Dermot. He followed Dermot.

151

When he entered Car 1, Dermot was half the car's length ahead of him, opening doors and switching on lights, calling, "Ahmad! Kasim!" From several of the rooms Hartley heard voices, startled, protesting. He narrowed the distance between himself and Dermot in Car 2. In the room near Darya's he heard Glendon cry, "Get out! My grandfather is ill!"

The train was running faster and the sway of the car, now the last in the train, together with Dermot's quick movements as he crossed and recrossed the corridor, would have made an accurate shot unlikely. But Hartley held his revolver ready for firing if Dermot lingered in the Abo's room. However, Dermot stayed only long enough to turn on a light and to call for Ahmad and Kasim.

Across the corridor Hartley saw Darya's door opened on her darkened room. Again Dermot turned on a light. After glancing through the room, he continued his search through the car and out to the rear vestibule. By the time Dermot started forward, Hartley was pressed against the inner wall of Darya's room.

Under the bright irrelevance of the Bulan song, which had continued through the stopping and starting of the train and through the contest with the freight engineer for right of way, he surveyed Darya's room, seeing first a few feathers of the kookaburra under a towel on Darya's bed, and then Darya's blue dressing gown beside it. The door of the narrow closet beside the bed was partly open. He pulled the door to its full opening. In the space which he would have thought could not hold even a child, he saw Darya, half-hidden by dresses on hangers, bending forward in the constrictive height of the closet.

"Darya!"

He drew her out of the closet, separating her from a suit and two dresses which had fallen from their hangers.

"How did you ever get into that space?"

"I was scared," Darya said. "I heard Dermot. I had to shrink in."

She rubbed her neck. "Probably a permanent crook. I couldn't stand up, but I didn't want to get taken back to Sammy. At least I had time to get dressed." She wore a black sweater and slacks and around her head a dark blue scarf.

"You did a good job getting Daoud to talk. You saw me, didn't you?"

"Yes. Was I ever glad to! I gathered from Sammy that some of the cars had been uncoupled, and was afraid you'd been in one of them. What happened after I left?"

"More talk. Dermot and Ali and Daoud." He added, "I must return the revolver General Percy lent me. Glendon has your handbag. I thought it would be safer with her."

"You have another revolver now?"

"Kasim's."

"How? What happened to Kasim?"

"I put him over the side. Don't look shocked. I'd knocked him out, but I don't think he was much hurt."

"Did you," she hesitated, "put Ahmad over the side too?"

He nodded. "I had to, Darya. If I'm ever going to reach the cab—try to reason with Sammy. I used to have some influence over him."

"So did I. But he's awfully strange. Very unglad to see me. I thought it was wild when he was all heated up about racing camels, but it was nothing like this."

"I wish we had some camels to distract him," Hartley said.

"They wouldn't. He's even more fanatic about trains."

The train wheeled forward. Dresses swayed on hangers in the open closet, and a jar clinked against a brush on the cabinet top.

I must go forward, Hartley thought. I must delay the train.

"Hartley, if Ahmad and Kasim had been badly hurt, would you still have thrown them overboard?" Darya asked.

"I don't know. Do you think I enjoy any of this?"

"No. But after seeing what's happened to Sammy—"

"I'm not Sammy," Hartley said.

Darya touched his hand and said, "No. Not at all like Sammy."

Hartley closed his arms around her. During the few seconds that he held her he felt a widening of the narrow imprisonment of the train and a freedom from the urgency of his mission and its thwarting obstacles. "I must go," he said, releasing her.

Darya looked beyond the partly opened door into the corridor and shivered. "Ghostly, all those blank doors. People behind them as quiet as ghosts."

"Good girl," Hartley said. "You've given me an idea. About a way to confuse the enemy, and maybe even delay the train."

He explained.

7

GHOSTS

Once more, starting from what was now the last car—
he thought of it as square one in his advance and
retreat—Hartley unopposed had reached the rear end
of the dining car and had slid down between the aisle
chair and the last table on the right side. He had waited
to move the chair until another of the long blasts
Sammy was blowing would make the sound inaudible
to Daoud, who had taken over Kasim's unfinished work
of making sandwiches in the galley, and to Ali, lounging
in the vestibule beyond. Why Sammy was blowing the
whistle, Hartley did not know. By now the freight train
would surely have reached its siding—if it had gone the
ten miles it had to go, if the switch had been thrown,
and if the long line of freight cars had been edged into
the spur and the switch rethrown—that is, if the freight
engineer in his state of shock had remembered to have
the switch rethrown. However, the action would

probably have been instinctive; he would have been aware of what would happen if the switch were left open. Perhaps Sammy was celebrating his humiliation of the freight engineer, or merely exulting at his command of the locomotive.

Two of the hijackers, three with Lady Mary, had been inactivated. But in addition to Sammy, Dermot, now probably in the cab, and Ali and Daoud, were left. Ali's rifle leaned against his knees, and even the more peaceable Daoud had a revolver in his belt. The odds against him were still great enough to keep him from trying to reach the cab. He would wait.

A long whistling sounded. Ali muttered words that Hartley could not hear.

Answering in Malayan, Daoud said, "Sammy is either proud or hungry."

Ali spoke again. It was a question.

"How do I know?" Daoud said, uncapping a bottle of beer. "I can't tell you where Kasim and Ahmad are. Dermot couldn't find them." Again, answering Ali, he said, "No. I do not think any passenger attacked them. The passengers are unarmed—and cowed, as far as we know. Not like Malays. Can you imagine forty or fifty of us sitting in our rooms and not coming out to see what was happening? Yes, I know, the disappearance of Ahmad and Kasim is very strange."

Ali uttered words that Hartley thought were in agreement with Daoud.

"Now," Daoud said, still speaking in Malayan, "will you take this tray to Sammy? No—I know you have been on the roofs. Yes, I know Dermot will want food. All right. I will prepare more." Another protest from Ali. "All right," Daoud said. "When you come back, you can eat." He made more sandwiches, and bent to take another bottle of beer from the refrigerator. At a word from Ali he said, "All right. Sugar." He turned to face the car behind him and lifted up a bowl of sugar cubes when he screamed and dropped the bowl.

What they saw with obvious horror was a wheelchair being propelled by its occupant through the rear vestibule of the car. The occupant of the wheelchair was a slight, stiff figure wearing a stained canvas windbreaker, a dirty felt hat pulled low over dark glasses, knees covered with a blanket, one hand on the head feathers of a bird protruding above the blanket, and the other hand outstretched, clutching a pipe leveled at Daoud like a gun.

Both Malays fled into the baggage car.

A moment or two later Dermot ran into the dining car, halted, and cried, "Holy Mother!"

As Dermot stood, daunted, a sound from the wheelchair made him cry out again. It was Hartley's turn now to be shocked. Had he imagined it? Was he filling in a Gestalt pattern involving sound? Was he sharing the Malays' and Dermot's panic? Or had he actually heard a faint, beyond-death sound, a travesty of the kookaburra's laughter—empty, dismal, mocking?

The hand of the figure in the wheelchair holding the pipe wavered only slightly.

Was it possible that the kookaburra was alive?

Dermot, transfixed, a frog facing a snake, had drawn his revolver.

The wheelchair moved toward him. Hartley's hand was on his own revolver. When the wheelchair was a few feet away, Dermot shrank away from it and ran

157

into the baggage car.

The train stopped in another savage concussion.

At a signal from Hartley the wheelchair was rolled back to the vestibule. It passed out of sight into the club car.

Seconds, less than a minute later, Sammy stormed into the dining car. Dermot was behind him.

"Damn and blast!" Sammy cried. He wrenched at his red cap. "There's nothing here. Have you gone out of your wits—imagining ghosts?"

"He was there!" Dermot cried. "The old dead man and the dead bird. I tell you—he was there!"

Behind Sammy and Dermot, Hartley saw Ali and Daoud hovering at the doorway. Sammy, his face gaunt and tense and angry, turned toward them. "You brought me here for nothing, you pack of idiots! Don't you know every minute counts? We've got to reach the Land Rovers! We're late!"

Behind him Daoud spoke.

"Sammy, we all saw it. The old man. The bird."

"Then you're all imbeciles." Sammy pulled off his cap. "Why did Sir Ian ever saddle me with such sickly, stupid beasts!"

Dermot, somewhat recovered from fright, rallied. "Beasts you say? How would you have got this far without us?"

"And how far is this? And by God, why can't you find Ahmad and Kasim? Did you think you'd get more reward throwing them off the train so there'd be fewer of you?"

Daoud placed a hand on Sammy's shoulder. Sammy tore it away.

"Stay away from me, you cur."

"Sammy," Daoud said, "how old are you?"

"I'm twenty-seven. What's that got to do with this crazy act? Superstitious bunch of morons."

"If you are really twenty-seven," Daoud continued, "then stop behaving like a boy of nine."

Sammy slapped Daoud's face. Hartley saw Daoud's hands clench into fists, but the voice that answered Sammy was quiet.

"Then you are old enough to understand that we are all here on a mission. We are not here to satisfy ourselves—in running trains."

"Who else could run the train?" Sammy demanded. "And who's running it now while we're losing time?"

"All right," Daoud said. "Run your train. But stop abusing us for seeing what we saw."

From the far end of the car Hartley saw Sammy. Daoud's hands were still fists, but his voice stayed calm. Dermot was wiping sweat from his forehead. Ali indecisively clutched his rifle a few feet behind Sammy.

Too much to hope, Hartley thought, that they would turn on Sammy. They knew Sammy, knew his violences and his turnabouts.

"Go back to the cab, Sammy," Daoud said. "You are doing very well. Leave us to do what we must do." He offered the tray of sandwiches.

A strange relationship between them, Hartley thought. Each disliked the other, each was bound to the other not only by the bonds of their mission but by some underlying respect or even affection, something too durable to be broken by his intervention. Even if circumstances drove them to kill each other, they would die without sundering, or understanding, their linkage.

Sammy had taken a sandwich from the tray. "And

159

now—" he raised his voice. "Daoud, you and Dermot move. See what trick was being played on you. Look everywhere for Kasim and Ahmad. I want Ali in the cab with me. We haven't passed the siding. That bloody engineer—" he broke off, staring at Dermot.

"No!" Dermot shouted. "I will not go back into those accursed cars."

"Then the devil eat your eyeballs!" Sammy roared. "If you can face up to live men with guns, why in hell can't you hunt down a dead man—if he *is* dead?"

"He was dead and so was the bird," Daoud said.

"Then go get proof," Sammy cried.

"Sammy," Dermot ventured. "I've just gone through the train. I couldn't find Ahmad or Kasim. I won't go again."

"Yes you will. You want me to think you're as white-livered as these Malays?"

Ali, not understanding, turned toward Daoud, who motioned to him to be still.

"Sammy," Daoud said peaceably. "We don't have time to quarrel. Whatever trick there was, maybe it was Rhys."

"Impossible!" Dermot cried. "He was on Car 3 when it was uncoupled. What do you think he is, a magician?"

"No, but I think he may be"—Daoud hesitated as if trying for a word that he had read but not spoken—"an acrobat."

"You mean he got across? But why the hell weren't you watching!" Sammy cried.

No one answered.

Sammy tasted the sandwich, and threw it down as if it were bitter. "Where is the boy—the hostage?" he cried.

160

Again Daoud spoke quietly.

"The boy ran away when you stopped the train so harshly. But Sammy, a hostage is valuable only if the holder is ready to kill him. You wouldn't kill a small boy. And if you had wanted hostages, you had a whole train to choose from. A whole train."

And this whole train, or what was left of it, Hartley thought, had still not passed the siding. Darya's impersonation had not, then, delayed the train.

Sammy picked up the discarded sandwich and looked at it and at the opened beer bottles with hate.

"Open. Flat by now." He found an unopened bottle and pushed at the objects on the counter, jerking open a drawer so violently that it fell out. "Get me a bottle opener!"

No one moved.

"Are you all bewitched?"

Daoud, moving like a sleepwalker, found a bottle opener behind a jar of pickles on the counter.

"Make another sandwich," Sammy ordered. "At least you can do that. Bring it into the cab."

But the three other men were still immobilized.

Sammy slapped Ali's face. Ali reacted by leaping on Sammy. Dermot pulled Ali away, and Sammy, staggering against the refrigerator, picked up his fallen cap, righted himself, and struck at Ali, who, freeing himself from Dermot, sprang at Sammy's throat. Daoud caught the claws.

"Stop!" Daoud shouted. "Stop—and remember why we are here. Listen! You hear those words?"

The Bulan anthem was still playing.

"I will go back into the other cars. I will go alone, if Dermot is afraid to go with me."

"Oh, I'll go," Dermot said reluctantly.

"Then hurry," Sammy ordered as he left the car on his way to the engine. "Follow me, Ali."

Hartley hoped Darya had had time to put away the trappings of her masquerade and was in some relatively safe place, though where that would be, he didn't know.

Daoud and Dermot passed the table behind which Hartley was hidden. They did not see him, but Ali, searching for sugar, came to the next table. As he took a handful of cubes from a bowl, he looked down and saw Hartley. Ali's shout brought the other two back from the vestibule door at a run, with drawn revolvers.

"Out from there, and drop your revolver!" Dermot cried.

Ali, who had leaped toward the forward door, came running back with his rifle.

Hartley crawled from behind the table.

"Don't shoot him, Dermot!" Daoud cried.

"We'll throw him off the train."

"Not at this speed—you'd kill him."

"Serve the bastard right."

"No more killing, unless we have to." To Hartley, Daoud said, "Turn around. Walk until we tell you to stop." He took Hartley's revolver and searched him for other weapons. "Ali, open the door opposite the stove in the galley." He handed Ali a key ring.

"Stop here," Daoud ordered when Hartley reached the galley. Dermot pushed him through the narrow doorway so forcefully that Hartley fell into the unlighted space beyond. He heard the door being locked behind him.

What dismal hellhole have I got boxed into, Hartley

wondered as he stood up. The compartment smelled acrid. He swung his arms in arcs to feel out obstacles in the darkness as he searched for a light switch. His left hand encountered the edge of a bunk, his right hand came into contact with shelf edges, and his feet stumbled against boxes. He found a switch which turned on a ceiling light. Two bunks on his left, running athwart the car, held the bodies of three men. All three were inanimate. Drugged, he thought. Their breathing was heavy, but there were no gags or bonds.

The compartment was both a bunkroom for the dining crew and a storage room. The shelves along the right-hand wall were filled with jars and cans. Under the window more cartons were ranged. Between the end of the bunks and the car wall stood a metal cabinet, similar to the one in his compartment which enclosed a toilet and washbowl. He opened the lockers under the lower berth: men's clothing in one, cleaning supplies in another. A small space beyond the shelves was filled with mops and a broom. A wall bracket held a fire extinguisher and an axe.

An axe. Hartley pulled it from the bracket and immediately felt less naked then before. He set himself to considering how he could get out of this room.

The window, centered between the fore and aft partitions, would not open. He broke the double panes with the axe and looked out. On his right, not more than six feet away, light shone from the forward end of the dining car. Leaning out, he saw that the glass in the nearest window there had been broken, possibly for ventilation.

Six feet—at worst, seven feet to that window.

But I am no acrobat, he thought. A leap from the

163

window in this compartment to the window in the dining car area? Can't make it. Not without support of some kind—a lifeline.

I told Farnsleigh I wasn't a hired killer. I might have told him too that I wasn't a Houdini. Not even an acrobat, no matter what skill Daoud credited me with. Combat skills, yes, and a fair sense of balance.

He thought of the leap he had made when the rear cars had been uncoupled. Yes, but no angle had been involved. Here he would be moving around the near window and again around the angle of the dining car window. If he tried to move from this cell. Also, he would have to contend with the irregularity of Sammy's driving, with the possibility of one of Sammy's violent stops.

By now the train would have passed the siding; that fact should have brought him more satisfaction than he could feel at this moment. But he tried to dwell on it, to measure his predicament against the carnage that would have resulted from a collision with the freight.

Sammy was still blowing the engine's whistle. Ali would probably be with him in the cab, the other two searching for two men whom they would not find. If they found Darya, what treatment would she receive from Dermot even under any restraint Daoud might try to exercise? Or if they took her to the engine's cab, how vengeful would he be toward a sister who had defied him? Physical abuse? Hartley could not think it impossible, although he knew how unpredictable and contradictory all human relationships could be.

He couldn't remember in any previous assignment having felt so completely stopped as he was now, confined in this brief space, subjected to the savage halts and starts of Sammy's driving. He had tried to reach the engine cab, to talk with Sammy, to use force if necessary. But he had regressed. If the hijackers held the *Cutlass*, where was she? He knew little about the southern coastline of Australia. And Darya, who had valiantly been his ally, was now beyond his help. Macrimmon—stop there, he told himself. I can't bear to think of Macrimmon. Not now. Six feet, seven feet, he thought. His own height was six feet one. Was he going to let a foot or two of space keep him prisoner?

One of the answers from conflicting sources within or under his consciousness reminded him of the cruel sharp gleam of the cinderbed beside the swiftly moving train. Get back into *your* hell hole, he told the reminder; and listened for a less murky prompting: go through the window. Yes; but how to reach the window in the dining car? Find something from which to make a lifeline. Yes—but what? I've never believed in the ropes people in books easily make from sheets. I don't now. And answer this—whatever you are: How do I know what—whom I will find in the dining car?

And what would he find if he escaped?—Ali with a rifle in the dining car? Dermot and Daoud returning from their search through the rear of the train?

He remembered something, Lady Mary's revolver. In the dark room, Hawkins's office, where Lady Mary and Dermot had attacked him and he had forced Mary to the floor, he had searched the floor for the revolver she had dropped, and had not found it. But if he could not find it, then probably no one else could. And when the lights returned, there was, he thought, a good chance that no one had thought of hunting for it. With that revolver he could force his way forward and maybe reach the cab of the engine.

The previous odds against him had been lessened.

There were four men left, but one was busied with the engine. That all four were armed he did not doubt. But in the narrow approach to the cab, one man with a revolver could do the job.

He stood at the window, breathing the night's freshness against the fetid smell of the drug under which the three men around him slept. He looked into the shadowless breadth of the Long Straight.

If he got out of here, even if he could not find Lady Mary's revolver, he could borrow General Percy's again. You, he thought to himself, must be the champion of the train.

The moon, such as it was, showed more clearly the glint of cinders and rocks on the rail bed when he looked down from the window. All right, he thought. Shine. You're down there on the ground. I'm here.

But the train was running fast.

One of the men in a bunk groaned.

He looked out again toward the window in the dining car. Had six or seven feet ever seemed so long a distance?

Again he thought of the revolver in Hawkins's office.

Yes, but if he reached the dining car, he would still be without a revolver. Could he use the axe, a caveman's weapon against firearms? Something answered him— could you be worse off than now? He remembered the murder-lust in Dermot's eyes. Then find some way to get out of here. How but by way of the window? Then it will have to be the window, over the vicious and swift passage of the sharp, murderously sharp, points of the rail bed.

God, he thought. I can't do it. Then, having stated the impossibility, he reacted against it. I *will* do it.

On the top of the cabinet he had seen a partly full

bottle of brandy. He drank a few sips.

He went back to the window. How much longer would the train be running through the Long Straight? Where would the hijackers rendezvous with transport for the gold? Was he going to be immured here while the sacks were off-loaded, while the hijackers forced their way to the seacoast? Would he have to wait here ignominiously, all his efforts thwarted, the *Cutlass* not located?

Then find something. *Get out of here.*

He was sitting on a large carton labeled "Tangy Plum Jam from Tasmania," and roped with stout cord.

Cord. A lifeline? He tried to lift the carton, but it was too heavy to lift. How to cut the knotted rope? He found a packet of razor blades on top of the metal toilet cabinet and hacked at the rope. Not long enough. But behind it was another carton marked "Regal Raspberry Preserves—Queensland's Best," and a third containing cans of tua tua fish from New Zealand.

Rope from the three cartons when knotted together measured well over his height. He added another section from an anonymous carton for the lifeline, and stripped rope from a wooden crate of canned apricots to attach to the axe at one end and to fasten around a packing case at the other.

Leaning through the window, he made two tries at heaving the axe. On the third try the axe penetrated the dining room window. He imagined himself as another pendulum—if on his lifeline he missed the window and fell—but he would be lucky to be a pendulum instead of being dragged over the teeth of the cinderbed. His ungainly weapon was secure in the dining car. Now he had to catch up with it.

He backed out of the storeroom window, leaned as

far as he could to his left, and grasped the frame of the dining car window. His rope was holding.

For a moment, above the fast-passing ground below the windows as the train drove forward, he clung against the side of the car. Then his left hand, aroused in urgency, took tight hold of the other window frame. He released the grip of his right hand on the storeroom window, forced that hand to join the other, swung his body to follow, hung over the passing ground, levered with his feet, reached the other window, and dropped through. He landed on a table. But as he got down from it and stooped to pick up the axe, his lifeline broke. If it had broken seconds sooner, he would have been either a pendulum hanging over the side of the car, or a bloodied object dragged over the roadbed. But he was neither.

None of the hijackers was in the dining car. As far as he could see, the galley was empty. Briefly he savored freedom. And now to hunt for Lady Mary's revolver. Until he found it, he would go primitively armed with the axe, which he now fastened around his neck by the remant of the broken rope. He followed the too-familiar route into Car 2, yielding his proximity to the engine. He had the heart-warming hope of finding the revolver, then of finding Darya.

In Hawkins's office the carpet was still wet from whatever had spilled from the pitcher he had thrown. The chair was overturned. He searched under the chair, under the table, at the edge of the carpet below the window. When Lady Mary had fallen, he remembered, something had been knocked from the table. In the broken shards of a plate mingled with fragments of biscuits, he found the revolver. Bloody Mary, thank you, he thought. He would wear the axe a little longer: he had become—oh, already was—attached to it.

He read the time from a clock on the table. By schedule the train should reach the end of the Long Straight in about an hour. But the train was far behind schedule.

Darya's room was empty. Hoping that he would not find it, he looked for any indication of a struggle. Nothing. He went out and knocked at Glendon's door.

"Hartley!" Astonished, she looked at the axe. "A fire?"

"Just something I picked up—I'll tell you about it later. Have you seen Darya?"

"No. I hoped she was safe with you."

"She wouldn't have been safe if she'd been with me. I must find her."

"Do you have a revolver. Do you need Grandfather's?"

"I have one," Hartley said. He uncorded the axe. "Mind if I leave this relic in your room?"

"Of course not. I might want to cut down a tree. Or that lout of an Irishman. He stormed in here looking for somebody."

"He didn't hurt you?"

"Not by half. I threw a bottle of shampoo lotion at him. He went out all foaming."

Hartley saw the picture and laughed. "You might, though, have enraged him."

"I had another bottle of shampoo."

"Nasty in the eyes, what?"

"Nasty anyway. How soon can I go to a hairdresser?"

"Well, not tonight. But as soon as this train gets to Sydney."

"Sydney," she said wistfully. "And the others, Tommy?"

"By the time you have a shampoo in Sydney. Maybe sooner."

"Sydney? When? Oh well, we've got this far—if only Tommy and the others are all right."

"I think they are," Hartley said. "You'll be meeting Tommy in Sydney."

"City of my dreams."

"Mine too," he said. But, Hartley thought, how far away. And how much could go wrong here on the train. Don't think of that, he told himself.

"I wouldn't mind if you shot the Irishman," Glendon said.

"I may have to," he said as he left her.

Apparently asleep, the Abo lay on his back covered to his head by a sheet, to his shoulders by a blanket. Another blanket lay rolled between him and the wall behind the berth. Cool air flowed from the Straight through the broken window.

From the floor Hartley picked up the discarded skin of the banana he had brought to the Abo. Warm enough, he wondered? He started to unroll the blanket at the back of the berth, then stopped. Someone was lying under the blanket.

With his right hand Hartley drew the revolver from his belt; with his left he flung back the blanket. He saw midnight-dusky hair. A white face. Troubled, fearful eyes looked up at him.

"Darya!" he cried.

Darya raised herself. In her arms she held the towel-swathed kookaburra.

Hartley lifted her out of the berth.

"I didn't know where else to hide."

Hartley hugged her.

"If you ever—ever—Hartley—"

"I never would," Hartley vowed. "Good brave girl."

The Abo was muttering. They listened. "No want girl. Tonight."

Darya gasped. "He was *awake*!"

Hartley gently laid the kookaburra beside the Abo's right arm, under the sheet. He hugged Darya again. "Did they come looking for you?"

"Yes. Dermot and one of the others. I hardly had time to try to give the kooka water and then hide. I think the kooka is alive."

The Abo was muttering again. "Kooka alive. Him and me cure us."

"There's your answer," Hartley said.

"And you, what has been happening?"

Hartley told her.

"And now?" Darya asked.

Hartley was asking himself the same question. The distance between Car 2 and the engine was as great as ever, except when he had been grounded. Now it seemed that he was starting over again. Once, he had reached the baggage car. He would get to the engine.

During the silence while he thought, he heard the clicking of the train's wheels which sounded like an imperious cricket, an immense, metallic cricket. The sound had become familiar, intimate; it promised no cessation. Nor would there ever be an end to the haunting he would feel when he remembered Macrimmon's twisted figure in death.

"What will they do, Hartley?" Darya asked.

"Go on to some rendezvous with a vehicle—Land Rover, jeep. Something to carry off the gold. Probably at a point near the end of the Long Straight, near roads.

Maybe they'll head for Port Augusta or Port Pirie. Maybe to load the stuff on a ship." The *Cutlass*, he wondered? Would they have brought the junk so far east if it were involved in the Bulan scheme? A junk at either port would be conspicuous, even if reports of the missing vessel had not been circulated from Singapore.

"If we let them go ahead," Darya said, "what will happen to us?"

"I don't know. They might wreck the train after unloading. Not a nice picture. They might simply move off with their catch."

"You think Sammy might wreck the train?"

"Darya, you know him. What do you think?"

"I know," Darya said unhappily, "that he can be reckless. Ruthless? I don't know. He has never been able to match up his objectives with other realities. He sees things in straight lines not related on the side to others, like that awful meeting with the freight train when he almost wrecked us. He might—I hate to say this—feel something, some satisfaction in wrecking a train. He used to build machines. And destroy them."

"Never mind," Hartley said.

He hugged her again. This was becoming a habit. Very pleasant. Darya turned the embrace into a comfortably unsentimental demonstration of camaraderie by hugging him briskly in response.

Hartley looked at his watch.

"How much more time in this endless Straight?" Darya asked.

"Less than an hour, if we were on time. But we must be at least an hour late. Maybe more. Right now we haven't much time. The others probably know by now that I've got out of the storeroom. They'll be looking for us again. It's like a merry-go-around. But not merry. We

172

evade them. They hunt us. If only I had a safe place to stow you—"

"No stowing," Darya said. "I stay with you."

"Remind me later to tell you what I think of you."

"If there is a later. Oh, I don't mean that we'd not see each other, just that later might not mean we got out of this nightmare. Because—let's face it—I am Sammy's sister, and we've always got on well, but Sammy hasn't ever been fond of anybody. Not until the Malay girl. Our uncle and aunt used to apologize for favoring me in all kinds of things. They said they couldn't help liking me better because I—well, I guess I responded. Sammy, never. We got on well because he thought I was intelligent enough to share some of his interests. If I am an obstacle in this mad scheme of his, he will think of the scheme, and to hell with obstacles."

"Also facing it," Hartley said, "we don't know what control Sammy has over Dermot. All the more reason for stowing you."

"Listen," Darya whispered.

She drew close to Hartley.

"They're coming," she whispered.

Hartley heard Dermot's voice. For himself, he would have risked staying amd meeting two of the enemy. But not with Darya. He checked the sheet covering the Abo and the bird, then took Darya's hand.

"Come along."

He led her to the rear of Car 2 and closed the door behind them.

"We go up."

"No, Hartley. I can't."

"I'll help you—just to the top. You won't have to walk along the cartops."

"Heaven forbid! And you?"

"I couldn't either. Not along the top. The Malays are cats. They don't mind heights or motion. No, we'll stick to the end of the car. I'll go first and pull you up. When you get up there, lie flat. Pretend you're on a horse."

"But there's no neck."

"Mine will be there. No—safer if you hold on to my belt."

He removed the revolver from his belt and put it into his pocket.

"When you land, you'll be facing forward. Don't try to turn around. I'll have a grip at the end of the car. I'm not going to fall off. Just hang on to my belt and don't let go for a second. Be ready for a sudden stop."

"I don't think I can do it," Darya said. "Isn't there something else we could do?"

"No. But you *can* do it. Nothing for you to do but hang on to my belt."

"You won't fall off?"

"No chance." I'd damn well better not, he thought.

With hand and foot holds on the coupling gear, Hartley got to the top of the car. He leaned over, caught Darya's upraised hands, and pulled her up beside him. "Lie flat. All right now. If they come out here, I can pick them off."

"What if Ali comes along the roof?"

"We'll see him before he sees us and I'll shoot him. He can't hit us lying down. By the time he gets near enough to fire from above, *I'll* fire, or catch his legs and throw him off."

"But you're facing the wrong way."

"*You're* facing the right away. You'll see him. I'll turn."

"What do I hold on to while you're turning?"

174

"Keep your hold on my belt. Loosen it up enough so I can swing around."

On both sides of the car top where they clung, the unconcerned Long Straight unrolled. Dark sky. A few stars. The constant clicking of the wheels.

"Are you all right?"

Darya's answer was faint but determined.

"As long as you are." She lay on her stomach, facing forward. Hartley lay beside her, gripping the end of the car.

"If Sammy jolts us, I'll fall off," Darya said.

"Not if you hang on to me. You're great, Darya. Anybody else would have gone into a flap."

"Not great," Darya said. "I'm scared to death."

So am I, Hartley thought.

"Don't talk—somebody's coming."

Below them the vestibule door opened and a man came through. A squarish figure, Hartley saw in the light from the corridor. Dermot.

Hartley released his right hand from gripping the end of the car, drew the revolver from his pocket, and fired.

At the steep, downward angle the shot missed, but Dermot drew back into the doorway. Hartley heard Ali's voice behind Dermot, who fired uselessly.

Seconds passed. Then Dermot's voice cried, "Break it off—shoot it off!"

"What are they doing?" Darya whispered.

"I hope it's not what I think," Hartley said. But it was. A shot.

"Try to get in!" Dermot shouted. "You just try!"

The vestibule door slammed shut.

"I think" Hartley said, "they've broken the handle

175

that opens the door from the outside."

"You mean we won't be able to get inside?"

"We'll get back somehow."

He replaced the revolver in his pocket and patted Darya's shoulder.

"Well, it's a good way to get better acquainted, Darya."

"Very well planned," Darya said faintly.

"Don't be bitter. With better planning I would have had rugs and cushions up here."

"And a wall," Darya said.

Trying to distract her, Hartley asked, "Have you ever been in the Southern Hemisphere before?"

"No."

"Then you ought to see the Southern Cross before you leave. It's overrated, but still not a bad show. Can you scrunch around, turn your head?"

"I don't think so. And I don't want to see any stars. They'd make me dizzy."

"But they wouldn't show any motion, good old steady stairs."

"I don't want to see any good old or bad old stars."

"Well," he said, "it's optional. You don't like stars?"

"I can take them or leave them. And I din't like that broken-down old moon I saw on the way here."

"Not at its best, it isn't," Hartley agreed. "But tough on any moon to shine down here with nothing to shine on. Nothing to make shadows."

"You think moons want to make shadows?"

"To make themselves felt, yes."

"Like Sammy blowing the whistle. Why does he do it? He wouldn't care what was on the track."

"What about a kangaroo?" Hartley asked. "But I don't think there are any kangaroos in the Straight.

What would they eat?"

"Other kangaroos?"

"Good heavens, no! You've never known a kangaroo!"

"Have you?"

"No," Hartley admitted. "But I know they're not cannibals."

"You like them, don't you?"

"Very much. Wish I could jump the way they do."

"You do all right," Darya said. "I don't think you told me half of how you got out of the bunk room into the dining car."

"Oh well, I had to get out," Hartley said. "You want to hear a train story?"

"I'm not sure. But try."

"Railroading friend of mine told me about a freight train crew member, an out-and-out atheist. Made a big deal of it. One night this atheist was going along the tops of box cars. Then his foot went over into space. 'God help me!' he yelled. Seconds later he said, 'Don't bother, God, there's a flat car ahead.'"

Darya laughed faintly. "How far do you think we've come since we've been up here?" she asked.

"Seven, eight miles at least. Nobody's fallen off yet. Do you speak Spanish?"

"A little," Darya said. "Why? Do you suddenly want to speak Spanish?"

"No. Just remembered a horse story. Years back, when I was studying Spanish, I used to read a Mexican news magazine. *Hispano*, it was called. One week there was a story about a Mexican farmer whose farm was on a tourist route to pyramids. He got tired of having tourists flock all over his place, feeding his animals. So one day the tourists found a sign on the corral railing which said, 'Please do not feed the horse.' It was signed 'The farmer.' Next batch of tourists found another sign under the first. 'Please disregard the above sign.' This one was signed 'The horse.'"

Darya's laughter was a lot more vigorous than before. Touching her shoulders with his left hand, Hartley thought that she was at least somewhat relaxed. She had caught on to the anti-tension game that he was trying to play.

"Tell me," he said, changing the subject, "does Sammy like many people?"

"No. Hardly anybody. He doesn't like animals, either, unless he can race them. Except of course, Selby, his sheepdog. That's the one I had to take to Honolulu because Sammy wanted to see him. And do you know what happened? After all the trouble I had getting Selby to Honolulu, he wouldn't even look at Sammy. Just stuck to me. Sammy pretended the dog was in travel shock. Jet lag or something. One night—" Hartley felt her shiver. "One awful night Sammy came into my room—climbed over terraces—he had the room next to mine. He was carrying a whip. Before I recognized him, I was on the phone giving the desk an S.O.S. about an intruder. Then I recognized him—didn't know whether he was going to whip me or Selby. Selby bit him. Sammy got away before people came. When they came, the darn dog bit one of them. Luckily I had his rabies shot records. Awful night."

"Where's Selby now?"

"I'd hoped I could leave him with Sammy. No go. My uncle and aunt were in Florida. So poor old Selby had to live with me in a small apartment near Columbia. He's with my uncle and aunt now in Greenwich. Actually a nice dog. But why couldn't he have been decent to Sammy?"

The train whistle sounded again feebly. They heard a hammering.

"If it's going out of order," Darya said, "why doesn't Sammy just let it *go*?"

"Because he likes to blow it," Hartley said.

"He could see anything ahead of him on the track, couldn't he?"

"I think so, though we're behind schedule. I don't know what could come barreling along."

"Whatever it was," Darya said unhappily, "he'd probably make it back to a siding. Who does he think he is, Alexander the Great?"

"If you can think of Alexander running a diesel electric locomotive—"

"I wouldn't put it past him. But Hartley, tell me where you live, what you do for fun."

"I live in an apartment in Singapore. Wonderful Chinese neighbors. I had a larger apartment when Jewel, my wife, was living. She died—about three years ago."

"Was she English?"

"Her father was English. A colonial administrator before Singapore became independent. Her mother was the daughter of a sultan of a Malaysian state."

"You have no children?"

"No," Hartley said. "Jewel died trying to have a child. Afterward, I moved into a smaller apartment. I've got some pretty wonderful Chinese neighbors. And as for fun, as you say, there isn't much time. What do *you* do for fun?"

"In New York—ballet, plays, opera. And friends of course. Though I'm awfully busy at the University. I'm working on Turkish. Picked up a little when I was on the dig. You know Malayan, don't you?"

"More or less," Hartley said.

"More," Darya said. "I don't think you half-do anything."

"My boss probably wouldn't agree. I'll make a bet with you, Darya. If I manage to find the *Cutlass*, Farnsleigh's first comments are going to be objections to the claim I'll be making for the cost of my ruined jacket."

"Your poor hands," Darya said. "They must be ruined too!"

"No. I rotate. Take pressure off one hand and then the other. Like shifting a suitcase from one hand to a fresh one."

"What's that noise?"

"That," Hartley said, "is the dying or dead gasp of Sammy's whistle. Hold tight. He may stop the train. That's all right, though. More delay will help us."

"Keep us treed up here longer too?"

He had decided what he was going to do if the train stopped but did not tell Darya. Not yet.

"Next time you come out here, you might want to visit a gigantic old Buddhist temple near Jogjakarta. Borobudur. Supposed to be the biggest in the world. Looks as if it had grown out of the mountain it's on."

"Gosh," Darya said, "that I'd like to see."

Before she could dwell again on the danger and discomfort of their cliffhanging, he tried another gambit.

"What's your favorite musical instrument?"

"Harp, I guess, or flute. What's yours?"

"Gongs, drums. Balinese orchestra instruments."

"Got any with you?"

"What do you think I carry around in my pockets?

An orchestra?"

She laughed but added soberly, "No. Revolvers. But you've had only one at a time, right?"

"I carry a derringer in reserve," he said, "but I gave it to Merriam when he was commuting through all those dark cars."

"Merriam. He seemed awfully nice."

"The kind of person," Hartley said, "you hope to heaven you'll know again when nobody needs revolvers or derringers. But it's not likely. He's always on tour through Asia or who knows where. Restless life."

"Yours seem to be too. And mine—I hope it will be. I can't wait to get at the marvels still buried underground. Turkey, Iran, Egypt."

"Malaysia?"

"I don't know much about Malaysia. Or Indonesia."

"You won't be going to Iran very soon, will you? Unsettled there. Conservative Moslems rioting all over the lot."

"Still," Darya said, "archaeological teams have a neutral status."

"You mean you'd risk going there now?"

"Yes. I'd go anywhere."

"You aren't," he asked, "anything like engaged or married?"

"No." As she spoke, the train stopped. The halt was not one of Sammy's worst.

Immediately they heard hammering.

"Oh, the fool, the fool!" Darya cried. "Why does he have to fix it?"

"Never mind. More delay. We want that. All right, Darya. We're going downstairs. Good chance."

"You mean it? Off this ghastly perch?"

"I mean it. I'll slide to the end of the car. You move

181

along behind me and keep your hands on my belt until I jump down. When I jump, you hold on to the end of the car, just until I can reach up and lift you down. Ready?"

He lifted her to the vestibule plate. "Sit back against the door. Can you reach the door handle sitting down?"

"Yes."

"You feel all right? Not dizzy?"

"No, but I don't want to look at the stars."

"Close your eyes. Lean back. Count to twenty."

"Why? I'm not enraged."

"I know you're not going to fight me. Just count. Think of your favorite color."

"All right," she said. "It's purple and I've got as far as thirteen—but thirteen whats?"

"Anything—lizards, nightingales, chocolate eclairs."

He put the revolver through his belt, took off his jacket, and wrapped it around her shoulders.

"All you have to do," he said, "is sit there. Hold on to the door handle. Brace your feet against the side of the door."

"Hartley! What are you going to do? *Not get off the train?*"

He leaned down and kissed her. "I'm going to the engine. I'll get there before Sammy fixes the whistle. Don't worry."

"Don't *worry*!" She held his arms. "Don't try it, Hartley! What if the train starts while you're out there?"

"I've been out there before and got back. If the train starts, I'll get back now."

"But if you're not near any steps—and it's going too fast—oh, Hartley, *please*!"

"Stay warm—as warm as you can." He kissed her again and ran down the steps on the right side of the train.

8

RACE WITH A BEHEMOTH

The lowest step seemed to hold Hartley's feet; it was like the brief security of the end of a diving board for an inexperienced diver. He forced himself off the step, felt the cinders of the roadbed underfoot, and saw the misshapen moon in the sky ahead of the stopped train. The hammering still sounded. He started to run toward the engine. His ears strained to hear the smallest sound that would signal the train's resuming motion. The hammering wasn't a guarantee of continued halt. The farther he ran from the haven of the steps at the rear platform, the tighter his muscles became.

He reached the midpoint of Car 2, saw a light in the window of the room that he thought was the one in which the Abo lay, and felt enraged at what had happened to the Abo, to Macrimmon. He hesitated and lost a few steps, wanting to get into that room to protect the Abo, wanting to be *inside* the train to continue his progress toward the engine. But inside the train—no. He had no time now to climb aboard and to risk opposition from the hijackers, no time for a resumption of his forward and backward quest. Sammy would need all his thinned ranks, but might spare one, even two, if they guessed that Hartley would be making another attempt to try to reach the engine.

Looming beside him, the train was only deceptively at rest. It was a behemoth that might suddenly heave into movement. Even if it would not leave its metal path, even if it would not attain its full malevolent speed for twenty, thirty seconds, the monster could as effectively defeat him by outracing him as if it had lurched from its path and attacked him.

The night air in the Straight was cold, but sweat poured over his forehead. In brushing it from his eyes, his fingers caught on a loosened tape and tore it from the cut it had covered. A gnarl of cinders underfoot made him stumble and reach toward the side of Car 1, but he did not touch it.

He thought of Darya huddled in the vestibule at the end of the train, and in a second's flash of recollection remembered what a friend had told him of traveling on trains with her restless father. At every station he had disembarked to buy papers or food or merely to disembark, leaving her in painful apprehension, braced against the starting of the train and her abandonment.

Beside him as he ran, a few lighted windows showed in Car 1. It was hard to believe that so many people could have stayed so quiet, pent-up in their rooms. Precious few had had the courage or the curiosity to open their doors.

As he passed the rear end of the club car, the

hammering stopped. He could all but feel the behemoth gathering force for the spring, could imagine the beast sliding its bulk past him, until only the tail, that final platform, remained for a dubious gripping. But by the time he reached the middle of the car, he heard the hammering start again irregularly and more lightly. The hammering stopped before he reached the forward end of the dining car. He counted the seconds of the acute silence, the silence of the Long Straight, where nothing grew, nothing moved.

It seemed to him that he had been running for hours, but the moon had not moved from the position in which he had seen it from the roof of the last car. He cleared the forward end of the club car and now ran alongside the dining car, from which lights showed the broken glass of wide windows and farther forward the small shattered window through which he had escaped from the bunk and storage room. A section of the severed rope still dangled from that window.

If the moon told the truth, he couldn't have been running for more than a few minutes. Of course the rough and jagged cinderbed, the slide of fragments of cinder or rocks, cut down speed and caused more effort.

Why did I try this? he asked himself. What thin chance made me think I could reach the engine? But how, staying locked out at the rear vestibule, could I have even *tried* to reach it? It would be worse, he thought, if I were *under* the train, the only place I haven't been.

In the baggage car, which he was now passing, someone moved inside a lighted window. Hartley ran closer to the flank of the behemoth. If somebody saw

185

him and shot at him again, the downward angle would give him some protection, though his being sighted would work against him when he tried to board the engine. Work against him? It could annihilate him. To hell with annihilation, he thought, running with new speed toward the midpoint of the baggage car. He had not quite reached it when he heard the engine's whistle cough out a tentative sound, then perhaps a second later, muster up a loud choke which grew into a blast. Sammy, he thought, had finished the repair. If I can reach the front of the baggage car—

Four running steps, five, six at most, to the end of this accursedly long baggage car. Oh damn you, legs! Make it! And damn you, train, don't start until I do! he said to himself. But he was still the third of the baggage car's length away from the engine when the behemoth moved.

The monster's first motion was deceptive. Then under the grating howl of the engine's whistle the baggage car slid past him and before he had realized it, the part of the baggage car which he had just passed, passed him.

He gained furiously on the lost distance, reached the midpoint of the baggage car, and pressed on, now almost at the vestibule. The train's speed quickening but not yet full, he drove himself to match the train's momentum and saw the moon's gleam on the handrails at the vestibule, the entrance to the engine. He leaped for the steps at the vestibule and missed, but his right hand caught a handrail.

His feet dragged over the cinders. He reached for the left handrail with his left hand, moved his right hand to the other side, and lifted his legs and feet. He set one foot on the lowest step, then the other foot, and crouched on the steps, clinging to the handrails as the behemoth sprang into blazing speed. He had reached the entrance to the engine. But he was not yet on board.

Ahead, when his breath returned, his eyesight cleared, and his legs hardened, he made out the convex forward end of the engine, and on either side of the housing of the generators he saw a catwalk leading to the cab. Outside, above him, the eaten-away moon was partly hidden by the cloudbank. He felt for the revolver at the belt of his slacks. Raising himself, he climbed to the vestibule and looked into the engine.

On his side of the engine, a dimly lighted catwalk passed the generator housing. Beyond, more brightly lighted, the catwalk opened into the cab. A red-capped figure—Sammy's?—sat at the controls. Beside him Hartley saw another figure, which he thought was Dermot's. Where were the other two men? He was partly answered when Ali, whom he recognized, moved behind Sammy. And then he saw Daoud moving through the vestibule, carrying something on a plate. Daoud's thin, bare ankles were on a level with Hartley's head. Hartley could have reached up, caught Daoud's ankles, dragged him down, and thrown him from the train. But he couldn't do it.

All right, Farnsleigh, he thought. I could have reduced their numbers to only three against me. But I couldn't.

Anyway, the moment was gone. Daoud was already in the catwalk. Blast you and your *Cutlass*, T. L., Hartley thought. Well, not quite. He hadn't given up.

Surprise? They wouldn't be expecting him. Sammy was busy at the engine, Dermot was ready to kill, and so was Ali.

Daoud was one of the enemy, but Hartley could

never kill Daoud. And he didn't think Welles, his predecessor on this case, could have killed Daoud, no matter what Farnsleigh had said. Could *you* have killed him, T. L., after he had saved your life, as Daoud saved me from Dermot, back there in the dining car? No. You, T. L., give orders—and loosely enough so that you can escape the feeling of guilt from any agent's action.

Oh, quiet down, Hartley told himself. I'm not in Singapore—I'm here in the Long Straight, ready—yes, ready—to halt the hijacking, ready for the men and cars at the point of rendezvous.

How many men would come with the cars? One, two cars? Two, maybe more men? They would swarm on board the train, dragging off the grey canvas sacks. Two sacks in Hawkins's office, the rest in Macrimmon's room.

And would they reach Bulan?

No, by God, Hartley thought, they aren't going to reach Bulan.

He dragged himself to the vestibule. For the first time he was firmly on the engine.

9

CONFRONTATION

Ahead of him Hartley saw the humped shapes of the generators in their housing, on either side of which narrow catwalks ran forward to the cab. The controls and the engineer's seat were on the right. He had to use the catwalk on the right to move on to his final destination and the confrontation with Sammy.

The catwalk was lighted but not brightly; the dimness, he supposed, was necessary to eliminate glare from the cab. Wearing the red cap of the hijackers, he might be mistaken for one of them, if only briefly, at least for enough time to give him an edge of surprise.

He felt little elation at reaching the engine after so many attempts. He was still outnumbered and out-weaponed four-to-one. During his interrupted passage into the engine, he had been preoccupied with reaching Sammy. He had at times been slowed by realizing the outnumbering but until now had spent no time in estimating its meaning, its risks.

All right, he thought. I am here. No backing off.

The wound above his cheekbone which had been exposed and opened when the tape had come off was bleeding. But the blood was below his eyes. He wiped it with a handkerchief and flexed his hands, which were still stiff from clinging to the edge of the rear car. He tested his steadiness, his balance. Nothing wrong there. He would need all his resources in this final encounter, from which there would be no retreat. But he waited for a flow of strength and determination to return.

Looking out through the open vestibule, he saw that at last the laggard moon had cleared the dark flat cloud and had risen perceptibly toward the zenith. Darya would be seeing, if she could look without dizziness, the same moon's progress.

He considered, then gave up the idea of uncoupling the engine from the remaining cars as preposterous, as mad as one of Sammy's nightmare escapades. No, he thought. He couldn't set adrift the passengers remaining on the train. And it wouldn't take long for whatever vehicles waited at a rendezvous to drive west a relatively short distance to locate the train. He didn't know how to uncouple cars, and the noise would bring hijackers to stall him. If he displaced Sammy, which he thought he could do, he could run the engine. On a mission in Malaysia he had ridden in the cab of a spur-line engine to a port, and had learned from the engineer how to operate the controls on the small shunting engine. He thought the basic procedure would be the same on a large engine. But he was ahead of himself, already imagining the displacement of Sammy. And the others?

He thought again of what might be happening on the cars left on the track behind them. Would anyone have thought of looking for conductors drugged or bound and stowed into lavatories or shower rooms?

He could not stay here. Dermot and Ali might have returned to the cab or would come soon, and there was no shelter, except perhaps in the catwalk on the left side of the generators.

Staying close to the rail of the generator housing, he moved forward toward the cab. He heard a soft voice singing the Bulan song, with its harsh words and gentle tune. The song was interrupted by the whistle. Perhaps Sammy needed the whistle now, to alert whatever vehicles were waiting for the train and its gold.

Then he heard Sammy's voice over the clacking of the wheels, between the blasts of the whistle.

"Stow it, Daoud," Sammy said. "It gets on my nerves."

"You always told us you have no nerves." Daoud's answer was smooth but mocking. "What about *my* nerves, with that whistle always blowing?"

"We aren't far from the Land Rovers," Sammy said. "Can't tell exactly where they'll have broken up the track."

"We aren't at the end of the Straight," Daoud said. "We've had delays. Will they wait for us or drive back to meet us?"

"Either way," Sammy said, "we'll find them. Or they'll find us."

"When we leave the train," Daoud said, "what do we do about it?"

"Do about it? We leave it. What else?"

"If that's it, all right. But you have no plan to blow it up? You know we have those plastic explosives."

"Oh, if we have to. Why?"

"How many people are on this train? Thirty? More?"

191

"So there are thirty," Sammy said. "Do you want a free Bulan or not?"

"Not at such a cost," Daoud said.

"Well, idiot," Sammy said, "would our people go to the trouble of tearing up the track if we were going to blow the train?"

"I don't know," Daoud said.

"All right, while you are brooding, go back and get me another sandwich. What do you think that last one was, something you'd dish up at a women's club meeting? Or doesn't that mean anything to you?"

"I have read about such things," Daoud said.

"Oh, you can read?"

"I believe so." He added derisively, "Tuan."

"Shove it," Sammy said. He blew two blasts on the whistle to reinforce his words. "If it won't interfere with your reading, bring me real food. I can't leave this bleeding engine. And while you're back there, see what's happened to Dermot and Ali. That goddamned Rhys—why can't you nail him down? And my crazy sister? She's going to wish she hadn't tried that frigging ghost act. And I want food! Got that through your thick skull?"

"Slow down, Sammy," Daoud said. "We all want food. But Malays don't change into beasts when they are hungry."

"They wouldn't need to change far," Sammy said.

"Sammy," Daoud said, "don't alienate me."

Surprisingly, Hartley heard Sammy chuckle.

"I'll see what I can find," Daoud said. "But there is little left. No cooked meat."

"There must be something—cheese, bread, eggs— must be something in the freezer.

"There are limits," Daoud said. "I am not here as a cook."

"Open cans. Do something, you sodding beast. Well, why don't you move? Don't sit down."

"You might go back there and find something for yourself," Daoud said.

"And who would run the ruddy engine?"

"I will," Daoud said.

"*You* will?"

"You heard me."

"How can you run an engine? Tell me!"

"Allah would help me."

"How many engines has Allah ever run?"

"A really penetrating theological question," Daoud answered, half-laughing. Hartley heard him leave the cab and start along the catwalk, whistling the Bulan song.

When the steps and the whistling sounded near him, Hartley reached for Daoud's legs and pulled him to the catwalk and struck his head with the revolver butt. He pulled Daoud from the catwalk into the space at the end of the generator housing, and propped him against a generator because there wasn't room enough to lay him flat.

On that back platform, in the darkness barely touched by the slow moon, was Darya waiting? Where else could she be?

The way now was clear to the cab. Hartley asked himself whether Sammy and his allies should not be allowed to get away with the gold and the *Cutlass*—if they had it—and secure the independence of their island. He knew a good deal about the treatment rapacious overlords gave to small, vulnerable peoples.

My God, he thought, am I becoming senile? Am I feeling sympathy with these people who should be the enemy? But when I joined the Sword Company, I didn't foresee anything like this.

However, his allegiance was clear, no matter what his sympathies. The death of Macrimmon and the near-death of the Abo were not to be, could not be, forgotten. You're forgetting, too, he told himself, that you and Darya, and the other passengers, are not out of the woods.

Ahead he heard Sammy roaring the Bulan song, which he had angrily stilled when Daoud sang it.

Stepping cautiously on the gritted floor of the catwalk, Hartley came to the opening into the cab. He saw Sammy in a chair on the right side at the controls, and beside him was the chair for an assistant engineer. The engine's eye pierced the darkness ahead.

Sammy, now wearing an engineer's cap, was swinging his feet in the space at the left of his chair and still singing thunderously.

Hartley spoke. "Stow it, Sammy. It gets on my nerves."

Without turning to look at Hartley, Sammy said coldly, "Thought you had no nerves."

"I have a revolver pointed at your head. Slow down."

"No way. You shoot me, and who runs the engine?"

"I run the engine," Hartley said.

"All-American boy," Sammy scoffed. "This isn't a ship, you know." But he reduced the engine's speed.

"Now," Hartley said, "you listen to me and give me answers. Where is the *Cutlass*?"

"For God's sake," Sammy said, "is this drill all about that miserable tub?"

"We'll start with the *Cutlass*. Where have you hidden her?"

For an answer Sammy began to hum the Bulan anthem.

Hartley pressed the revolver against the back of his neck.

"You shoot me, and the train goes off the track," Sammy said.

"No. I shoot you, and my hands replace yours on the throttle. The safety on the revolver is off. I don't want to kill you. But I won't be able to help it at this range."

"Who's making you? Why don't you want to kill me?" Sammy taunted, prodding at Hartley's vulnerability.

"Because I'm not out for murder, like you and your gang."

"You've got it wrong! We aren't out for murder."

"What about Macrimmon—and the Abo?"

"I don't know anything about them. Are you trying to make me believe they are dead?"

"Macrimmon is dead. The Abo is near death. Also an old man with a heart attack."

"Oh, blast."

"Your hatchet man Dermot isn't particular."

"He'll come back here and slice you into threads," Sammy said in renewed defiance.

"You couldn't stop him?"

"I *wouldn't* stop him," Sammy said. "You're in our way, but you're alone. You made my sister help you, but she's not with you now. There are four of us, maybe more. But you won't shoot me, Rhys. I heard Farnsleigh say you were the best man in the company, except in the rough and tumble you couldn't be counted on to be

195

rough. You'd rather tumble. Besides, what would Darya say if you shot me? You can drop people off this train as if they were empty match boxes. But you couldn't shoot into a man's neck."

In the half-light Hartley saw Sammy's ears, small and delicately tooled like Darya's. The smell of hot metal and diesel oil and the sight of Sammy's meager neck, the impersonal click of train wheels, merged as a sharp external point of focus. He held to one certainty: his determination to protect lives and to make valid the work that he had started.

"Sammy, you didn't think the *Cutlass* was a miserable tub when you got your job on her. How far are you going to scrap values?"

"Some values get to be obsolete. Like steam engines."

"What about the value of human life? Does that get to be obsolete?"

"You preach like an old woman," Sammy said. "But yes, if some human lives build things that crush down more human lives, they *ought* to be obsolete."

"Are you arrogant enough to think you can judge which human lives or how many have to be sacrificed."

"I'm not an adding machine," Sammy retorted. "But you know how people without defenses can be exploited. Copra, for example. Some poor workers slave to get out of a shipment of copra, then the rulers take it, steal it, for a wretched few dollars, and sell it for hundreds. Thousands. Same is true of spices."

"And oil," Hartley said. "But if you think your islanders can buck Jakarta, you're out of your mind."

"Even if we were, is that a reason for not trying?"

"For trying, maybe. But how does that stack up

against what you've done here? To people that have nothing to do with Jakarta or any other colonial predators?"

"We gave them reasonable terms. They saved their hides by doing what we told them to."

"Macrimmon? What did he and the Abo do?"

"I tell you I don't know who killed Macrimmon! I don't even know if he's dead."

"He *is* dead," Hartley said again. "The Abo would have died because of you and your people if we hadn't found him. He was left with a deep wound. Would have bled to death. And," Hartley added, "how do you justify the way you put everybody on this train in danger when you almost rammed the freight? Haven't your games gone far enough?"

"They aren't games!"

"No, they are not games—they are brutalities. Does Sir Ian know how much he depends on the impulses of a sadist?"

Sammy did not answer.

"Wasn't there an easier way for you to get to run a locomotive?" Hartley asked.

As an answer Sammy pressed the throttle and drove the engine forward at full speed.

Hartley prodded the revolver deeper against Sammy's neck.

"Stop the engine. Stop all of this intensity. Stop before any more people are hurt or killed. Too many people know about this. You aren't going to get away with it!"

"Yes I am. We are. If I were standing behind you with a gun, I'd shoot. But *you* won't."

Hartley struck Sammy with the revolver butt on the side of his head.

Sammy swayed to the left, and his hand slid from the throttle. Hartley gripped the throttle bar with his left hand, and with his right thrust the revolver under his belt. Then he dragged Sammy into the narrow space between the two chairs.

But the blow had not been hard enough. Sammy clawed at Hartley's legs and jerked him away from the engineer's seat.

Good God, Hartley thought. If I wreck this train—

He fought to keep hold of the throttle, kicking at Sammy with his left foot and leg. With his right he sliced down at Sammy's throat, but the angle was wrong. He heard Sammy make a gurgling sound, but felt Sammy's hold on his left leg tighten. He felt the downward pull, felt his hand loosening on the throttle.

With his right hand he drew out the revolver and beat at Sammy's head. Hartley's arms were crossed, and because he was gripping the throttle with his left hand, the blow was too soft. Sammy was struggling toward the engineer's seat, his arms flailing.

Hartley pressed the brake control for a gradual halt; then as the engine slowed to a stop, he took his left hand from the throttle. Both hands were free, but Sammy, struggling up to a crouch, dragged him from the seat. Sammy's hands clutched Hartley's throat. Hartley tore at the grip with his left hand. With his right hand, he struck Sammy again with the revolver butt, though Sammy's fingers pronged into his throat. Hartley felt a pain and blackness crowding out consciousness. With the revolver he beat again at Sammy's head, felt the fingers relax, and saw Sammy slip to the floor of the cab. Hartley leaned over the controls again.

With air again flowing through his lungs, he bent over Sammy, who, wedged between the two seats, was breathing gratingly. At the tapered front of the cab, below the window, Hartley saw a low door whose top was level with his elbows as he stood. He opened the door and looked down into a small lavatory compartment which a man could enter only by bending almost to a crouch.

He drew Sammy to the opening, lowered him to the floor, and propped him against the wall at the left, but there was too little space to allow him to sit in a recumbent position. Hartley closed the door and wedged the handle with a wrench that had been left on the floor of the cab. Sammy would be out of the way if, as Hartley expected, he would have to stand off Dermot and Ali. As a possible move to gain time, Hartley put on the engineer's cap that had fallen from Sammy's head. In the low light, leaning over the throttle, he might at first be mistaken for Sammy.

He started the engine slowly and felt a brief exhilaration at the response of the engine and at the pull of the cars behind it. He understood something of Sammy's excitement about engines, but not sufficiently to sing the Bulan song or any other song. He adjusted the cap to the angle at which Sammy had worn it and experimented with increasing the engine's speed, then slowed it again to the cautious rate at which he had started. In the brilliant circle of light that scanned the track, he looked into the flat darkness of the Long Straight.

Somewhere along here the train would reach the rendezvous of which Sammy had spoken, probably, Hartley thought, before the end of the Long Straight. Beyond, in more populated areas, the transport would risk interception if alarms had been sent out. The Indian-Pacific by now was about equidistant from

Perth and from Port Pirie on the southern coast. It seemed unlikely that the gold would be carried to a ship on the east coast or even to a port as large as Pirie. Probably at least two drivers would meet the Indian-Pacific at the rendezvous.

Hartley considered the possibility of backing the train in order to delay it further. By now the freight must have left the siding and be well on its way west, but if he backed, he would still be taking a chance on colliding with the freight. More safely he could halt the train here. Enquiries or alarms must have been sent from stations at which the Indian-Pacific should have stopped. He tried not to think of dispatches, undelivered from these stations, which would have affected the train's progress. If he stopped here or backed, Dermot and Ali would come forward all the sooner to find out what was wrong. But they would come anyway, and at any moment.

He decided to back the train very slowly, at a speed which would be lower than that of the freight. After braking, he brought the engine to a moderately smooth stop. Then, locating the reversal control, he set the train into motion slowly back toward the west. Let Dermot and Ali come.

On the chair next to the engineer's someone had left a leather jacket. With his left hand Hartley searched the pockets. In a breast pocket he found a wadded blue handkerchief and a packet half-full of Turkish cigarettes; in side pockets, a worn rosary, a key ring attached to a Celtic cross and three keys, three sticks of American chewing gum, and a pocket knife embedded in tobacco crumbs and dirty lint. He confiscated the knife. Listening for steps behind him, he thought of the anomaly of Dermot and the rosary.

Nothing changed in the dark flatness. The train might just as well have been moving forward. He increased the speed slightly. And as he had expected, he heard steps behind him and Dermot's voice.

"What the bloody hell, Sammy? Why are you backing? We're over an hour late."

Hartley whistled the start of *Bulan Forever*, then muttered, "Out of my way."

"You fool—put her forward! Are you mad?" Dermot said.

"Train ahead," Hartley improvised.

Dermot shouted, "We have to get to the junk before daylight. Ram the damned train!"

Hartley shook his head. He whistled the refrain of the Bulan song and substituted his left hand on the throttle so that he could draw the revolver from his belt with his right hand.

"Stop if you have to, but don't go back!" Dermot cried.

Hartley continued to back the train and to whistle.

"How can a train be coming?" Dermot shouted. "The track's wrecked, beyond the rendezvous. Oh, you crazed fool, how far are you going to back?"

Hartley whistled more loudly.

"Go forward! We can't have a bloody train blocking the rendezvous!"

If only we could, Hartley thought.

Dermot lunged toward him.

"If you stop me, who'll run the engine?" Hartley growled.

Dermot halted. "By God, I'll run it!"

"You don't know how."

"You think you're such a great Bulan patriot, but all you want to do is run this engine!" Dermot shouted.

201

"I'm not getting paid. I'm not a mercenary," Hartley said, turning around.

"*Rhys!*" Dermot cried. "*Where's Sammy?*"

Hartley pointed the revolver at him. "Take out your revolver and throw it across the cab," Hartley said.

Dermot's revolver fell across the empty chair and dropped at the opening into the catwalk on the left side of the cab.

"Keep facing me and walk back five steps. All right. Now turn and unwedge the door handle. Drop the wrench. Don't try anything with it. Now open the lavatory door." As Dermot opened the door, Hartley braked and stopped the engine.

"God, Sammy's in there!" Dermot cried.

"Go in," Hartley ordered. He ran to the door as Dermot stumbled over Sammy's body inside the narrow compartment, and slammed the door and wedged the handle. Then Hartley went back to the controls and restarted the engine in its backward movement.

He had been driving only a few minutes before he heard pounding and banging from the lavatory. Hartley held his revolver ready for any emergency.

A few minutes more of guarded backing. And then, as if the controls had been torn from under his hands, he was thrown from the chair. Someone in one of the cars behind had thrown an emergency brake.

Was there something on the track behind the train? He thought of Darya's exposed position on the rear platform.

The pounding was louder against the lavatory door. I cannot leave the engine, Hartley thought. I can't start over again the battle that got me here.

The train had been stopped; someone had been

watching the track. Or had Ali on his own initiative halted the train? And if he had, if he had not been watching the track, if the Indian-Pacific were threatened by a rear collision, what about Darya and the people inside Cars 1 and 2?

If he left the engine, Dermot would break loose. Sammy, reviving his own frenzy, would again unpredictably menace everyone on the train. All he could do was to blow four, five, six long blasts on the engine's whistle to warn any possible traffic on the track behind. He waited a few seconds and blew four more sustained blasts.

He started to count to fifteen before using the whistle again. At twelve the lavatory door buckled, the wrench clanged to the floor, and Dermot, scarlet-faced from heat and exertion, exploded from his imprisonment. Dermot's body was wholly in motion; he seemed to be executing a dance, behind whose gyrations Sammy emerged sheltering himself.

Hartley shot at Dermot's right leg, but missed. He fired again at Dermot, but splintered the cover of the toilet seat.

Three feet behind Hartley a fire extinguisher hung in a bracket on the forward wall of the generator area. Hartley transferred the revolver to his left hand. With his right, he pulled out the fire extinguisher, pressed the control, and sent a stream of foam against Dermot.

Gasping, Dermot dropped his shield, clawed at his eyes, staggered back, and fell through the opening into the lavatory. Before the fire extinguisher was empty, Hartley directed the stream against Sammy.

"You are going overboard. Off this train if you don't give up," Hartley told him.

"I'll—never—give up," Sammy gasped. "Damn your

soul, Hartley. You've blinded me."

"All right, then off the train." Hartley, still holding the revolver in his left hand, struck Sammy below his right ear and dragged him toward the catwalk. Sammy kicked at him weakly, but his hands caught the railing at the cab end beside the catwalk and held.

Hartley heard steps on the catwalk. Dropping Sammy, he faced the rear with the revolver in his right hand.

It was Darya who ran through from the baggage car.

"Hartley, something is coming along the track behind us!"

"A train? But how—"

"I couldn't tell—lights. Far back."

She saw Sammy crouching, coughing, covering his eyes. She protected her eyes and nose from the extinguisher fumes with her scarf. Hartley was wiping his eyes.

"Where is Ali?" he asked her.

"At the back—with a flashlight—signaling to what's coming."

"How did you get through?"

"Oh, Hartley, when I saw those lights, I beat on the door with a shoe and yelled and yelled for Glendon. Finally, she heard me and ran up but couldn't open the door. Then she came back with an axe—I don't know where she found it."

"I do. Go on."

"She broke glass in the door and helped me climb through. Then Ali came, but I managed to make him understand that he had to signal with his flashlight, to warn whoever was coming. He threw the emergency. Then I ran here—I didn't know where you were. Not even—"

Suddenly, Sammy, who had come from behind him, lurched toward the controls. Hartley leaped at him and jerked him away from the throttle, but their feet slipped on the foam. Sammy staggered against Hartley, who threw him to the floor of the cab.

"Talk fast! Where is the *Cutlass*?"

"Go to hell," Sammy gasped.

Hartley bent over him, forced his face into the foam, and struck the back of his neck. "Harder next time if you don't tell me."

"Hartley!" Darya cried. "Dermot is behind you!"

Hartley wheeled. Unhesitating, he shot at Dermot's legs. Dermot fell to the left of Sammy.

Darya ran past Hartley and lifted Sammy's head from the floor.

"Hartley—don't—don't kill him!" To her brother she cried, "Sammy—tell him—tell him where the ship is!"

Sammy raised himself to his knees. "I'll never tell him!"

"You *must*!"

"No. He won't kill me. Doesn't have it in him."

As Hartley reached to pull Darya away from her brother, footsteps sounded from the catwalk. He turned, expecting to see Ali. Instead he saw Glendon's grandfather, who walked briskly toward the cab, glanced coolly through it, and introduced himself casually.

"Owen Percy, General, retired. Rather a full docket here, haven't you?"

He drew a silver flask from the pocket of his white linen jacket. "Have some of this. Brandy. Will help."

Hartley, his eyes still stinging, tearing, drank brandy gratefully. Unreal, though, he thought—this echo of a British officers' club in all the shambles here. The

205

General might have been a good actor playing the part of a British officer. He returned the flask to the General, who offered it to Darya.

"No, thank you." She was still hovering over Sammy.

Dermot groaned, clutching at his knee.

Hartley moved past Sammy, past Dermot, to recover Dermot's revolver, but Sammy kicked the revolver from his hand. At the same moment, Glendon came running along the catwalk.

"Hartley!" she shouted. "I can't see the lights behind us, but something is coming—from ahead!"

Hartley, stooping to pick up the revolver that Sammy had kicked from his hand, heard Glendon but could not answer. Sammy went for Hartley's throat. General Percy retrieved the fallen revolver and dealt Sammy a blow on the neck, handed Hartley the revolver, then looked through the broken window of the cab.

"She's right, you know. Something—a vehicle—is coming along toward us."

They didn't wait any longer, then, Hartley thought—not after the long delay at the rendezvous. And whatever was coming along the track from behind—maybe help—might have been warned off by the flash signals.

Sammy lay still, and Dermot still groaned. The wound in his knee, Hartley thought, must be horribly painful.

"Glendon, you have a first-aid kit?"

"Yes. I'll get it."

"No, Darya, will you? And look in on the Abo."

"Sit down a moment," General Percy said. He offered the brandy again. "Tell me. Are these bastards working for Ian Richland? Old Tick-tock—we called him that because of his cough. I knew him when I was fighting in Malaysia. He was, well, not exactly fighting. Doing a desk job. Rather likeable fellow."

"The hijackers," Hartley said, "are his people. Adopted. Glendon, where's Ali?"

"Still at the rear."

"Bring us a tablecloth, Glen," her grandfather said.

Is he going to serve tea? Hartley wondered. But the General's purpose was practical. The tablecloth that Glendon brought he used to tie Sammy to prevent him from attacking them again.

Afterward, carefully adjusting his well-creased white trousers, he seated himself in the engineer's chair and calmly lighted an English cigarette. Glendon, with an arm over his shoulders, stood looking through the broken window. "The lights are still far off," she said.

"In this terrain," her grandfather said, "lights show at a considerable distance." He seemed indifferent to Dermot's groans but presently handed his flask to Hartley. "Give the man a drink, and stop sweating."

"I'm going to give him a sedative."

"Yes—against the books to give both—but advisable now."

As Hartley returned the flask, he was alerted again by the opening of the door from the baggage car, but was relieved to see Darya. He shook out three tablets from a bottle in the kit.

"I'll give you these," he said to Dermot. "Just as soon as you tell me where the *Cutlass* is."

"We could shoot his other leg," General Percy said conversationally, "if he won't tell you."

"I'll tell you," Dermot muttered through grayish lips.

"Off Head of Bight. About five miles east of it. About sixty miles directly south from the end of the Long Straight."

Hartley gave him the sedative.

"But it won't do you any good," Dermot said. "The Land Rovers will come here—they had orders not to wait more than an hour at the rendezvous. Four men. Armed. And the track will be torn up at the end of the Straight. Give me a cigarette."

Hartley reached for a bulge in Dermot's shirt pocket.

"No!" Dermot screamed. "Don't touch me. Cigarettes"—his teeth chattered—"in jacket. On chair."

Hartley brought the cigarettes and lighted one. The smell of Turkish tobacco was strong.

General Percy tapped a finger twice on the throttle. "Too bad we can't deploy this vehicle. Yes. Might work. Hartley, when I give the word, turn out the cab light. Let me handle the men in the Land Rovers."

"Do you—" Hartley broke off. A shuffle of feet sounded in the catwalk, and a laugh.

"The Abo!" Darya cried.

In bloodstained trousers and shirt, with throat bandaged under his haggard, dark face, the Abo unsteadily entered the cab.

"How are you feeling?" the General asked.

"Want food."

"I'll get him something," Glendon said. She ran lightly down the catwalk.

Leaning back in the chair, the Abo looked benevolently at the General and said, "Who you?"

"A friend. Helping out."

The Abo looked at the two men on the floor, then drew Hartley toward him and whispered to him.

"What! Are you sure?" Hartley exclaimed. The Abo

started to speak but stopped and made a sniffling noise.

"Smell," he said, frowning. "Smell."

On the catwalk footsteps sounded. Glendon was coming back.

But she was not alone. Behind her Ali held a revolver pressed against her throat.

10

END OF THE LONG STRAIGHT

Hartley switched off the cab light. Moving swiftly and soundlessly, he stepped over the two bodies on the floor and started down the catwalk on the port side of the engine. He pocketed his revolver. In the darkness he would not be able to use it without risk to Glendon. As he approached the end of the generator housing and the juncture of the two sections of the catwalk, he tightened his muscles for the attack he would make upon Ali.

He put out his hand to feel for the end of the housing.

Instead of metal, his hand touched the arm of someone standing at the end of the passage. The impetus of his movement carried him into collision with a man's body.

The man reacted to the contact more quickly than Hartley. His hands gripped Hartley's throat.

Hartley fought the grip and kicked, but as if warned by communication from Hartley's muscles, the other

210

man—Daoud, it must be—sprang and leaped to Hartley's shoulders, and clung to him by knees and legs.

Hartley kept balance by grasping the housing rail. Although the figure that had fastened itself on him was light, the fingers and legs ground into his body with a tenacity which Hartley's hands could not loosen.

Daoud had made no outcry, but the sound of their feet must have warned Ali of the struggle; Ali could not, however, know who would round the end of the housing. He might, Hartley thought, have moved forward into the silent cab. And he would still be holding the revolver at Glendon's throat. Hartley heard Ali's voice, near him, cry, "Put on the light, or I will shoot the girl!"

Hartley leaped toward Ali, tore the revolver from his hand, beat his head with the butt, and kicked him until his body collapsed against him.

At that moment Hartley heard the braking of cars and saw headlights shine against the engine's darkness. Land Rovers. He groped for Glendon, raised her from where she had fallen, and drew her with him toward the cab.

Halfway along the catwalk they heard General Percy's voice, cheerfully calling out in Malayan, "Welcome, friends!"

Hartley had heard that cough, that time-gaining palliative mannerism, in the Hilton bar in Singapore.

"Ian Richland here," Percy said. Decided to come along for the sport at the last minute."

Could the General get away with it? Maybe, Hartley thought. Just as Malays all looked alike to Westerners unfamiliar with them, perhaps Britons all sounded alike to Malays. He hoped Sir Ian spoke British Malayan. The

General had the right words but not the tune.

"A little delay. A bit of trouble from some passengers," Percy continued. "Not serious."

"Tuan," a man's voice speaking Malayan called from the first of the two cars. "Do you need help?"

"No," Percy answered.

Hartley, now in the cab, said clearly so that the Malays outside would hear, "Sir Ian. One moment."

"Wait for my signal," the General ordered the drivers.

Hartley whispered that Glendon was safe, and he relayed what the Abo had told him. Then he added, aloud, "Two of the sacks are in the first room on the left in Car 2. The rest in rooms 5 and 7."

Another voice called, "Tuan, why do we wait? It will be daylight before we reach the ship."

General Percy posing as Sir Ian called back, this time with an enthusiasm that was not simulated. "When did daylight ever defeat a Malayan? By day or night, Bulan will triumph!"

From both Land Rovers howls of elation rang out. Someone started to sing the Bulan song, and others joined. Percy-Ian was talking again rapidly.

Was the General stalling for time, to delay still further the progress of the Land Rovers, or to allow more time for the arrival of possible help from behind the train? Or merely to encourage the drivers?

A voice from the rear car asked where Lady Mary was, another asked for Sammy, and a third for their comrades.

"Do you think," the General's voice thundered between two small coughs, "that *I* would not care for all of them?

The waiting Malays acclaimed him, but a voice from the first car said, "Tuan, there are no lights in the engine."

"Of course not! Lights interfere with driving an engine."

The driver of the first car called, "Tuan, we wait for your signal. But the time, Tuan! We are ready to load the gold and to start. A piece of track at our rendezvous, where we waited two hours, has been destroyed, as Sammy ordered."

"Good, then," he called to the men outside. "This is the signal." He blew the whistle. "You will drive to the front of the last car of this train. Stop outside. Then all of you will enter that car. Car 2. It is marked. Two of the sacks of gold are in the first room on your left as you go in. Break the window, throw them out. Then go on to rooms 5 and 7 on the left. The rest of the sacks are there. The window in room 7 is broken. You will throw out the remaining sacks. Then go outside again and load them." The ticking cough was slower. Two beats, Hartley thought, not the usual three. Would the men in the car respond?

A man in the first car spoke. "Our comrades— Sammy, Lady Mary, you—will all go with us?"

"We will all join you," he said, then added confidentially, "You know we had expected to find supplies of food on the train. Not enough here. You will need much food for that long voyage."

"And fuel oil," another voice from a Land Rover said. "You said *you*. Won't you be with us, Sir Ian?"

"Do you think that Lady Mary or I or Sammy would *not* be with you?"

"No," the man said. "But we need Sammy on the junk

213

as soon as we get there. For the loading. The fueling. And Dermot if there is trouble with the Australian Coast Guard."

"Men of Bulan. Either you trust me, or you do not trust me. Which?"

Hartley heard cries of trust.

"So," the General said. "Fuel oil, food, water—we will supply everything for the voyage."

"But—" the objector was speaking again, "—what if the Coast Guard threatens us?"

"We have arranged for that possibility," the General said loftily. Hartley's hold on his revolver relaxed. "Haven't you heard of the power of bribery?"

"Yes, but Australia is so enormous a country, Tuan."

"With all the more possibilities for finding officials that can be bribed and oil depots where we will not be asked for papers."

Through the cab window Hartley saw four men, two from each Land Rover, disembark. Why didn't they move faster? He clutched the back of the engineer's chair behind General Percy's rigid figure and heard the General mutter, "Get along, you bastards." But when he called again, his voice between short punctuations of coughing was smooth and supercilious. "What is delaying you, friends? Why aren't you loading the gold?"

Three of the men moved toward the rear. The fourth called up to the window. "Sir Ian."

"Yes? What is it now?" A small cough.

"Sammy said if anything went wrong, we should talk to him."

"I will tell you where Sammy is. He is taking care of a passenger who was unwise enough to oppose us and who had to be subdued. You know how merciful

214

Sammy is. Ah, yes, Sammy arranged for a password. He told me. A word that would make you sure our plans were safe. Another word that meant danger. There is no danger. Are you asking me to bring Sammy now—for a word—when you have mine?" His voice grew sterner. "Which of our men are you?"

"I am Hassan, Tuan."

"Yes, I remember you. You are a loyal and cautious worker for Bulan. When we all return to Bulan with the gold, I hope to be able to praise you. But," he coughed, "I will not praise you if you continue to delay us."

The General turned toward Hartley. "There they go. How was the impersonation?"

"Masterly. But how did you get into that bit about Bulan sunsets?"

"Nothing gases up these boys like a whiff of the natural beauty of the homeland. They'd go miles on an empty tank if you threw out a good word about the ruddy scenery."

"All quiet on the catwalk?" Hartley asked Glendon, who stood beyond Darya at the rear of the cab.

"All quiet."

"But Hartley," Darya protested in a whisper, "you're letting them get away with the gold!"

The General was leaning out of the window.

"Lights behind us," he said to Hartley. "Coming on. Too close. Handcar? With help? But what arms? Can't have them stirring up the Malays. Getting shot up. Getting *us* shot up. Whistle? No good. They might think we were calling for fast help."

"I could run back along the track to warn them," Hartley said.

"No. Need you on board. We're not in the clear. Won't be till the Land Rovers push off. No. Tell you what." He coughed Sir Ian's identification. "Thing's habit forming. Hartley, you shove along to the vestibule, front end of Car 2. Keep out of sight. Wait there. Watch out for trouble."

As Hartley moved toward the passage on his right to avoid the bodies of Ali and Daoud on the other side, the General said, "Glen, you and Darya get down. Away from windows."

The Abo uttered a croaking sound.

"You sit low. You be quiet," the General told him.

In the vestibule of Car 2 Hartley, with revolver still drawn, stood on the port side and heard the General advance toward the opposite side of the vestibule.

"Men of Bulan!" he called loudly, then uttered a fragment of the Ian cough. "Proceed with your work. If you see lights behind us, do not stop. We'll be having a doctor coming on. As I told you, a passenger is hurt, the one that Sammy is helping. No trouble for you."

"But Tuan," a worried voice said. "How will you and the others reach the ship if you do not come with us?"

The weak point, Hartley thought.

"A helicopter will bring us." The General spoke with a strained patience. "It will also bring supplies—rice, lamb, tea, fruit, bread. These have been trucked to a point near where the ship is anchored. The fruit will not be what you like best, but this is not Bulan. We will bring whatever food there is on this train."

Another voice said hesitantly, "Water, Tuan?"

"But of course! Water where we get fuel oil."

The inventiveness of the man! Hartley thought. "Stay out of sight, General, here they come."

He and the General retreated a few steps into Car 1 as the drivers boarded Car 2.

"Load up now, men. We're on our way to Bulan. Insha-Allah!" the General yelled.

"Insha-Allah!" voices answered him.

Hartley heard the window in Hawkins's office break, and heard the thud of heavy sacks falling to the ground from there and a few minutes later from the window of Macrimmon's room. He waited. The front Land Rover turned left into the Straight and the second followed. The Abo was still laughing when Hartley and the General returned to the cab.

"He's delirious!" Darya said.

"No. I'll explain later."

The General was holding the Abo's shoulders.

"Now you stop it. You be quiet. Those men on the floor—they could be listening. Hartley, get along to the rear. Light showing again. See what's up. Everything seems under control here. Land Rovers steaming south. Almost out of sight. Stubborn, those bastards."

"General Percy," Hartley said, "you'd better try some of your own medicine. Out of the flask."

"Damned if I won't. Want some, anybody?" The General flourished the flask.

The Abo put out a bearlike paw.

As Hartley left, he heard the General say, "You've earned it, boy. And double."

He hurried through the dismantled dining car to the end of Car 2, where he found the glass pane in the vestibule door shattered and the axe leaning against a wall. Through the broken window he saw in the light of its own lantern a handcar as near as a hundred feet away.

The door would not open. He ran to the forward end of the car and disembarked, for the first time with a reasonable expectation that the train would not move away without him.

Halfway along the car he met the men who had descended from the handcar. Hawkins, in the lead, said, "Mr. Rhys, is everything all right?"

Behind Hawkins, Hartley heard Tommy's voice. "Hello, Hartley. Having any fun?"

"Not exactly. What took you so long?"

"Long!" Hawkins exclaimed. "If you knew—but here are Engineer Riggs and his assistant, Guard Ellis from Cook, and Mr. Armitage."

"Where's Merriam?" Hartley asked. He waited for the others to pass and fell in beside Tommy.

"Back in Cook, with his crowd," Tommy said.

"Thank heaven! I didn't know where he'd got to when the cars were uncoupled."

"In Car 3—he'd been dodging the Malays. All gone now? The gold—what about it?"

"Never mind the gold," Riggs said irately as he followed Hawkins aboard. "I'm taking over the engine. Train's almost three hours late."

"We've had some trouble," Hartley said.

"You think *we* haven't?" Hawkins muttered. "Freight had to push us back to Cook. Nobody there ready to help us."

"Who would be ready this time of night?" Riggs growled as he pushed past Hawkins into Car 1. "Routed out of bed, in my free time."

"Use the left catwalk," Hartley called. "Right side isn't clear."

When they reached the dining car, he wasn't surprised to hear Hawkins's cry of outrage.

The assistant engineer and the guard had already reached the baggage car.

"Great heavens, Mr. Rhys, *what* happened here?

Windows broken, dishes smashed!"

"It looks as if you'd had a real bash," Tommy said. "Where's Glendon?"

"In the engine cab," Hartley told him.

"What's in the other catwalk?" Tommy asked.

"Two Malays. Out of the action."

"You put them out?"

"Yes. Somebody had to."

Glendon, seeing Tommy, ran past Riggs and slipped in the residue of fire extinguisher fluid. Riggs caught her.

"Miss, please get out of the cab." To Darya he said, "you too."

Glendon was already on the catwalk, secure in Tommy's arms.

General Percy, meanwhile, sat erect in the engineer's seat beside the Abo, volunteering nothing.

"Two bodies on the floor!" Riggs yelled. "And what's this? Fire extinguisher fluid! And *this*!" He kicked with particular disgust at the broken toilet seat from the lavatory. "I want this cab cleared immediately."

"Sir?"

General Percy rose to a height far above that of the thick-necked engineer, and moved from the engineer's seat. Below that gaunt, impressive height, Hartley saw Riggs move a step backward.

"I am Owen Percy, General, retired from her Majesty's service."

"General Percy! Malaysian Percy?"

"If you wish."

After a moment of what Hartley thought of as a silent tribute, Riggs scowled at him.

"You responsible for all this?" Riggs asked the General.

"Young man," Percy said, "you would do well to stop

219

accusing anyone until you know what has been happening here."

"I can see what has been happening."

"The man you have just spoken to is Hartley Rhys, who represents the Sword Shipping Line of Singapore."

"And what's this?" Riggs pointed to the Abo, who seemed to be dozing. "What's he representing?"

The Abo, awakened by the noise, raised his head. Before the General could hold him back, he lurched from the chair and lunged at the assistant engineer. "You—that smell—you kill Mac!" The Abo shouted.

Hartley pulled the Abo away. "Down. He's just now come on. Couldn't have killed Mac."

"I kill!" The Abo thrust past Hartley and fell upon Dermot.

Hartley caught his hands before they could encircle Dermot's throat.

The Abo looked up at him, half-snarling, half-grinning. "You look in pockets! You find. Opals. He take from Mac. When he kill. I smell that smell."

Hartley released the Abo, turned down the blanket that someone had covered Dermot with, and drew from Dermot's shirt pocket a red-striped pouch. He shook it. Opals glimmered on the foam and blood-stained floor of the cab.

Hartley gathered them up and gave them to the General.

"So," General Percy observed, "there is your murderer."

"Get him out of here!" Riggs shouted, pointing toward the Abo.

"Go easy on him," Hartley said to the assistant with whose help he carried the Abo into the baggage car and laid him on a packing case. The railroad guard passed them and returned, carrying a broom, a mop, and a pail.

Tommy, at Hartley's request, went aft in search of blankets.

In the cab the assistant had thrown the toilet seat into the lavatory and was gathering up wreckage. The guard was sweeping. Riggs now surveyed the immobile figure of Dermot groaning in his sleep, and of Sammy, beside whom Darya knelt.

"Christ! You blokes have a crust—to talk about saving lives and property!"

Tommy came back into the baggage car while Hartley, the assistant, and the guard were moving Dermot and Sammy.

"Proper hospital ward here," he said.

"And two other bodies beside the generators," the guard said. "Should we bring them in here too?"

"No," Hartley said. "Better not move them." The guard looked at Hartley with mingled distrust and admiration.

"Good old killer Hartley," Tommy commented cheerfully. Coming from Tommy, the characterization was not offensive.

"I could have used your help, Tommy."

"Yes, well, next time. Last cars were sliding back loose when I saw you lying at the edge of that vestibule. Bad moment. Thought you'd fall off. You'll have to clue me in sometime on all the massacres."

"Over a Scotch in Sydney," Hartley said. Tommy grinned.

"Sydney. Glendon will be there."

Glendon, who had been covering bodies with blankets, echoed him. "I'll be in Sydney!"

Darya was leaning over Sammy. Neither Sydney nor

any other goal, Hartley thought, would at this moment lessen the trouble that had dulled the old brightness in her eyes.

Hartley returned to the cab. "The engineer," he said, "was forcibly ejected."

"Where is he?" the General asked.

"Probably stowed away somewhere. Unless the hijackers threw him out."

"Threw him out? Off this train?" Riggs asked. Riggs, who seemed to share the Hawkins syndrome of the inviolability of the Indian-Pacific, threw himself into the engineer's seat. "God! It's impossible! Hijackers? More likely some drunken brawl!"

"Look," Hartley said, "several men need medical care urgently. Please start the engine."

The General reinforced him. "Push on to the nearest station as ruddy fast as you can."

"I'm in charge here!" Riggs shouted.

"Then you'll be responsible," Hartley said, "for the death of one man, maybe two, because of a delay in getting medical aid."

"You should have thought of that before you half-murdered them," Riggs muttered.

Hartley gave him a few minutes before saying, "Somewhere ahead the track may be torn up. Probably near the end of the Straight."

Riggs, perhaps soothed by the familiar process of driving the engine, confined himself to muttering, "I've seen everything."

His assistant, seated beside him, said, "She runs all right."

"She better," Riggs growled.

In the baggage car Hartley found Hawkins indefatigably bearing a tray with teapot and cups.

"Meet Florence Nightingale," Tommy said.

As Hartley had noticed before, Hawkins looked at Tommy as if he had been a toy in a shop window, and not a toy that Hawkins wanted to buy.

None of the others wanted tea, but Glendon took a cup, saying, "I don't know how you found tea things, Mr. Hawkins."

Hawkins turned to Hartley. "The dining car, the galley, the crew—how we are ever going to serve breakfast tomorrow?"

"You'll manage," Hartley said. "You find any of the other conductors?"

"Oh yes," Hawkins said dolefully. "In shower rooms. One in a lavatory. Drugged. I can't believe it. This train—how could it all have happened!"

"At least," Hartley said, "the passengers haven't been hurt. Except Macrimmon and the Abo. Your first duty is to the passengers, isn't it?"

"Yes—but Mr. Macrimmon. I haven't gone into his room—is he—"

"Yes. He is dead."

"Oh, poor Lady Mary!"

"Watch it," Tommy said. "You're spilling tea."

"Anyway," Hartley said, "*you* weren't drugged. Early in the game I think the hijackers with drugs were busy with the messmen. But there's something I've wondered about—that dispatch. Wasn't there radio communication from the engine?"

"Yes, but the radio had been chancy. Important dispatches were sent to stationmasters along the route. When I think about that freight—"

"Don't," Hartley said. "No collision. Tell me something else. The man that got off at Cook—in such a hurry. It was Hall, Macrimmon's nephew, wasn't it?"

"Yes. It was Hall. When the freight pushed those three cars back into Cook, Hall was there. He had gone into Mr. Macrimmon's room, seen the body, and panicked. Then he got off the train. But where could he go? There was no way of getting out of Cook. So he gave himself up to the police. They were holding him when I was there."

The train was running smoothly under Riggs's driving.

"Can you see any landmarks? Know how soon we'll come to the end of the Straight?" Hartley asked Hawkins.

"No landmarks. But the stars—" Hawkins looked through a window. "Can't be exact about this, but I'd say we were near the end." He took Glendon's cup and started to go toward the dining car. "Mr. Rhys," he said, halting. "About Lady Mary. I can't believe she had anything to do with the others."

"Do you remember what happened in your office in the dark after you were untied?"

"I remember there was some shooting. But all I remember about Lady Mary was that she fainted when you took her into that room, and that she thought her father was dead."

"Hartley," Darya said when Hawkins had gone. "Sammy wants to talk to you. Alone."

"Come along to the club car," Tommy said to Darya and Glendon. "Maybe I can make some Singapore Slings. One good thing about Malays is they don't guzzle liquor. Give me Moslems any day."

Hartley had already crossed the irregular aisle between boxed and heaped baggage and was looking down at Sammy, at another of Sammy's selves, this one without flamboyance, a boyish Sammy.

"You used to be my friend," Sammy said. "Maybe—oh, I don't know. But I want to make a deal. Listen, will you?"

"What deal could you possibly make?"

"I can tell you that Dermot lied. The *Cutlass* isn't where he said it was. I could save you a lot of time hunting. I could tell you what they're going to do with the gold if they can't load it today and take off."

"And you could be lying too," Hartley said.

"You could check it. If I tell you, will you put in a word for me with the Company or the law, and tell them I had nothing to do with murder?"

"How can you prove it?"

"I couldn't have done it. I was up front even before the stop at Cook. We had to clear the cab and the dining car. I don't know who killed Macrimmon, but I know I didn't."

"Who of your men wasn't with you, just before the train got to Cook?"

Sammy shook his head. "I'm not ratting on any of my men."

"Then what's your deal? And hurry."

Sammy rubbed his eyes.

"I'm going to trust you, Hartley."

"Oh, for God's sake, what's trust got to do with any of this!"

"Maybe not much," Sammy admitted. "But Dermot *did* lie."

"If you had nothing to do with Macrimmon's murder," Hartley said, "the Malays who were with you could clear you."

"The Malays will be scurrying to protect themselves. And Daoud will want me caught. He wants my girl."

"If Dermot killed Macrimmon, maybe they wouldn't

225

rat. But it *was* Dermot, wasn't it?"

"Even if I were sure," Sammy said, "I wouldn't tell you. I told you I wouldn't rat. Not for murder. But I didn't kill. I don't know who did. The whole thing is such a mess. All I'm sure of is I didn't kill."

"Why did you go into such a mad scheme?" Hartley demanded.

"Because I believed the people on Bulan deserved their freedom. They hated the Indonesians. The Indonesians were trying to take over everything. The Portuguese were bad enough, but not as bad as the Indonesians. We've found oil and tried to keep it a secret, but all we needed was money to develop the wells.

"You stole the *Cutlass*," Hartley said. "Planned to steal the gold. Hijack the train. You think you have any help coming from anybody?"

"No. Only that I didn't murder Macrimmon. I can face all the other charges. Not murder."

"I'll do what I can. No promises. So what can you tell me?"

"If I had the materials," Sammy said, "I'd draw you a map."

Hartley took out a small notebook and pen from his pocket. He ripped a piece of paper out of the notebook.

"You draw a line south from the end of the Long Straight," Sammy said. "Then another thirty miles east along the Bight, to a cove, where the water is deep enough for the *Cutlass* to anchor. Empty land. No road. Cave hidden by mulga. Wreck of a wagon. Bleached tree trunk tilted to the west. You got it?"

"Yes."

"If there's interference, the Malays will bury the gold before they get to the coast. They'll mark the place with red caps. Can't tell you more. There isn't any more."

He roused himself. "Yes, there *is* something more. The Malays mustn't start off without food. No supplies on the *Cutlass*."

"Your Malays," Hartley said, "aren't going to start for Bulan."

"Oh, poor dogs!" Sammy cried.

Hartley calculated. Say it would take the train a half-hour to reach the point where the track was destroyed, and another half-hour for him to bypass the uprooted track and reach a telephone. Then how much time to call for ambulances and notify police and the Coast Guard? And how long before they could be combing the coast to find the *Cutlass*? How long would it take for him to hire a hydroplane or a helicopter to get to it?

The train was now apparently running at full speed. He lighted a cigarette and put it between Sammy's lips.

"Cold?"

"Well, yes," Sammy said. Hartley went into Car 1, to the room that two of the Malays had occupied and brought blankets.

"Lie down." He covered Sammy. He crossed the aisle and put his hand on the Abo's forehead. A new stain crimsoned the bandage on the Abo's throat. "Now you lie quiet. Understand?" Hartley told him.

"No—want whisky."

"I'll find some," Hartley said.

"I say, Hartley," General Percy said, standing beside him. That man over there is feverish. Don't like it. How long before you can get an ambulance?"

"Soon as I can. After we get to the place where the track is torn up."

Dermot, deeply asleep, still groaned. His forehead was hot. In the cab Riggs was bent over the controls, his assistant in the chair beside him. The railway guard was still swabbing out the cab.

"Piece of track torn up near the end of the Straight," Hartley reminded him. "You'll be watching for it?"

"I'm running this engine!" Riggs roared. "Get out of here!"

"Not till you get it through your thick skull that track is *torn up*. Slow down. Now. Before you get to the end of the Straight."

"Get back," the assistant muttered. "Maybe the old man will do."

"If the old man won't do, he'll wreck us!"

The engine's speed dwindled and presently the assistant engineer announced, "Lights ahead. Probably workmen repairing track."

Hartley ran back to the baggage car to General Percy.

"Quite a ride, what?" the General asked.

"Nothing like it. Good-bye, Sir. See you in Sydney?"

"Wouldn't miss it. You off now?"

"Yes. I've got to get an ambulance. Then I have to telephone the police, the Coast Guard, and my company."

As they gripped hands, Hartley heard the edge of a cough, something like Sir Ian's tick-tock."

"Have to stay in this climate to get rid of this bloody cough," General Percy said.

In single file Hartley and Darya started toward the rear.

"Think we'll ever get used to walking side by side?"

"We'll try."

She followed Hartley into his compartment. "Can I help you pack?"

"Thanks, no." He was crowding anything that came

to hand into his suitcase and the bag. He stopped long enough to scrub his face and hands and put on a clean jacket.

"Take care of yourself," he said to Darya. "Sammy will have to be hospitalized—I don't know where. You'll want to stand by, but when you get to Sydney, go to the Menzies Hotel. I'll make contact with you there. If you need anything—checks cashed, lawyers—go to the Sword Line Office in Sydney. They'll help you." He wrote a note on one of his identifying cards and gave it to her. "Are you all right for money in the meantime? Before you get to Sydney?"

"Yes. I suppose Sammy will be arrested?"

"Yes. But he'll get medical care."

"And you?"

"First off, doctors, ambulances, then police. When I find the *Cutlass*, I'll have to get together a crew, provision her, and fuel her, then get her back to Singapore." He snapped shut the suitcase latches. "The four drivers of the Land Rovers—I'll have to get General Percy to help identify them."

"I'll take the Kooka to a vet," Darya said.

"And have Macrimmon's friend Jim Blake, the museum curator, look after the Abo."

"How long—" Darya hesitated.

"God knows. But I'll be in contact with you at the Menzies."

She followed Hartley into the vestibule.

"You think Dermot killed Macrimmon?"

"Yes, I'm sure. But God, what a lot of litigation. I hope they'll let you make a deposition and get along back to New York."

"You're sure you'll be coming to Sydney?"

"I'll get there somehow if you're there."

"But Hartley, the hijackers have the gold."

He put down his suitcase and bag and put his hands on Darya's shoulders. "They don't have the gold," he said.

"But they took the bags—"

"You remember when you thought the Abo was delirious? He wasn't. He had just told me that the sacks were full of rubble. The gold was in packing cases in the baggage car, addressed to Macrimmon's friend in Sydney."

"Then it's still on this train?"

"Still here. The way Macrimmon always sent it. Cases marked *geologic specimens*. Addressed to Jim Blake."

"Hartley, what else could happen?"

"I could think of what else."

The train stopped.

"End of the Long Straight. I must go." He drew her tightly into his arms and kissed her pale, smudged, beautiful face.

On the bottom step he halted and looked up at Darya.

"One thing—could you be happy living in Singapore?"

"Yes," Darya said.

An insect chirped wanly as Hartley stepped down to the cinders of the track bed. The moon which had seemed paralyzed was high toward its zenith. Back along the serpentine train, from which all venom seemed to have been drawn, rectangles of light showed at the windows. From ahead he heard the impact of metal on metal. Was a work gang already repairing the track? The alert would have gone out from Cook to stations near the end of the Straight.

He did not look back toward the vestibule where he had left Darya. The one kiss could not be dwelt on now. A Malay proverb edged into his mind: "Daripada ta'ada, baik ada". Something is better than nothing.

He stepped from the gritted roadbed to the hard, sandy earth. Seeing the cars' headlights beyond the engine, he hurried toward them.

POSTLUDE

Letter from Hartley to Darya:

Dear Darya:

Yesterday I mailed you a note on more personal matters; this letter will bring you up to date on what's been happening to the people on and off the Indian-Pacific.

I don't know how thoroughly your newspapers have covered the mass of legal complications. Underneath these, there probably are details you'd like to know about specific individuals.

It's been over a year now since we took what General Percy called "quite a ride, what?" in the Long Straight, a long year since you and I had those few days in Sydney.

Good thing you didn't take me up on that bet I offered you about T. L. Farnsleigh and the Cutlass and my ruined jacket. He got his Cutlass back intact—she's been inspected and is now in service again. But when I saw him for the first time after the junk got back to Singapore, he'd already had reports from me while I was tied up on legalities in Australia. First thing he said was, "Hartley, how do you justify your claim for 100 Australian dollars for damage to one jacket?" Very first thing, I swear. He said I should have bought a jacket in Singapore where it would have been cheaper. I ought to have taken that jacket to show him. He wasn't moved when I reminded him of my trip's timing. He still hasn't O.K.'d the claim, but I've been too busy to care. First, the Australian courts are all in a flap because crimes and damages took place in Western Australia and South Australia. The National Railways are involved, and there are insurance claims and damage suits coming in from passengers from the U.S., England, France, and Japan, for shock if nothing worse. Probably all directly laid at the door of the Bulan outfit, though the railway is involved too. As if the railway could have helped what happened!

First you'd want to know I went to see Sammy in jail in Singapore last week. He was in good shape. Completely unrepentant. Not glad to see me, but he wouldn't be even if he didn't hold grudges. He asked me to get him some books. Seems he's working on the invention of some kind of rotating transport machine. Entirely recovered from what I had to do to him on the Indian-Pacific. I honestly believe he's forgotten the bloodshed and fiasco of the hijacking. I told him what I'd heard from you—part of it—and all he said was that he wanted to see Selby. *Selby!* Does he expect you to bring Selby to the Singapore jail to see him? Maybe bite him again? Somebody should consult Selby. But you will.

I asked Sammy if he'd seen Munah. He brushed off

the question as if she'd become obsolete. But surprisingly he had seen Daoud. More about him later. He visited Sammy, who gave the impression of being able to take or leave Daoud. Preferably leave. I took him cigarettes, and remembering his terrible appetite, chocolate bars and biscuits. He didn't like the brand of biscuits.

As you probably know, he's serving a sentence in Singapore for piracy. There are suits pending against him in Australia. I understand the engineer of that freight train has been raising hell.

I didn't go into those charges with him. Sentences there might run into years. I hope your uncle and aunt are bearing up. I know you are. At least, Sammy doesn't seem to have been involved in a murder charge.

But Dermot is. All the other hijackers managed to produce convincing alibis. But Dermot's possession of the opals and the Abo's astonishingly clear testimony about the smell of the Turkish cigarettes turned the trick. I heard part of it. The Abo wasn't in the least intimidated by courtroom procedures; he was out for vengeance. The defense laywer tried to foul him up on the tobacco smell. He smoked in court several kinds of cigarettes, including the Turkish, three times. Each time the Abo picked out the Turkish tobacco. The prosecuting attorney pointed out that anybody else might have taken one of Dermot's brand, but the jury was impressed by the Abo's unshakability. Devious, lovable old character. I needn't have strained myself talking pidgin English—how did he learn so much English? Macrimmon wouldn't have seemed exactly a teacher. Only irrelevancy in the Abo's testimony was about the Kooka. Violent and irrepressible, that.

But the Kooka is flourishing. Hall has him. More later about Hall.

Macrimmon's friend, the curator of the museum in Sydney, looked out for the Abo while he was in the hospital. Macrimmon didn't leave a will. Never could, I imagine, envisage that one would be needed. And it mightn't have been for years. He was one of those frail, tough old guys that would hang on and on. Especially with the Abo's support. And maybe the Kooka's.

Funny thing about the trials in Australia. Sometimes they seemed to be as much concerned with minor details as about graver things. Damage costs. Broken windows, dishes, toilet seat. Wasted food, spilled fire-extinguisher fluid. Sometimes they made Farnsleigh seem like a spendthrift.

But to go back to the Abo. Poor old chap, they found he had a head injury. Nothing grave. You should have seen him in court, towering over everybody else in the courtroom, looking in his bandages like a turbaned Mogul emperor. He hugged me once in a recess, and nearly broke the rib Lady Mary had kicked. (It's all right now, so don't worry.)

Macrimmon's curator friend is quite a guy. Had known Mac for fifty years. Told me Mac's wife had been an angel. He liked Lady Mary—said Macrimmon doted on her! Hard to believe. Told me Lady M. was always sending gifts to her father. Like really great shirts and jackets and pajamas. Mac always brought them with him, wore them in Sydney. He was immensely proud but also scornful of them. Jim, the curator, had met Sir Ian. A brain, he said. A visionary. Devoted to his wife. It shakes one's belief in judgments, when you think how Lady M. and her father wrangled on the train. Still, I'll never forget how Lady M. fainted when she saw her father dead in that bunk. She wasn't the kind of person to faint easily.

And speaking of judgments—after that short visit you and I had with the curator, he told me you were the most beautiful woman he had ever seen! He said you were like what used to be called a *grande dame*, only young.

The Abo kept after Jim. You'll have to let him do it, Jim said to me. Do what? Let him take you to dinner. What—the Abo take *me* to dinner?

"He can't think what else to do. He says you saved his life. Which you undoubtedly did." I objected to this. How let the Abo take me to dinner?

"You'll have to let him do it. Let him pay. He has money saved. Mac paid him well. You can handle reservations and ordering. But let him do it. Get me off the hook."

I think I said something like for God's sake. Not that I didn't want to have dinner with the Abo. But after all! In the end, the Abo took me to dinner at the Coachmen's Inn in Sydney. You and I would have gone there if there'd been time. Odd old place—wine cellar under the roof. Abo still looking like a Mogul potentate. It didn't seem real, but then what *did* seem real about that whole business in the Straight? Anyway, the Abo and I had caviar, chicken breasts in wine, and heaven knows what else. When we got back to Jim's house, Jim had news for the Abo: the vet said the Kooka was going to be all right. Might not fly again—some wing damage—but it was croak-laughing already. I was afraid the Abo would hug me again. I'm not the Kooka, I told him. You should have heard him laugh.

T. L. Farnsleigh would disapprove of my attachments to people I've made contact with. For years, if I stay with Sword, I'll be hearing about derelictions, like giving my derringer to Merriam. Oh, Merriam returned it—T. L. gave me credit for that, with a warning not to be so profligate (that was his word) in spreading around firearms furnished by the comapny. He wasn't at all impressed by what Merriam did for us. More about Merriam later.

And Darya, if you have the slightest worry about your hiding place in the Abo's bunk, you needn't. He's never mentioned it. He never will. One lawyer I talked to said the Abo showed what the Australian policy toward the aborigines had resulted in. I hope so. How far, though? I don't think there could be another Abo.

And while I'm talking about unrealities, Darya, maybe you could have believed it. I could scarcely. Not long after you had made your deposition and the lawyers let you go back to New York, two little beautiful nuns came from Dublin to testify as character witnesses for Dermot! All that distance—a sister and an aunt. And Dermot already well launched toward conviction.

The younger nun was Dermot's sister. Her name was Sister Ursula. She was too harshly scrubbed, a red-cheeked girl, excited about being out of Ireland for the first time. The older nun, Sister Monica, was oval-faced, ivory-skinned, and hadn't been out of Ireland either. But her eyes showed that in studying, reading, perhaps praying, her experiences had transcended geography. People in their parish had raised money to pay for the trip. Dermot had written to his Dublin bank to draw out money. News stories had reached Dublin. I met them in the lobby of the Menzies Hotel. They asked me how to find the restaurant. We talked a few minutes, and it ended in my taking them to lunch, but with some misgivings. They were to be witness for the defense, and I was of course on the other side.

A good boy, they said Dermot had been. Never failed to write to them, to send contributions to the chapter. Dermot a mercenary? A murderer? Impossible, they declared in their lovely, lilting Dublin-English. Dermot—a murderer for a treasure of opals? No. He had helped people in trouble all round the world.

But the opals would be a court exhibit.

"He would never have wanted them," the sister told me.

Had the defense lawyer put up the two nuns at my hotel, perhaps planning to have us meet, perhaps sensing my underdoggism?

"Opals mean bad luck," Sister Ursula said.

They had indeed for Dermot.

That lunch was a miserable ordeal. What could I say when Ursula asked me whether I hadn't found Dermot to be a good Christian boy?

"He had a rosary in his pocket," I said unhappily.

"They couldn't do anything like convict him, could they?" she asked. The aunt seemed to read my eyes.

She stayed silent while Ursula, schoolgirl on holiday, chattered about wanting to see kangaroos. After lunch I arranged at the desk to have them take a tour including a zoo. Ursula seemed to be in a non-religious ecstasy. The aunt sadly thanked me, mercifully saying nothing more about Dermot. I did not see them again outside the courtroom.

They saw Dermot once, maybe twice. I hated to think of the feelings on both sides.

I don't know what Dermot's sentence will be.

To go back to Singapore—Sir Ian lorded it over his questioners. Had he planned for the stealing of the *Cutlass*? He claimed it was borrowing. And of course, he had Farnsleigh on his side. No criminal charges against him. He was fined. In Australia he has not yet been tried as instigator of the conspiracy. But he has testified that Lady Mary took no part in the hijacking for the theft of the gold. Hawkins, of course, suported this testimony. Their lawyers played up the fact that indeed the hijackers had not stolen the gold. The sacks they had taken contained only rocks, stubble. And as to intent, if, as Lady Mary claimed, the gold was only to be borrowed from her father—was that a theft? Of course it was, I would say. But legally? And I didn't think this should be a factor. But did Lady Mary, as heiress now to her father's wealth, have some claim to it? Or did her title throw weight into the proceedings?

The opals have been impounded for the duration of the probation procedures. I understand that Lady Mary plans to return them to Hall.

I hope that the probate will not take too long, that she *will* return the opals and that Hall's father will live long enough to enjoy them.

Hall came close to having a murder charge pressed against him in Australia. He was held, along with Dermot, for months. Long past the date for his wedding. Why had he left the train in such haste? It happened that the chief constable in the district including Cook, where Hall turned himself in, was his cousin.

Remind me to have relatives in the constabulary if I'm ever unlucky enough to be charged with a crime. Not, of course, that I think Hall was guilty. A strange man. But during the hearings, when he was free on bond, we met. I couldn't help liking him. When we were both in Sydney, he took me to see Morsel, his fiancée; her aunt; and the undistinguished family of cats whose mother was supposedly the male Tomcat. The aunt teaches history in the university; Morsel works in an architect's office. They urged me to go to the wedding in Kalgoorlie, but I had too much on the docket. Hall preserved his mysteriousness, but Morsel seemed happy to be mystified. Very likable, the three of them; and maybe the cats would have been if I had known them better. The only cats I've ever liked are kittens owned by the two children of my Chinese neighbors in Singapore.

I don't think I told you, but when I finally got back to the apartment in Singapore in a rather fragmented state, I found my Chinese housekeeper very much on deck. I'd sent her a card about my return. There she was, the apartment shined, chicken and shrimp cooking, mail sorted, and a letter from you on top of the pile. Before there was time for her to make a drink, my neighbor was knocking at the door. He took me downstairs for a rum punch and a reunion with him and his wife and the children. But they were sympathetic. After one rum punch my friend's wife detached a child curled around my neck and a kitten from my knee and said, "You need rest." My housekeeper fed me not only chicken and shrimps but eggplant and western rolls which she had baked. I read your letter, of course, before dinner and afterward. Later I slept. I think I would have slept for twelve hours. But at eight the telephone rang.

"Hartley?"

"Yes, Mr. Farnsleigh?"

"How soon can you come to the office?"

Wouldn't you know?

He had another assignment which he said nobody but I could carry out. This was dangerously near praise, but there was a motive. I reminded him that I might be called back to Australia at any moment, but he rumbled something about being able to fix that. The new assignment, fortunately, has nothing to do with trains. I have to go to Penang, where one of our ships broke down; he wants me to supervise repairs. Plenty of other people in the company could do the job, but I imagine Farnsleigh feels the leash has been too long and wants to put me to work here right off.

You may have heard about the supposed oil deposits in Bulan and its satellite islands. Sir Ian and his followers had tried to keep that hushed up, but it all came to light during the trials; and as we foresaw, Indonesia pounced on Bulan, and tightened up what had been loose control formerly shared with the Portuguese. So Sir Ian's and the Malays' dreams of independence for Bulan have been stopped.

General Percy's cough turned out to be non-habit-forming. You've probably heard from Glendon and know that she and Tommy will be married as soon as they get back to England. The General seems pleased. Tommy says that his uncle, the Consul, dislikes agreeing with anything Tommy says or does. He feels that Tommy is too undisciplined, but the General is dispensing charm and authority. I've an idea that under his flippancy Tommy may be a pretty sound fellow.

I saw Merriam while I was still in Australia, and asked him if he had escaped from being latched onto by the French girls. Merriam said yes. He sounded relieved but a little regretful. He was slated to escort a travel group through Malaysia and Burma and Thailand on his next outing. His old man with the heart attack and a collapsed elderly lady reached the end of their tour in good shape.

The two Malays I had to eject from the train didn't

come off so well. Some broken bones. But Ali and Daoud were all right. And so was Dermot, after an operation and two months in a hospital in Sydney. All the missing train crew members turned up from lavatories and shower rooms, and my three drugged roommates in that bunk-storage room came out all right.

The Australians got the first shot at Ali, whose trial is still in progress. In Singapore investigations are going on about the death of Welles and his informant. Ali is involved. A cantina girl put him near the scene of the crime.

Daoud will probably come off with the lightest sentence. I testified about his saving my life and generally trying to restrain his confederates. I skipped any mention of his attack on me in the catwalk. He certainly wouldn't have killed me. Of all the people involved he was the most broken-up about Bulan. I saw him in Australia right after the Indonesian pounce. I told him I would send him any books he wanted to study in jail. He's looking forward to going on with his studies in Singapore after he's free. We didn't talk much about Bulan, mostly about his studies. He did speak of Sir Ian, wondered what he would do. We couldn't see Sir Ian operating the gold mine at Kalgoorlie, or Lady Mary either, though Lady Mary is unpredictable. Somebody, Hall, I think, told me that a conglomerate has been wanting to buy the gold mine.

Long enough letter, Darya.

Every time my housekeeper dusts, she stops in front of your picture, entranced. No wonder.

Wish I could help with all your massive work.

Love,

Hartley

Letter from Darya to Hartley:

Dear Hartley:

You're an absolute angel to write me that letter! I've been practically out of my mind wondering about what's been happening. After some splashes at first, the news coverage here tapered off, except for stories about the Bulan oil. Glendon has written me, but naturally he is so madly absorbed in Tommy and their plans that she has said almost nothing about the other people. She did say she'd found your once-handsome blue jacket, which I must have dropped when I got into Car 2 and went racing forward to tell you about the lights on the track. She was saving the jacket, but thinks Hawkins collected it and threw it away. Glendon forgot to tell me about this when I saw her in Sydney. But in Sydney I don't think I'd have noticed if a hundred jackets had come parading self-propelled into the Menzies. I'm glad you didn't need the remains of the jacket as an exhibit for Mr. Farnsleigh. He probably would have given you hell for disgracing the Sword Line's image by wearing such a wreck.

It was good of you to go to see Sammy. I've written him twice. No answer. I can't see myself dragging Selby almost halfway around the world to visit Sammy. Weird idea. Selby would probably bite Sammy again, if he could come close enough in a jail visit, or into the jail at all. Our uncle and aunt are holding up. I think they've been resigned for ages to anything Sammy might do. Maybe it's a kind of relief now—what can he do in jail? No, don't say that he might try to escape! But the worry they don't show about Sammy comes out on me. They say I'm working too hard, that I'm too thin. But under the circumstances, I'm all right, though terribly bogged down in the last of the course work for the doctorate.

Orals coming up. My uncle is trying to help me pin down a subject for my dissertation.

I got through the Turkish courses and now am in a frenzy over epigraphy, which is fascinating in a ghoulish kind of way.

A friend of mine here at Columbia is a girl from Kuala Lumpur. Chinese-Malayan. Very nice, intelligent, but so homesick for Malaysia that she doesn't think she can stick it out. She met Tommy's uncle at some party in K.L. (her favorite initials) and says he's a straight. If she stays, we'll get an apartment together and she'll teach me Malayan. Maybe some Chinese.

I took my language exams—French, German, Turkish. Passed. Committees went into a hassle about accepting Turkish, but in the end they did.

Your housekeeper sounds dreamy. And your neighbors. I wish you'd had time to stay at home for a while instead of hustling off to Penang. But tell me about it. What's your housekeeper's name? You're a scoundrel, Hartley. I have no, repeat, no, picture of you for my friends. Or me. Just repulsive old photographs of artifacts hauled out of Turkish sites.

My Malaysian friend raves about Singapore whenever she isn't raving about Kuala Lumpur. She's a Moslem but hasn't any religious hang-ups.

What happened to Munah? Is she waiting for Sammy or for Daoud? And how is the dancer who was Welles's girl?

Last week I went to the Metropolitan Museum to see the lovely old temple that was rescued from the Egyptian dam.

You asked me in one letter what my favorite stone was. Amethyst, I think. Not opals, gosh no.

I'm now off to a seminar. Other things I'd rather do.

Love,

Darya

Letter from Hartley to Darya:

Dear Darya:

Don't, please, work too hard! But congratulations on passing language exams.

Had time only for brief notes to you these past two weeks. First, Penang, where I finished up in eight days. Then, a similar assignment in Borneo. In Penang I stayed as usual at the Merlin Hotel. No wizardry noticeable.

News from Australia: Daoud was sentenced to three years in prison, Ali got six and faces trial later in Singapore, Ahmad and Kasim got four years each, and Dermot—a life sentence.

I saw Sammy for a few minutes between assignments. He's all right, still buoyed up, I think, by his railroading feats.

While I was on Borneo I had the idea, believe it or not, of visiting Bulan. Not sure why. I don't think I told you that I met Sir Ian in Singapore. Didn't expect him to be cordial, but he was. Made noises about my just doing my job. Under the lordly manner, he seemed not exactly apologetic but aggrieved by the behavior of his men. He probably wouldn't have been if they had got the gold and brought it back to Bulan.

Anyway, I used one of the ship's boats to go to Bulan on Friday when Moslems at the port would not be working. Larger island than I had expected, ringed by a coral reef cut through at the harbor, where a couple of freighters were loading copra. Little islands raising indigo mountains in the offing. The whole layout

245

looked somewhat like pictures you may have seen of Tahiti. Larger than I'd expected. Copra warehouses at the port. Clusters of fishing boats. A generating plant.

A friendly old man with a pickup truck took me uphill past stores, a school, a hospital, a mosque, a small Chinese temple, and a Catholic church. Off to one side I saw rice terraces and water buffalo. In a level area we passed a sports field, then up higher, nearer a spine of mountains, came the main settlement made up of native huts with thatched roofs and larger houses of wood and stucco. People were working in gardens, women were in sarongs doing laundry in a clean-looking canal, and children were playing with dogs still unwesternized, ribby and mangy. Several houses in compounds had small Hindu shrines and a smell of incense. Palms and flowering trees everywhere. Atmosphere clean and orderly. I wondered how much of this Sir Ian was responsible for.

We drove on toward the mountains into the clearing where Sir Ian and Mary have their house. One of those houses—and I haven't seen many—that seem to have grown out of and become part of the luxuriant beauty of a tropical paradise. I don't think that's too strong a word. Long, low, white, with a roof that looks thatched but is probably of a sturdier material. And the view—blue water far below, spending strength against the reef. And to the north, coming right up from the water, a blue-violet mountain, its probable underlying islet invisible, if there at all.

Sir Ian in alabaster-white slacks and shirt, looking like nothing less than a colonial governor, came from the patio to meet me.

"Hartley Rhys! So you took up my invitation to visit us! As I hoped you would."

We sat on white iron chairs on the patio. A Malay boy brought three rum punches, and after a few minutes Lady Mary joined us. I had a shock seeing her in a white and gold-embroidered kind of Chinese cheongsam, but was pleased to notice she wore soft, gold-colored backless slippers, not those stout boots with which she had kicked me in Hawkins's office. Can you imagine her looking feminine? A different person there with Sir Ian, and perhaps still tamed and saddened by her father's death.

I found it incredible, though anything might have been believable under the spell of that idyllic setting, that they both spoke frankly and almost indifferently about the Bulan episode. I tell you, Darya, I expected to hear the Bulan freedom song played somewhere in the background. But they didn't go that far. Music there was, distant, the shining beat of gamelan instruments.

"Of course," Sir Ian said, with the little cough, "there was a lot that was regrettable, tragic." He looked at his wife, who nodded. "But now that it's over, one can't ignore some of the comedy, such as Owen Percy's impersonation of me." He sounded as if he had been flattered by that imitation. "Some time back, old Percy told me I would go too far, come down in a heap. What was the issue—you remember, Mary?"

"Was it your plan to make a tourist resort on that little island near here?"

"Believe it was. Good show, too. Still think it would have worked. Oh, well. Another drink, Hartley?"

The Malay boy was summoned. He refilled our glasses.

"This boy," Sir Ian said, "is Ahmad's brother."

God, I thought. Ahmad, whom I threw off the train. The brother, rather sullen and sad-looking, nodded.

Either he didn't associate me with what had happened to Ahmad, or was caught up in the generally unreal and dreamlike atmosphere. I didn't know what to say to him. What could I say?

Sir Ian resumed. "I didn't exactly come down in a heap this time. Oh, I grant you, a near heap. I must say I made some pretty bad choices."

"You couldn't have known about Dermot," Lady Mary said. "From your point of view, he was hired for a simple job—back-up, stiffening for the Malays." To me she said, "The probate is over. I have returned the opals to William Hall for his father."

"Decent chap," Sir Ian said. Then he added reflectively, "Even if that effort with the train and the *Cutlass* had come off, I suppose the geologists' report on oil deposits couldn't have been kept secret. Trouble was, we'd been dragging along in a kind of twilight zone between Indonesia and Portugal too long. Nobody wanted us and we wanted it made clear that we didn't want *anybody*. Portugal had pulled out. But Indonesia was still a threat, satisfied for the present by cheating us on copra. No definite administration."

"Was there the beginning of a nationalist movement before you became their leader?" I asked.

"Yes. Students—and there were a lot of bright chaps that left the island to go to universities like Daoud, whom I think you knew."

"You helped most of them, Ian," Lady Mary said.

"Yes, well, these aren't stupid people, you know."

Lady Mary turned to face me. "My husband is paying for all medical and legal expenses for the Malays." She added, "Will you stay to have lunch and dinner with us, Mr. Rhys?"

"Thank you, but it's impossible. I must go back to a

248

ship I'm tending."

She asked, then, about you.

No word so far about Sammy. Too sensitive a subject? I risked touching on it.

"I saw Sammy Javenel the other day. In prison."

A silence. Sir Ian set down his half-empty glass.

"Sammy," he said. His voice still sounded through a screen of unreality. You know, Darya, in some ways he seemed to me like Sammy, given over to pursuits of visions, remembering ephemeral triumphs rather than basic defeats. He had a lot of Sammy's charm, but as far as I could tell, none of Sammy's urges toward violence.

"I don't know what to say about Sammy." He spoke with candor, real or pretended. "I didn't know. He was so gifted, genuinely a patriot in our cause. My god, Mary, we were fond of that boy, weren't we?"

"Yes. And Sammy wasn't greedy for anything like opals. Not anything material. Violent? I didn't suspect it. Driving that engine—" She left the sentence unfinished and went on to another. "You couldn't have known, Ian, how that experience—he'd apparently yearned for it—would unlock what it did unlock."

"The duel with the freight train," I said.

I didn't know how we would move from there to anything else. I very much wanted to steer the talk to the night when Welles was killed. Investigative training goes deep. I made a start by picking up what Sir Ian had said about the Malays' intelligence and education.

"Your boy Daoud seemed the most promising of the Malay nationalists."

"Certainly was. Is, I hope."

"I knew him best. Of the others, I wondered about Ali."

Sir Ian called for another drink and waited to answer

until it came. When fortified, he said, "If you are leading up to the death of your colleague—and, by the way, is your visit today part of an official inquiry or, as I assumed, social?"

"The latter. But you will understand—Welles's death hit me hard."

Sir Ian drank again. Moslem he may have become, but his conversion excluded the edict against liquor.

"Welles," he said, "and the seaman from the *Cutlass* who turned informer—their death was no part of my plans."

Lady Mary raised a hand apprehensively as if saying, "Don't rat."

"They had to be silenced," Sir Ian said slowly. "But by some means less than death. Kidnapping, perhaps. My orders always forbade killing. Ali and Ahmad were entrusted with that mission. I know that a girl from a cantina has identified Ali from a photograph as having been in that alley behind the bar. I know too that Ali will face charges in Singapore after serving his term in Australia. As for Ahmad, I believe he was not noticed. He's not a noticeable person. Beyond that, there's nothing I can tell you."

It was true, I thought: anyone meeting Ali and Ahmad would be impressed by Ali's height and his blackly scowling face. Ahmad was small, neutral-looking, except for the piercing black eyes.

Ahmad's brother brought a bowl of macadamia nuts and a plate of fruit.

Behind him came the girl Munah, whom I recognized from the snapshot you showed me. A pretty girl in a green sarong, she looked more oriental than in the photograph. She was listless and without expression, barely acknowledging our introduction.

"Munah," Lady Mary said, as if to forestall anything further I might say about Ali, "is Ali's sister."

Munah sat on the arm of Lady Mary's chair and examined her green nail enamel.

"Too bright," Lady Mary said in a low voice. Munah nodded. "Yes. I'll change it."

I wouldn't go so far as to say that Lady Mary's attitude toward the girl was maternal, but it was certainly affectionate.

"Has the car been repaired?" Munah asked Sir Ian, who shook his head.

"Hard to get spare parts here," he said to me.

"I've had an idea," Lady Mary said. "Mr. Rhys, could your ship take a passenger back to Singapore?"

"No, I'm sorry. It doesn't carry passengers."

"Munah needs a change, needs to get away from here. I thought—well, if you can't."

"You couldn't smuggle her on board?" Sir Ian asked.

"Impossible, I'm afraid. But at the port in Borneo there are other freighters. She might be able to get passage on one of them."

"And how would I go to Borneo?" Munah asked.

"I could run you over there when I go back this afternoon. There's a hotel, in case you have to stay over. How soon could you be ready?"

"Twenty minutes," Munah said.

Sir Ian followed her into the house and came back a few minutes later with a wallet. When Munah returned he gave her some bills. Indonesian money, I noticed.

"Thank you, Sir Ian. When I can—"

"Never mind, child. You'll be staying with your cousins in Singapore?"

She nodded.

The driver of the pickup was sleeping under a tree

when Munah and I left the house. She wore pearl-gray slacks and a white shirt and carried a gray jacket. I stowed her suitcase at the back of the truck and sat on a makeshift bench, letting Munah sit with the driver.

The run to the Borneo port would take about three and a half hours. It was a little after one when we embarked on the launch. I wanted to make the run before darkness. I suggested a seat under the deck awning for Munah, but she came into the wheelhouse and sat stiffly on the cushioned bench around the bulkhead, from where she watched me, still expressionless and noncommunicative. She refused ice water or lemonade from thermos jugs, but just sat there staring at what my hands were doing, though I tried to talk with her about diversions in Singapore: visiting with her relatives, shopping. She listened stonily without answering questions. Naturally I wondered whether she planned to see Sammy, but did not ask her. I did speak of Daoud, however. At the mention of his name though, I saw in her black eyes a flicker like that in a cigarette lighter about to expire.

The wind grew strong, the sea choppy. Munah pulled on her jacket, tied a white scarf around her head, and held on to the bench with both hands. At my request she closed the windows.

"Warm enough?" I asked. "There are oilskins in the locker."

She was ash-pale, but not the green-pale of seasickness.

We were running into a storm. The sun was obscured. Lightning. Thunder, I suppose, but it was inaudible over the sound of the engine. Nothing to worry about. The launch was as tough as they came. Far ahead on the port side, beyond the storm, I caught occasional glimpses of the blurred line of the Borneo coast, just often enough to show that it was there, before swirls of vapor and rain reduced our horizon to the launch's width. Odd effect too, there was: purplish blackness closing against the white vapor.

I thought of the violet-blackness of your eyes, Darya.

Beside me, a little behind me, Munah spoke. "I'll take an oilskin," she said. "Will it smell?"

"They always smell. Like varnish and fish."

Holding the wheel with my left hand, I leaned over to the locker on my right, pulled on an edge of an oilskin, and brought out, unwanted, a pack of cigarettes, a book, an opened packet of biscuits, and a dirty towel. Then, as I was withdrawing the oilskin, against that purple-darkness that walled the windows on my right, I saw a narrow flash, but not of lightning.

If I hadn't seen it, if I hadn't swung around and gripped Munah's wrist, I would not be writing you this letter. For the short, steel-bright dagger in Munah's hand was pointed at my neck.

The launch skirted off course while I pinioned Munah, wrenched the knife from her hand, and threw it overboard. I then pulled out the oilskin, fastened it around her, tied the sleeves, thrust her down the few steps into the cabin below, and shut the hatch. Her handbag was on the bench. I opened it. No weapons. I removed a folder of matches.

The Long Straight had put out a long tentacle for that attempt.

When I reached port, I freed Munah (and myself) by turning her over to the ship's second mate and asking him to try to find her a passage to Singapore, or if he couldn't, to take her to the hotel. Before leaving her I asked why she had tried to kill me.

She looked at me with loathing and said, "Because you ruined *everything*. You ruined Ali, my brother. You put Daoud in prison. Right now he's probably being tortured, maybe dying."

I told her Daoud was not being abused, was indeed well and studying. She didn't believe me. Later that night the second mate reported that he had put Munah on board a Norwegian freighter, which would sail for Singapore the next afternoon.

Back in Singapore I told Farnsleigh about this incident.

He said quickly and haughtily, as if daring me to disagree, "You can't blame Sir Ian for *that*."

I gave him a long hard look.

"Well?" He bristled, ready to quell mutiny in the ranks.

I let him bristle for a minute or so, then said, "I don't think Sir Ian ordered Munah to kill me. I do think he may have implied that he wouldn't be displeased if I were removed from any further connection with him or Bulan. A little late, of course. I think, behind his hedges, he was counting on Munah's vindictiveness to carry out his wishes. Generously, I must say."

"Have you any vindictive plans?" he asked, obviously foreseeing and shrinking from legal involvement with Indonesia. I told him I just never wanted to hear of Bulan again.

At that, he served cognac.

For some time he has been hinting darkly about a mysterious gift. I hadn't known whether it was something he intended to receive or to give. I didn't think he expected me to have brought him any souvenirs from my trips to Australia, not with what I *did* bring, which, aside from the *Cutlass*, was largely trouble.

The mystery came to light the other day when his secretary, an amiable woman, decided she couldn't keep the secret any longer. She made me promise to be surprised when Farnsleigh made his announcement.

Farnsleigh, she told me, had been brooding for more than a year over the fact that he hadn't given you and me a wedding gift. "You can understand," she said, "that he was in a flap, several flaps, at the time you were married in Sydney. It happened rather fast."

No question about that, since you, Darya, and I had only those three days in Sydney.

So Farnsleigh is now going to give us a three-month trip anywhere in the world. All expenses, no restrictions.

Come as soon as you can, darling.

Meanwhile I'm working on a project for you. Several universities with grants from archaeological societies, mainly in England, are teamed up for some digs out here in Malaysia. Good chance you can dig with them, and maybe pull a thesis out of the rubble.

But before you do any more work, let's take the Farnsleigh trip. Not using any trains, though, right?

Love,

Hartley